NEVER SAW IT COMING

BERNADETTE MARIE

5 PRINCE PUBLISHING

NEVER SAW IT COMING

Bernadette Marie

5 PRINCE PUBLISHING & BOOKS, LLC

PO Box 16507

Denver, CO 80216

www.5PrinceBooks.com

ISBN-10:1-63112-193-6 ISBN-13:978-1-63112-193-7

NEVER SAW IT COMING. Bernadette Marie

Copyright BERNADETTE MARIE 2017

Published by 5 Prince Publishing

Cover Credit: Bernadette Soehner

First Edition May 2017

5 PRINCE PUBLISHING AND BOOKS, LLC.

Stan,
First day of college, under my dorm window...
I Never Saw It Coming!
27 years after that day, I'm glad you're still by my side.

ACKNOWLEDGMENTS

To my favorite 5:
I had no idea 5 was going to be my most favorite number!
I love you all. I'm so proud to be your momma!

To my mom, dad, and sissy:
Who could have known all those messes of papers would pay off.
Thanks for letting me take over so often! I love you!

Clare:
Thanks for the many, many miles!
You help keep my head on straight.

Cate:
Thank you for being on top of it all. You never see the mess
coming your way, yet you handle it gracefully!

To my RMFW IPAL sisters:
Without your love and support this past year, and your constant
urging to do bigger and better things, I think I would have gotten
a bit lost. I love you all!

To my devoted readers:
Every day that I sit down to write, I think of the love you have showered me with for the past seven years. Thank you for that! I love writing for you.

NEVER SAW IT COMING

Bernadette Marie

CHAPTER 1

With a foot of fresh and falling snow on the ground, business was slow. But it was Colorado, so there were enough patrons in the restaurant to keep it busy. After all, people in Colorado weren't afraid of a little snow. However, at the moment there were only two people at the bar.

Chandra was going crazy trying to keep busy enough to look as though she were in charge. Good thing Gabe, the owner of McGuire's, wasn't around. When things were this slow, he tended to get in the way.

Lucky for her, he was much too busy with his wife Holly and the pending birth of their second child. Chandra figured with the snow, and Holly's due date, she'd be lucky to see him even once this week—or so she hoped. She'd sent him away on paternity leave a week ago. After all, why put her in charge of the entire place if he was there all the time?

She waved goodbye to a couple leaving from dinner, and another man walked in. He certainly wasn't dressed for the weather, which meant he was from out of town or native to Colorado. Until he spoke, it was iffy.

"How are you?" she asked as she set a napkin on the bar.

"Cold."

From out of town, she decided. He'd flown in when it was sunny, which had been that morning, and now there was a blizzard outside. It could always catch a tourist off guard.

"Can I get you something warm to drink?"

He wiped his feet and dragged his hands through his wet hair, then walked toward the bar.

"How about a beer?"

"What kind?" she asked as he sat down.

"I guess I'm in the Coors territory, huh?"

"You're also surrounded by micro-breweries. I can hit ya up with about anything you'd like."

"Nothing heavy."

"I've got you covered." She pulled him a micro-brew that nearly looked like water to her. It was a good place to start someone who didn't quite know what they wanted. "Try this one. We can get darker and more stout from there."

"Thanks," he said looking down into the beer, but not drinking.

"Can I get ya something to eat?" She handed him the menu.

"What's your favorite?"

She rested her arms on the bar. "Prime rib sandwich. You can't go wrong."

"I'll try that."

"Good choice." She punched in the order on the computer screen. "It'll be out shortly. We're not too busy."

"Snow keeps everyone inside, huh?"

"Not usually, but it slows things down a bit. Where are you from?"

"California."

That explained the lack of a heavy jacket. "Hmmm, here on business?"

"Yeah. Was. Guess not."

He might be the entertainment she'd been looking for. It had been a long time since she'd had a sap at the bar crying into his beer. Who'd have thought she'd look forward to one. But the truth was this was the fun part. Bartending was only part serving up drinks. The other half was trying to get into someone's soul. Even better, he was from out of town, so if he were too sappy, he wouldn't always be hanging around.

He sipped his beer and held it between his hands as if maybe he were counting the bubbles in it. This one was in a dark place, Chandra thought as she took a towel to a mug to dry it.

His tie hung loosely around his neck. The top button of his shirt was undone, and the sleeves had apparently been rolled most the day.

The dark circles under his eyes said he'd been up worrying. The newly shadowed chin told her he'd been clean-shaven early that morning when the shirt looked crisp.

There was no wedding ring on his finger, though there might have been one not too long ago. That one was a hard one to judge. She knew he hadn't taken off the ring in the past few days, though. Usually, men who did that had not only a tan line, but there was a dent there too.

Her bet was a guy who had recently lost his wife, and now it looked as though he'd lost his job too. Add to that he was stuck in Colorado.

He took a second sip of his beer and now it was time to move in and get the specifics.

"What kind of business are you in?" she asked drying another glass.

He let out a small grunt. "Software. Was," he said as he had when he walked in.

"Your business meeting didn't go so well?"

"That I could forgive. Oh, no. They hire me. Offer me the entire world. I sell my house, my car, gave away my dog..." He stopped and took a long sip from his beer. "Came out here ready to change the world. I'm here exactly sixty-three hours, and the company is seized. Doors are locked, and signs are up that the government has them now."

Chandra felt the grip on the glass in her hand become tighter. "What were they into?"

He shrugged. "I researched them. They were a thriving company which developed software for doctors' offices. But it looks as though they'd never—ever—paid out a dollar in taxes. That crap catches up with you."

The sense of urgency took over, and she reached her hand across the bar to rest it on his arm. "I'm really sorry."

He looked down at her hand, and she yanked it back. It wouldn't be the first time she'd crossed a line like that.

When she looked up at him, his eyes had gone wide. Oh, she'd broken the cardinal rule. You can talk to the patrons—even dig into their past. But you sure as hell didn't touch them unless you wanted a stalker.

The man swallowed hard then took another drink. "How long have you worked here?"

"Forever," she said trying to busy herself, though she'd cleaned every inch of that bar since it was so slow.

"I like your tat," he said with a grin and blush.

Chandra knew every bit of ink on her body, but she looked down just to figure out what he was talking about.

He lifted a finger. "The one on your wrist. Does it say Jason?"

Oh, he was good. She was the one that was playing the game of uncovering the secrets and here he was working her.

"Yes."

"He must be pretty important."

"He is."

"Son?"

Ouch, she winced when he mentioned it. "Yep."

"Lovely tribute." His eyes had softened. That said a lot too.

"You have a son?"

He nodded. "Just turned nineteen. Moved out with some friends and goes to Southern California State."

"You must be extremely proud of him."

It showed on his face as he nodded again. He pulled his iPhone from his pocket and scrolled. "This is him," he said laying the phone on the bar and pushing it toward her. "He's six-three. I think he gets it from her side of the family. None of the men in mine made it past five-ten."

She noted the gorgeous blonde in the picture. "Is that your wife?"

His lips tightened at that. "Ex. We couldn't make it work. Tried for years, but I think we knew years ago it was over." He tucked the phone back into his pocket. "Now that Dane moved out it didn't seem as important to try anymore."

Her heart broke at that. What did she know? She'd never even tried to make it work with Jason's dad. They weren't compatible at all.

The server from the back brought out his plate and set it down. He thanked her, and Chandra gave her a grateful nod.

"Looks like you're all set. Can I get you anything else?"

He lifted his eyes, and she saw the sparkle in the deep blue, which she hadn't noticed before. Okay, so maybe she'd done her job and lifted his spirits a bit.

"I'm enjoying the conversation. I'd be okay with more of that."

Desperate. He was desperate. What had she started?

She put down her rag and leaned against the counter. What did it matter? This man, who looked like a cross between Bill Gates and a politician, sat at her bar, broken. He was from California, where his son still lived. Even if he came back every day for dinner, he'd only be in for the next week. It wouldn't hurt to talk to him and make him feel human. He wasn't her type. She obviously wasn't his, judging from the picture of his ex-wife. She could let down the bitchy exterior for one night—one cold, snowy, slow business night and be compassionate. Oh what would Gabe think of that, she chuckled to herself.

"What's your name?" she asked.

"Mike."

"Mike, the software developer from California."

He bit down on a fry. "That's me. What's your name?"

"Chandra."

"Chandra, the tattooed bartender from Denver?"

She hoped her face didn't show the disappointment she felt when she heard it. That was her, and it sounded so dull. "That's me."

"There's more," he said, and she stared at him. "You don't just work here."

"I manage the restaurant now."

He nodded. "I could tell you have authority." He ate another fry. "Not involved with the boss either."

She shook her head. "He's married with the second kid on the way."

That caused him to smile. "You adore him, though, and you'd take care of him and what is his."

"Sure."

"Polar opposite of his wife."

Okay, now he was playing her game, and she was spewing out answers. "Complete. She's a prodigy. Graduated college at twelve, or something like that. I have a GED."

"I have a masters. You have a job of authority. I have a hotel room for two more days. I don't think education matters when it comes to success."

"Don't tell my son that. It's hard enough to convince him to turn in his homework."

"Sixth grade?" he asked with a grin.

She pursed her lips. "Fifth, but that was close. How'd you know?"

That caused him to laughed when he lifted his sandwich to

his mouth. "That's when it starts. Boys have a rebellious streak when it comes to homework."

"He's making me a maniac about it."

"It's not too bad—that is, if he's a good kid."

She felt her body soften. "He's the best." And that was the truest statement she'd ever spoken.

Her mother had helped her raise him, and he'd turned out okay. Sure, what boy didn't meet the principal once or twice? He'd honor rolled a few times. He loved soccer. But he was usually in his bed when he was supposed to be, and he spoke to her with a kind tongue. She'd done okay alone.

"I can see it in your eyes. He's your world. No man has ever stacked up to him."

"Never tried. It wasn't worth it. He's mine."

"He'll be okay then."

Her heart was melting. That wasn't supposed to happen. He was supposed to order a beer and spill his story so she could entertain herself. Now here she was, wanting to hug him and that had disaster written all over it.

"How's your dinner?" she asked, picking up a rag and mindlessly wiping down the already clean bar.

"You were right. I couldn't go wrong with it."

From the corner of her eye, she noticed one of the bussers running toward the bar. She set down the rag and moved toward him.

"There's water," he said gasping for breath. "From the apartment, I think."

This wasn't what she needed, but it was what she'd signed on for.

She went back behind the bar and grabbed her set of keys.

"Trouble?" Mike looked up at her with his beer in his hand.

"I think I have a broken pipe in the apartment upstairs. Know anything about that?"

"I do."

He was already rising from his stood when she stopped to look at him. "You do?"

"Parents owned a B and B when I was growing up. I'm one handy dude. It might not look like it," he said looking down at his rumpled tie. "But I am."

Nothing seemed off about this guy, and that worried her more than if he'd walked in looking as though he were there to start trouble.

But she knew nothing about busted pipes, so if he could help her for the moment, she was going to let him.

"C'mon," she said giving him a nod toward the stairs.

Chandra hurried to the hallway that led to the inner staircase. Mike followed as she ran up the steps as water already began to trickle from under the door.

"Oh, shit. This isn't good," she said as she put the key in the door and pushed it open.

They all three stepped in, and Mike laughed. "Not as big a catastrophe as you thought."

There was water on the floor, but not the massive puddle she'd imagined.

Mike moved quickly to the sink and pulled open the cabinet. He knelt down in the water and reached in to turn it off.

"Yep, cracked pipe. If you can get the materials to fix it, I can do it," he said standing back up. "I don't know what's open or around here, but..."

"Nothing," Chandra said crossing her arms in frustration. "You're not headed back on a plane tonight are you?"

He chuckled. "No, I'm stuck here."

"Good," she said then thought better of it. "I don't mean good as in good that you're stranded."

"I get it. Do you have some rags and a bucket? I'll help get this cleaned up. You have a bar to manage."

"You'd do that?"

"You know I'd feel better being useful this week."

"Let me get some. You could use some dry pants too. I have some uniform pants for the bussers downstairs. I'll get you a pair. I'll be right back."

MIKE WATCHED AS SHE FLEW BACK DOWN THE STEPS AND HE smiled. That felt good too. He certainly hadn't had much to smile about lately.

Without moving from his position, he looked around the quaint apartment. It had obviously been empty for a while, but the furniture remained and even a few pictures on the mantel.

He could hear her running back up the stairs, and he watched her hurry through the door with a mop bucket in one hand and a mop in the other.

"There is a smaller bucket in here," she said as she set down the mop bucket. "You should be able to sop it up with the mop and use the other bucket…"

"Under the leak. I got it. I'll get busy on it."

She nodded. "I'll have dry pants for you when you get downstairs, and I'll have the kitchen make you a new sandwich."

"That's not necessary."

"Yes, it is. And it'll be on the house."

"Thanks."

"I owe you," she smiled a tight, threatened smile as she retreated and headed back down the steps.

Mike stood still for a moment longer. He'd been in a desperate mood when he'd walked into the bar. There had been the thought of getting shit-faced and passing out in the street, but it hadn't worked that way. He'd met a vibrant woman who made him want to hit the streets looking for a new opportunity tomorrow. Maybe he was the one who owed her he thought as he began sopping up the water on the floor.

CHAPTER 2

*J*ust as promised, there was a new sandwich on the bar, and a pair of black pants hung over the back of the stool.

"Thanks," he said, picking up the pants. "I'll be right back."

"I called my boss. He's going to bring the parts you need in the morning and leave them in the apartment. Would you be able to come by and fix it before we open? I'll make sure to feed you breakfast."

"I have nothing else on my schedule. I didn't go snooping around, but that's a nice place up there. Someone used to live there?"

"My boss when he moved here. It's been vacant since he got married and moved out."

"I'll have it fixed up in no time. I noticed the door could use some oil on the hinges and the knob is a little loose. I'll fix that up too."

"You are handy."

"Like I said, I just don't look it."

"Looks can be deceiving."

He scanned his eyes over the fairy-sized woman. Her stature

was tiny, but she walked with a no-nonsense gait. Her biceps were significantly more toned than his and covered in ink. A long brown braid hung down her back, and her ears were pierced from bottom to top. This woman looked as though she'd jump on the back of any man's Harley, but when she spoke of her son, he'd nearly wept. She was right. Looks could be deceiving.

Before he left, Mike changed his clothes, ate his dinner, and left a nice tip on the bar—under the plate to save from any argument.

He walked back to his hotel, now with a jacket that said Maguire's on it, which he'd return tomorrow as well as the pants.

The lights of the city glistened against the silver backdrop of the snowy night. It was beautiful. Maybe his adventure had only begun, he thought as he turned the corner and walked through the front door of his hotel. This could have just been the wake-up call he'd needed. Life needed a change once in a while, and well, being stranded in Colorado was a change, that was for sure.

He rode the elevator as a musical rendition of "Billie Jean" serenaded him, and the vision of Chandra filled his mind.

He caught himself smiling in the mirrored wall of the elevator. It had been a long time since he'd felt like smiling. She had been a breath of fresh air on a stormy night, he thought.

When the elevator opened, he walked to his room, inserted the card in the door, and let himself in. He hung the jacket on a chair. He'd called down to see about a laundry service for his wet pants and the borrowed ones. They'd be sending someone up to collect them.

As he changed into a pair of University of Southern California sweatpants, he thought about thanking Chandra for the wake-up call.

When he was done fixing the pipe tomorrow, he'd start looking for a job—in Colorado. No need to head back to where he'd left. There was nothing there for him now.

~

IT WAS MIDNIGHT WHEN CHANDRA QUIETLY WALKED THROUGH THE back door of her house. The light over the stove was on, and she smiled. All her life her mother had left a light on her for. Nothing had changed except her age.

The kitchen smelled of chocolate chip cookies, which meant her mother had been baking. Whenever it snowed, her mother wanted to bake.

Sure enough, there was a plate on the table covered with plastic wrap. Lots of crumbs and only two cookies remained. A glass of half drank milk sat there too. Compliments of her son, no doubt, and not because he'd left it for her to drink. He'd neglected to clean up his mess.

She growled as she picked up the glass and poured out the warm contents. Then she returned for the last two cookies.

With both cookies in one hand and the empty plate in the other, she put the plate in the sink, turned off the light and headed to her room.

The light under her son's bedroom door was a giveaway that he was still up. How this kid made it through a full day of school was beyond her.

She pushed open the door just as he crashed a very fancy car into the side of a building in the video game he was playing.

"Mom!"

"Midnight. You were supposed to be in bed over two hours ago."

"Mom, I don't need a bedtime."

"You need to go to bed," she said with a wink as he groaned and turned off the TV. "Grandma must have fallen asleep again, huh?"

He grinned up at her as he turned off his game. "Are those Grandma's cookies?"

"Well, they're mine, and I assumed Grandma made them."

"Can I have one?"

She looked at the two cookies in her hand and held one out to him.

"Thanks. You're the best mom ever."

She laughed. "If I were, I wouldn't make you go to bed." She pulled close the door and continued toward her room.

A light under her mother's door glowed too, but she knew she wasn't awake or Jason would have been in bed. Her TV was set to automatically go off, but her mother fell asleep much faster.

Chandra bit into her soft cookie, and it melted in her mouth. She never could bake like her mother could. One more reason to always keep her nearby, she thought, as she kicked off her shoes and fell on her bed.

Her entire body hurt. All part of the job, she thought as she bit into the cookie again.

She loved her job and always had. Gabe was the best boss she ever could have asked for. But the past few weeks had been harder than most. She'd been putting in nearly fourteen to sixteen hours a day since he was spending time with his wife, who was due to have that baby any day.

And Chandra had been clear with him that if she saw him at the restaurant before his paternity leave was over, she'd quit. He needed to be with Holly, their daughter, and the new baby, which she was sure was a little girl. It served him right to be surrounded by more women in his life. Gabe had four sisters, a wife, and one daughter.

She chuckled as she brushed the crumbs from her shirt and tucked her pillow under her head.

She was much too tired to even change out of her clothes.

Tomorrow was going to start early. She'd asked Mike to be there before nine, which meant she needed to be there earlier than she'd intended.

On a yawn, she rolled over and fluffed the pillow into place.

Mike. He was interesting, she thought. Very interesting.

❧

THE MOMENT CHANDRA DROPPED JASON OFF AT SCHOOL SHE DROVE straight to work. Once she parked, she sprinted down to the pedestrian mall to buy a bag of burritos. She'd promised Mike breakfast, and she was starving. It hadn't taken her long last night to realize that the cookie was one of three things she'd eaten the day before.

As she jogged around the corner to the front door of the restaurant, she was more than surprised to find Mike standing there with two cups of coffee in his hands.

"I said before nine," she said huffing.

"It's before nine." He smiled. "I brought you a coffee. It's just black because you didn't look like the kind of girl that gets all goofy for that fancy coffee."

She was sure she was just staring at him. Maybe the running had caused her to lose oxygen to her brain.

"Thanks," she managed as she dug her keys from her pocket. "That's how I like it."

He gave her a nod as she unlocked the door. With a generous nudge from her hip, the door opened. She held it until he walked through and locked it back up.

"Place is quiet when it's closed," he said looking around the dark dining area.

"My favorite time. Before everyone gets here with their moods."

Mike set the coffees on the bar. "I can get started now if you like."

"Right. I'm sure Gabe left everything upstairs." She set the bag on the bar and looked at it before she remembered what was in it. "I got you a burrito, for breakfast. Is that okay?"

"Wonderful. Thanks." He pulled a canvas shopping bag off his shoulder and handed it to her. "I have your jacket and pants. I had them laundered last night."

"You didn't have to do that."

"It wasn't a problem. I appreciated it." He picked up his burrito and began to unwrap it. "I also wanted to thank you."

"Me?"

He nodded. "I was very desperate last night when I came in here. I have a few thousand to my name. The rest is tied up in my son's college. This job was supposed to be my rescue. I thought everything was over for me. But you made me want to pick up the pieces and start over."

"How did I do that?"

"I'm going to call it fairy magic."

She narrowed her eyes on him. "Is that a joke about my size?"

"No. It's a compliment actually. I didn't mean it any other way."

He looked horrified. She hadn't meant to scare him. Sappy men never made much sense to her. Sappy women didn't either.

Chandra flung her braid over her shoulder and picked up the coffee.

"You weren't suicidal."

"No, I didn't say I was."

She nodded. "I know suicidal when I see it. I wasn't trying to save your life or anything."

"I know. You just gave me some hope that this is where I'm supposed to be."

She lifted the lid on the coffee. "What are you going to do?"

"Start searching for a job. It might take some time, but I'll find one."

She was getting itchy now. That meant she was thinking too hard. Her hands were shaking, and she hadn't even had the coffee yet.

"Can you fix refrigerators?"

"I've been known to."

"Maybe we could use your handy skills around here until you find a job."

He stopped mid-bite into his burrito. "You're hiring me?"

"I mean you can't live in a hotel without it eating up your money. You'll probably need first and last month's rent too. You'd better answer me before I realize that I made this decision without Gabe's approval and…"

"I'd appreciate that."

She nodded on a breath. "Good, I'll talk to him and tell him you're helping out for a bit. I'm sure you'll find a job in no time."

"That would be nice. Maybe I could take you out for dinner some night as a thank you," he said as he took another bite of the burrito she had been so hungry for, but now her stomach jittered and she wondered if she could eat.

"Me?"

He looked around the dark restaurant. "Yep, you. No one else here."

"I don't think I'm your type. I saw a picture of your wife."

His eyes grew wide. "Yes you did, and no, you're not my usual type. But you're friendly, and I need a friend. You're helping me out, and I'd like to repay you." He bit off another bite. "Maybe after we sit down for a nice dinner we can decide if we're a type that each other likes or not," he said with his mouth full.

Okay, now she felt like an idiot, and that was rare. So he wasn't interested in her? She could accept that. Most of the men who ended up at the bar weren't interested either. They were desperate. Mike might have been desperate, but not for a quickie with the bartender.

"I hope I didn't offend you."

"Not in the least," he said wiping his mouth with a napkin. "So you'll have dinner with me?"

"I will. I'm usually off on Wednesday and Thursday."

"I'm off those days too," he said with a laugh, and she found the tension in her shoulders ease. "I'll get started on that sink. Then I can look at the refrigerator."

CHAPTER 3

*M*ike turned on the lights to the apartment and shut the door. Just as promised, there was a bag from the hardware store sitting on the kitchen table.

He dug through it and found the pieces he'd needed to fix the sink. It wouldn't take long, he figured. He'd seen his share of broken pipes, clogged toilets, cracked windows, and anything else people could do to a residence. It amazed him how people could spend a few days in a place and ruin it all. His parents were saints putting up with that so that they could both be home for their kids.

In less than an hour, he was finished with his job. He could smell food from down the steps, and he wondered what the special would be today. If Chandra wasn't tired of him yet, he'd sit and have lunch before he went to the library down the street to work on his résumé. He'd print it out there and then take it to the Kinko's around the corner and make copies. Tonight he was having leftovers, which he was going to purposely keep from lunch, and surfing the internet for jobs. Denver was a hotbed for technical jobs. Surely someone had something they could offer him. His skills deemed him a high-end employee. His desperation had him content with taking an entry level job.

Mike cleaned up the area, put the spare parts in the bag, closed up the apartment and walked back down to the restaurant. He noticed, for the first time, that there were two doors that led to the staircase and up to the apartment. That was good business sense to have an outside entrance. Chandra had said the owner used to live there, but he assumed that might not always be the case.

They had a few more lights on now, and there were two people setting tables. Chandra was at the bar with a clipboard making notes. He assumed she was taking inventory.

"Sink is as good as new."

She snapped her head up and looked at him. "You were fast."

"Did what I came to do. You said you had a refrigerator that needed looking at."

"I did. It's this one under the bar."

She stepped back as if to invite him to walk around and look, so he did.

"What's going on with it?"

"I think it's a short or a fuse or something. It works, just not all the time."

"I can pull it out and look. When do you start serving?"

"Half hour."

He nodded. "How about I look now. Then we can get the parts we need, and I can come back in the morning and fix it. No breakfast necessary."

The corner of her mouth turned up into a smile. "I'll have breakfast for you, and I'll buy your lunch today if you'd like."

"Only because I'm desperate, I'll accept. Already decided I'd eat here anyway and take half of it back for dinner."

Her eyes softened. "I'd pay you cash if that was easier."

"I'll take food. After I leave here, I'm going to go work on my résumé."

"You're really staying in Denver?"

"I am if it works out. I told you, you inspired me."

Chandra bit down on her lip. "That is flattering. Tell me what you want for lunch. I'll have them get it ready."

MIKE HAD LOOKED OVER THE MENU, AND CHANDRA TOOK HIS order to the kitchen. He was jiggling wires on the back of the small refrigerator when she walked back to the bar.

"They'll have it up soon. I had them make you something for dinner too. Do you have a place to store it in your room?"

He shifted a look up to her. "There's a small fridge and microwave in the room."

"Handy."

He stood and pushed the small refrigerator back into place. "You didn't have to do that, by the way. This goes against the profits if you feed me. I know that."

She shrugged. "You're doing me a great service. So what's the verdict?" She gave a nod toward the refrigerator.

"You were right. Faulty fuse and a short in the cord. I'll swing by a hardware store and pick up the pieces. Is there a store downtown?"

Her mouth curled up into a beautiful, perhaps not used nearly enough, smile. "Of course. But you tell me what you need. I'll have it here for you."

"It wouldn't be a problem."

"I know."

A man walked through the front door, a tablet in his hand, and a patch on his shirt.

"Hey, Chandra."

"Hey. I thought you were going to be here an hour ago," she said to him as he walked around the bar.

"I-70 is solid. Accident out by Stapleton or something."

"Good thing I got everything done then."

Deciding this was his queue to exit, Mike began to move from behind the bar, placing his hands on Chandra's well-formed shoulders to pass behind her.

It was then he felt that sizzle between them. Maybe it was when she sucked in a deep breath as if she'd felt it too that made him suddenly light-headed.

"Want me to look at anything else?" he asked quickly.

She looked up at him, but she appeared to be slightly stunned into silence. After a few blinks, she looked around the restaurant. "Table eight is off balance. We have cardboard under the leg."

Mike smiled. "I'll go look at it. Which one is table eight?"

She pointed him in a direction, and he made his way to the table. He sat in the booth and jostled the table around, but sitting down was more to steady his shaking legs.

All he did was touch the woman, and both of them went into some trance. Maybe today he'd not only work on that résumé but look for an apartment. Something deep inside of him told him he wanted to stay in Denver for as long as he possibly could.

It hadn't taken too long for the restaurant to fill with an early lunch crowd, then turn again. Mike decided, though, that she needed the refrigerator, and it would be a good time to get the pieces he needed. A brisk walk would also do him good. He was still a little shaken from that exchange behind the bar.

He was man enough to admit he was just stupid. Yep, he was just a man who had nothing, and a pretty woman was keeping him around out of pity.

Although he did feel as though he deserved some pity, he had to admit that Chandra was the least likely to offer it up.

She seemed more down to earth than the women he'd met over the years. She worked hard and provided for her son, who was her light in the world. There was great respect for her boss.

And c'mon, any woman who proudly showed that many tattoos on sculpted arms like hers, you didn't mess with her. She could take care of herself.

He chuckled to himself as he walked down the Sixteenth Street pedestrian mall. There was something in that extensive armor that made him want to know all about her.

Checking the coordinates on his iPhone, he crossed the street and started his trek through town to find the pieces he needed. There was an Ace Hardware about ten blocks away. With the snow on the ground and his lack of proper footwear, he thought it would be just as easy to catch a cab. However, with his lack of employment, he thought it even better to keep walking.

He'd love to live in town. It sure would be convenient. The thought crossed his mind, as he looked at all the new builds cluttering the Denver skyline. Of course, he was sure that was going to cost a pretty penny. Nothing in comparison to living in California, but not cheap either.

Then he thought about the apartment above the restaurant. It had a separate entrance. There was absolutely nothing fancy about it. It could use some updating. It was vacant.

He stopped at a light and waited to cross as the thought of living there filled his mind. It would be perfect.

Then the image of Chandra flashed into his mind too. It might just be too close.

He crossed when the walk signal flashed, and ten minutes later he was entering the store.

"You look frozen," the man at the checkout said.

"Yeah, wasn't prepared," Mike said as he stomped off the bottom of his shoes. "I'm looking for fuses."

He directed him to the aisle, and Mike thanked him.

Another man stood looking at the same items Mike needed. He carried a sleeping toddler on his shoulder who was bundled up in a big pink coat.

"Always something needs fixing, huh?" The man joked as he scanned the shelves.

"Yeah, but it's getting me by," Mike offered as he reached for a fuse and then replaced it when it wasn't the right one.

"Working as a handyman?" The man asked and then gave him a look. "You don't fit the part."

"Kinda got stuck here, so I'm helping out. My tech job fell through."

The man turned to him fully and narrowed his gaze. Mike took a step back.

"You're not the guy helping out at Maguire's are you?"

Mike was certain he looked as surprised as he felt. "I've done a few odd things there, yes."

The man's face lit into a smile, and he extended his free hand. "I'm Gabe Maguire. I own the place."

"Oh, wow. I'm Mike." He shook his hand. "It's nice to meet you. Chandra talks very fondly of you."

"You too," he said, and that put a knot in Mike's stomach.

"She told you about me?" he asked realizing he sounded like some teenage girl trying to get the low down on some boy.

Gabe chuckled, then put his hand on the toddlers back to ease her against him. "She said you were helping out and she wanted to keep you around while I'm out. She didn't tell me you were coming for the part for the refrigerator, though."

Mike shrugged. "I was in the way."

"She's not fond of people in her way." They shared a laugh over that. "Why don't we get those parts. I know the doorknob to my office needs replaced and tile near the front door. Do you do tile?"

"I can do it all. As long as I can walk back with it," he said.

"You walked here?"

"I sold my car to move to Denver for a job that folded. Just making those ends meet until something comes up."

"Where are you living?"

"In a hotel for now. I'm going job hunting this week and looking for a place."

Gabe bit down on his bottom lip. "What kind of job?"

"Software development."

"Are you willing to keep helping out at the restaurant?"

Mike nodded. "Oh, of course."

"What I was thinking was, that apartment upstairs is run down. I never did much to it when I lived there, and that's been over two years. Would you consider some trade work?"

"Trade work for what?" he asked not wanting to assume anything.

"Rent for the apartment if you'll put it back together. It needs to be painted, flooring, plumbing—you name it."

Mike crossed his arms over his chest and studied him. "You're serious?"

"Very. I figure if you're working, it will take you probably six months. We can renegotiate then. Maybe you'll have a good job, and you'll be ready to move on. I'll have something I can rent out."

Mike wasn't even sure why he was contemplating it so hard. He knew his answer. "I'd like that," he said holding his hand out to shake on the deal.

Gabe shook his hand. "This will help me out a lot. I have my hands full as you can see."

"And another on the way I hear."

"Yep. C'mon, I'll give you a ride back. Since I have her, Chandra won't yell at me or quit if I walk through the door."

Mike laughed. He couldn't wait to watch her squirm, though.

CHAPTER 4

*T*he bar and tables were full, and they had a waiting list at lunch time. Didn't people notice the snow on the ground, Chandra wondered. Then she laughed at the thought. It was Colorado. Snow didn't stop anyone. Hell, half of the execs in their ties didn't even have a coat.

She looked up as the door opened again and she felt the heat rise in her cheeks as Gabe walked through the door with Madison in his arms.

"I warned you, Maguire," she said holding up a finger and pointing it at him as she served a beer with the other hand. "You'd better turn around and leave."

He only grinned at her. "First of all, I figured you'd keep your language clean and not yell at me if she was with me," he said taking the hood off his daughter's head. "Besides, my business is with Mike and not you."

"Mike?" she asked just as he walked through the door with his arms full of supplies from the hardware store.

"I found him walking the streets buying supplies." He winked at her. "Gave him an offer."

Mike walked up next to Gabe and situated the bags on the bar.

"So you two have met?" she asked looking at Mike.

"Yep. You were right. He's a nice guy."

Chandra grunted. "I'm sure I didn't say that."

Gabe smiled as he bounced his daughter on his hip. "I didn't believe him either. Anyway, he's going to be fixing up the apartment."

"Good. That place is a dump."

Gabe's brows rose. "He's going to live there too."

Chandra picked up the towel on the counter and wrung her hands in it. She wasn't sure how she felt about that.

He was a stranger. Then again, anyone Gabe rented the apartment to would be a stranger. What did that matter really? It had its own entrance. They would just lock off the entrance to the restaurant.

She knew what it was, but she didn't want to admit it to herself. When Mike had walked behind her and touched her shoulders, there had been an electricity that shot clear down to her toes. It was stupid.

The man was not her type, and she wasn't his. Why was she worried about it? Sure, he'd even offered her dinner, but that was because she was helping him out as much as he was helping her and Gabe out.

It would work. Mike was just now a daily fixture and hadn't she been the one to make it that way when she asked him to stick around and fix things while Gabe was away?

"Well, that'll be handy with you fixing stuff around here," she said throwing the towel back down and moving to the sink.

She glanced over her shoulder to see him smiling at her.

Gabe gave the bar a tap with his hand. "I'm going to take him up and show him what I want. Then Madison and I will head home."

"You'd better hurry, or I'm quitting. Holly needs you with her."

"She has her mother there."

Chandra turned and scowled. "Even more reason to hurry. That woman shouldn't be around your wife."

He laughed and started for the stairs to the apartment with Mike following behind, with his bags.

GABE UNLOCKED THE DOOR TO THE APARTMENT AND SET MADISON down to walk around. Mike followed him in, closing the door behind him, and setting the bags on the kitchen table.

"Are you sure Chandra will be okay with me living here?" he asked, and Gabe turned his attention from his daughter to Mike.

"Of course. Not much upsets her routine."

Mike wasn't sure Gabe understood, but that was okay. He'd noticed how nervous his new living arrangement seemed to make her. He'd just have to work to make sure she didn't have a reason to worry about it.

His plans had changed for the day, but if he had a place to rest his head, he could work on the résumé right there at the kitchen table. Once he found a job, he wouldn't be in her way at all. In fact, he probably wouldn't see her too much anyway.

"The apartment is fairly straight forward. Kitchen, living room, bedroom, and bathroom through the bedroom. Whatever is here is yours to use. You might need to buy some sheets, but other than that, you're set to go. This will get you started in the Denver housing market."

"You have no idea how much I appreciate this and I promise to do good work."

"I've seen what you can do. And the fact that you can handle the boss downstairs, that says a lot too."

Maybe she was even more of a spitfire than he'd already thought.

"I'll give you my phone number," Mike said. "You can just call me anytime you need anything done. I can do things for you at your house too if you need with the baby coming and all."

Gabe nodded. "I'd appreciate that. I know Holly has been thinking about painting the dining room. Of course, that's not going to happen until the baby is here and a little older, but..."

"I can paint. My parents owned a B&B. I was raised fixing things."

"You were a good asset that just happened in here then," Gabe said with a smile. He took the keys and handed them to Mike. "These get you inside the door at the end of the stairs and into your apartment. We'll lock the other door to the restaurant. Then no one takes a wrong turn and heads up here instead of the restroom."

"That would be good."

Gabe called for Madison, who had wandered into the bedroom. She toddled out and into her daddy's arms. "C'mon, let's go save Mommy from Grandma."

"Gam-ma!" she happily squealed.

"She spoils her rotten," he admitted. "It's funny how different parents are with their grandkids when they weren't all that attentive with their own kids."

"I can't say I understand that at all. My family life was very solid."

"Mine too. My wife's, well, with her being such a prodigy and all, it just wasn't as normal I guess."

"She sounds pretty normal to me."

Gabe nodded. "She's perfect. Thanks again. I'll check in with you tomorrow."

CHANDRA WATCHED THE STAIRS AND WAITED. GABE HAD BETTER BE coming down soon, or she was going to go up and get him. She didn't like the thought of him not being with Holly, and she disliked the thought of Holly's mother being with her any longer.

A few moments later Gabe emerged with Madison on his hip again.

"Okay, our new tenant has the keys to both sets of doors. You can lock up this bottom one."

"Are you sure about this? We don't know him."

Gabe chuckled. "If I put a for rent sign up we wouldn't know that person either. This one is at least beneficial."

She growled. "You need to get home."

"I'm going." He set Madison on the bar and zipped up her coat. "Can you believe in the next week I'll have another one of these cuties?"

"I can't believe you have that one," she quipped. "But you're a lucky man."

"Don't I know it." He picked Madison up and situated her on his hip. "Tell Chandra bye."

Madison rested her head on Gabe's shoulder. "Bye."

"Bye, sweetheart. Take care of your daddy."

Gabe gave her a wink. "You take care of our tenant."

She watched him walk out the door as three more couples walked in.

What did he mean, take care of our tenant? He was a grown man. He'd gotten there on his own. He damn sure could take care of himself.

As drink orders came in, Chandra kept her eyes on the stairs. He'd need to come down soon. He still had to check out of his hotel. What good was it to keep the room one more night?

She made sure the couples that had walked in were seated by the hostess in a timely matter. Four orders had printed out by her register for her to fill. It was just another day, so why did this one seem to be frazzling her?

It was another hour and a half before she saw Mike again and this time he was walking through the front door.

"Where were you?" she quizzed him in a tone she didn't even like hearing.

"Went and checked out of my hotel."

It was only then she realized he had a small suitcase with him. "That's all you have?"

He laughed. "The rest of my life is in a storage container being shipped here. Albeit a very small shipping container. It should arrive Thursday or Friday. I hate to ask, but are there a few parking spaces behind the building that we could block off for its delivery? I'll get it emptied out as quickly as possible and picked back up."

She blinked a deliberate, long blink. "Um, sure. Gabe keeps a few orange cones by the back door to block parking when we're getting early morning deliveries. Tonight just put a few out."

"I appreciate it," he said as he headed back toward the front door.

"Where are you going?" Chandra called after him.

"Around back."

She let out a huff. "Go through the restaurant. There's no need to trek around back if you don't have to. It's icy back there. You'll fall on your ass."

He chuckled. "I don't want to be a menace."

She thought he already was. She was seriously spending too much time worrying about him for her own good.

"Just go. The lunch rush is over by two. You should be able to get in here and look at the fridge again. I'll have lunch for you too."

"It's a date," he said, grinning as he trudged through the restaurant to the stairs that led to his apartment.

WHEN MIKE PUSHED OPEN THE DOOR OF THE APARTMENT, IT FELT good. Who would have thought a dingy apartment above a restaurant would be home sweet home? But it was exactly that.

Mike set his suitcase on the table and opened it. On top sat a picture of him and Dane taken outside Dane's dorm. It had been prominently displayed in his home in California, traveled with him anywhere he went, and now would be the first personal item he put into his new home.

The mantel over the fireplace would be the perfect place to display the picture. He set it on the dusty wood and stepped back. Yeah, this was a good place for a new beginning.

For the next fifteen minutes, he unpacked. Then looking around, he decided, he should have stayed in the hotel one more night.

He needed sheets, blankets, hangers, and a few plates to eat from. His shipping container wasn't due for two more days.

Now that he wasn't spending money on a hotel room, he could afford to eat in the restaurant a few days so that plates wouldn't be needed. A blanket would be nice, though. Surely there was a store down the street where he could buy one. At least he'd taken all the toiletries out of the hotel before he left.

In the small pantry closet by the kitchen, he found a broom and dustpan. He could at least clean up a bit.

Pulling open the blinds, he surveyed the street below. Pedestrians trudged through the snow. Some were bundled up, and others acted as if this was the norm. And did those kids walking from the Auraria campus have on shorts?

He'd like to open the window, but his California blood would certainly freeze if he did so. In time, he figured he'd be used to the snow, just like the rest of them on the street, but he'd never be caught dead wearing shorts in it, though.

His cell phone rang, and he pulled it from his pocket. That warmth he'd been thinking about filled his body when he looked at the caller ID and saw Dane's name.

"Hey kiddo. What's new?"

"Hey, Dad. I'm checking in on you," he mimicked Mike's voice. "How's the new job?"

"Fell through," Mike said as he sat on the couch. "So I'm job searching right now."

"Fell through? That's crap, man. How do they expect you to move out there and not have a job? Are you coming back? You could stay with us."

And that was why he loved this kid so much. "I just moved into a new place about twenty minutes ago."

"Seriously? You're staying?"

"Sure am. It's snowing, too. You could come ski."

There was a thoughtful hum on the other end of the line. "We could do that. What about a job?"

"Right now I'm doing some handyman stuff for a restaurant. I'll get my résumé out there this week, and we'll see what happens."

"Dang, Dad. You've been relegated to handyman?"

"Don't knock it, kid."

"Yeah, yeah. Are the women hot there?"

Mike laughed and leaned back. "I haven't met a lot of women. Just one."

"What's she like?"

Mike closed his eyes, and she came right to mind. "Small little thing covered in tattoos and a long braid down her back."

There was a groan. "Oh, ain't what I was talking about. I thought there were snow bunnies there. You got biker chicks."

First impressions were a bitch, he thought. "She might be, but she's the nicest person I've ever met. Took me in. Got me a job and a place. Feeds me."

The line went quiet for a beat. "Dad, are you sleeping with this lady?" Dane whispered in the phone.

"What? Where'd you get that? Pull your head out of the gutter."

"You said she took you in. Kinda sudden."

"I mean she took pity on me and helped me out. Besides, I'm a grown man and…"

"Yeah. Don't want to hear it. Hard enough knowing Mom's dating."

And that was the blow that knocked the wind out of his lungs. "Dating?"

"Thought you knew."

"None of my business."

"It's all creeping me out. So, if you're staying, can I come out on spring break?"

The pain of the comment before that eased. "I'd love that."

"Cool. I'm glad you're doing okay. Offer stands. If your biker chick doesn't work out. You can live with us."

Mike chuckled. "Love you, bud. Thanks."

"Love you, too."

Mike disconnected the call and slid his phone back into his pocket. He'd head down to the restaurant and see if there was anything he could help out with.

The door between the stairwell to his apartment and the restaurant hadn't yet been locked. For today, since she'd insisted he use it earlier, he'd go through the restaurant.

It wasn't quite two o'clock, but the lunch crowd seemed to have died down. Tables were cleared off, and the wait staff was busy cleaning up.

Chandra was wiping down the bar when he walked over to it and sat down. "How was your lunch rush?"

"Pathetic by normal terms. But this fridge is toast. I don't see any problems if you want to get started on it."

"Works for me. I'll get the bag Gabe had and the tools." He climbed down and pushed the stool in. "So is there a department store close by? I need to get a few things before my container comes."

"What kinds of things?"

"Blanket. Maybe some sheets and some towels. A few extra never hurt anyway."

She puckered her lips as though she were giving something

some deep thought. "Do you mind some loaners? I'd be happy to set you up with some bedding and some towels. Why buy things you have coming?"

"That's thoughtful of you. Are you sure? You're not off for hours."

She shrugged. "I can get it here. Do you like chocolate chip cookies?"

"Never met one I didn't like," he joked, and she laughed.

She had a beautiful laugh. He wondered how often it came out.

Tossing down her rag, she picked up her cell phone. "What do you usually eat for breakfast?"

"Coffee."

She lifted her eyes to meet his. "That's not healthy. You should always have breakfast."

"Just have been too busy the past few years to think about it."

"You're living in a health-conscious state now. Start thinking about it," she scolded. "Do you like cereal?"

"Always did."

"Choices might be limited to anything that has a prize in the box."

Now he laughed. "You're getting breakfast for me?"

"Until you get your shipment. There is a store about five blocks from here."

"I saw it on my journey to the hardware store."

"I have a lead on a car too if you decide you need one soon."

Mike leaned his arms on the bar. "I've never been without a car. It's a little bothersome having to think out my travel plans, but I don't have a paying job yet."

"Car will be there if you decide at any time."

"Are you this nice to everyone you meet?"

"No," she was quick to answer. "You're proving to be a solid asset around here. I appreciate it."

He gave the bar a tap. "Thank you. My son probably thanks you too. He's worried about me out here alone."

"You're a grown man. I think you can handle it."

"Sure. But if I can't, he's invited me to live with him."

Her eyes went soft, and she moved toward the bar where he was standing on the opposite side. "He's a good kid, isn't he?"

"The best. Called to check up on me. I didn't call first."

"That's very special." She looked back at the screen of her phone. "Your items will be here in time for dinner. Do you like meatloaf?"

He crinkled up his nose. "Let's say it wasn't one of my wife's specialties."

"It's one of my mom's. She'll bring it with the bedding, and we'll all have dinner upstairs at your place."

It squeezed at his heart that she was doing this for him. "Thank you. Are you sure about all of that? Is your mother okay to drive in this snow?"

That made her laugh as she tucked her cell phone into her back pocket. "She's a native of Colorado. She'll be just fine. It'll be a good break for me to be with them too. A few more weeks and I'll have my normal schedule back."

"Well, I really appreciate it," he said moving from the bar to gather his tools.

"I'll have some cheap labor for you too when you get your shipping container."

"Your son?"

She nodded. "Are you good with math?"

"Of course."

"He needs some help with his homework. It could be a very good trade for both of you," she said as she took an order off the printer and began putting it together.

Mike smiled as he walked away. Wasn't it funny that a lost opportunity turned into something new and wonderful?

THE REFRIGERATOR HADN'T TAKEN LONG TO FIX. IT WASN'T GOING to be a permanent fix though either. Gabe was going to have to shell out the money for a new one fairly soon. But judging from the constant stream of patrons into the restaurant, Mike assumed that wouldn't be a problem.

He'd just started working on the railing at the end of the bar when the door opened to the restaurant and a boy in a Denver Broncos hoodie, with a grocery bag in each hand, and a woman carrying twice as many bags, walked in.

The hostess greeted them by name but didn't try to seat them.

They both walked straight to the bar, passed by him, and behind the bar to Chandra.

"Hey, handsome!" Chandra put her hands on the boy's cheeks and gave him a noisy kiss, to which he shook his face as if he'd seen a bee. "Hello, Mama." She kissed the woman on the cheek and took the bags from her hands.

"Where's Gabe?" The boy looked around.

"Waiting for his new baby."

"That's taking forever," he said as he dropped the bags right where he stood.

"I'm sure Holly would agree." She turned to the woman. "How are the roads?"

The woman who had a gray braid that traveled over her shoulder, much like Chandra's, lifted her brows. "I drove a rig through the blizzard of eighty-two. This was nothing."

Chandra laughed as if she'd heard that story a million times. And then she shifted her eyes to him.

"Mom and Jason, this is Mike. He's the new tenant upstairs."

Mike put down the screwdriver and wiped his hands on the rag that Gabe kept in the bucket of tools.

Jason scanned a look over him from head to toe. "You live here?"

"Gabe rented me the apartment upstairs," he said extending his hand to the boy. "I'm Mike."

"Jason," he said giving his hand a firm grip.

The woman walked closer to him. "Chandra's mother," she said holding out her hand to him. "Esther."

"It's a pleasure to meet you, Esther. Did I hear you say you drove a rig?"

She laughed a deep laugh, perhaps an old smoker's laugh, though he didn't smell the scent on her now.

"Hauled lumber from Oregon to New Mexico."

"Through the Rockies?"

She smiled wide. "Best damn ride ever. Chandra was a tyke. She'd ride with me in the summers, and we'd camp along the way. Her daddy had his own rig," Esther said. "We lost him in Wyoming in a pileup. Some snow storms are worse than others."

Mike saw the flash of sadness move over Esther's face, and just as quickly Chandra turned her back to them and picked up her rag.

"Enough about snow storms. I have a meatloaf, some potatoes, salad, and a loaf of bread. I hear you have a place we can eat it."

"I sure do. I don't have any dishes."

"Jason has a bag of paper plates that'll last you until your stuff arrives."

"That sounds great. What can I carry?"

Jason picked up the bags he'd dropped on the floor and handed them to Mike. "Here. Carry these," he said as he handed them to him and walked off toward the staircase in the hallway.

Mike laughed. "Can I help you with any of yours?"

"I've got this," Esther said as she looked back at Chandra. "You taking a break to eat with us?"

"I'll be up in ten minutes."

Esther gave her a nod and started for the stairs.

Mike looked back once more at Chandra before he followed. He watched her wipe her eyes as she motioned to someone to cover the bar.

Losing her father must have been a traumatic event to still shake her up like that. It was obvious she was close to her mother, and they evened the weight on each other's shoulders. Something told him, Chandra wasn't the kind of woman to take that kind of relationship for granted.

CHAPTER 5

*J*ason walked through the door to the apartment, and his grandmother and Mike followed behind him, carrying all the bags.

"This is where you're going to live?" he asked with his nose crinkled up.

"Yeah. You don't like it?"

He shrugged. "It's really small."

Esther nudged him out of the way. "It's a nice apartment, and I guess Mike will make it even better. Trust me, kid, when you grow up, you'll beg Gabe to let you live here."

"I doubt it," he said as he pulled his cell phone out of his pocket and plopped himself down on the couch.

Esther turned to Mike and shook her head. "I despise those damn phones. Minecraft is all I ever hear about."

"I'm fairly sure if they were around when we were kids we'd have looked the same," he said knowing full and well he too would have been addicted to Minecraft.

"The meatloaf needs a warm up. Can you start the oven?" she asked as she pulled the dish from a canvas bag.

Mike studied the oven for a moment and then pushed the

buttons he assumed would kick it into gear. "I think that's it. I wonder how long it's been since this has been on."

"At least two years. That's when Gabe moved out."

"Perfect bachelor pad, that's for sure."

"Now he's having a second baby." She smiled wide. "Lucky man to have found Holly."

"Haven't met her, but between Gabe and Chandra, I've heard good things."

"It was a one-night stand kind of deal," she whispered as if to make sure Jason wasn't hearing her. But when Mike looked his way, he knew that he was engrossed in what he was doing.

"I suppose that works out sometimes," he said.

"She was pregnant when she came looking for him. Didn't even know his name. Wasn't either of their styles to have done that. I suppose sometimes our hearts know what we want long before our brains do."

"I couldn't agree more."

Esther took a set of sheets from another canvas bag and handed them to Mike. "We have a closet full of these. So don't worry about returning them—ever. It'll save you some money too."

"I appreciate it."

She looked around the apartment. "I have an entire window of plants too. I'll bring you one. You need something homey here. I see you have one picture."

He chuckled. "I'll have about three more when my storage unit arrives."

Esther walked toward the mantle and looked at the one picture he'd put there. "Your son?"

"Yeah. Dane. He's living the dream on my dollar."

She laughed. "Going to college huh? What's he studying?"

"Engineering. He's either going to be an astronaut, a video game designer or teach middle school history."

"None of it sounds too shabby," she said as the door opened and Chandra walked through.

"Meatloaf is going to warm up," Esther told her. "Go help Mike get his room together and take that bag there," she pointed to another bag they'd carried in. "It's got some toiletries and necessities."

Chandra nodded and walked straight to the bedroom. Mike took that as his cue to follow.

"Thanks for all of this."

"You're helping me out. It's the least I could do."

She stood on one side of the bed, and he on the other. He pulled out the fitted sheet, and they managed it on the mattress, but not without some difficulty.

He learned a lot about her as they made the bed. She was a hospital corner kind of woman, and he was a throw the blankets on the bed kind of man.

She fluffed up the pillow they'd brought him when she put the pillow case on it and readjusted the quilt after he'd simply pulled it up over the sheets.

Chandra then took the bag into the bathroom, and he followed.

"She thinks of everything," she laughed as she opened the medicine cabinet. "You have everything you need in here. Toothpaste, toothbrush, mouthwash, Advil, a razor, and shaving cream. What does she think you've been doing, coming in dirty and unprepared?"

"Your mother is a very kind woman. I've picked up that much in the few minutes I've been around her."

Chandra's expression softened. "I'd be lost without her. She's taken care of Jason and me. I couldn't do what I do if she weren't with us."

He'd never mention it, but he was sure he'd just seen her eyes moisten.

"Do you have a shower curtain coming?"

He looked at the small shower. "No. I had a door on my last shower."

She nodded and dug into the bag. "She thought of everything," she said as she pulled out a brand new shower curtain.

"I didn't want her to have to buy things. I need to know how much to pay her back."

Chandra laughed. "You think she went out and bought this? No. She hoards this kind of stuff just for this reason."

"Just in case a man like me comes along."

Her cheeks grew pink. "You have no idea how close you are to getting that right."

Chandra reached for the shower rod, but she'd have had to jump to pull it down.

"I've got that," he said moving in behind her, brushing up against her as they had in the bar. As quickly as she moved away from him, he knew she'd felt that spark again. How could he even blame her?

"Here," she handed him the curtain. "I'm going to help Mom with dinner."

Mike continued to attach the curtain to the rod after Chandra had run out.

"Can I use the bathroom?" Jason stood in the doorway and looked at him.

"Yeah, let me just put this back up," he said pushing the rod, now with the curtain hanging from it, back up between the walls.

"My mom must like you," Jason suggested as he leaned against the wall with his hands behind his back.

"What makes you say that?"

Jason shrugged. "She's only dated a few guys, and she's only ever brought home one of them. That's why I think she likes you. She's letting us meet you, and she brought you all this stuff."

"Your mom's a nice woman. And, I'm not dating her, so I suppose it's okay if she's nice to me and I get to meet you."

"You're not dating her?"

"No. I just met her. She's been very nice to help me out."

"She sure talks about you a lot," he offered as Mike moved out of the bathroom and Jason closed the door.

He stood there for a moment thinking about that. What could she have possibly said in two days that would make her son think he was a boyfriend?

The thought gave him a little jolt of happiness. At least someone appreciated him.

The small table set up in the small kitchen of the apartment had been set for dinner. A warmth, which Mike hadn't felt in a very long time, washed over him. Once Dane had become busy in high school, he and his wife—ex-wife—had stopped having family meals. He couldn't even remember the last time he'd sat at a table like this.

"Everything is ready," Esther gave him a nod. "Sit. We will eat in just a moment."

"Is there anything else I can help with?"

"Tomorrow, you can count on it. Tonight, just enjoy."

Jason ran from the other room, pulled out a chair, and sat down as if he were playing musical chairs. Mike pulled out the chair closest to Esther, and she sat.

"Thank you."

"My pleasure."

He quickly moved and reached for the next chair at the same time as Chandra. She snapped a look at him. "Were you going to sit here?"

"No, I was pulling out your seat for you."

The crease between her brows eased. "Thank you. I'm not used to that."

"You should be," he said as she took her seat and he took the last.

He'd caught the approving grin from her mother and the look of confusion from Jason.

Perhaps there was something still to teach a young man. He

thought of Dane and his offer to let him live with him. There was proof he'd done a good job with one kid—but then the thought backfired.

He looked at Chandra who scooped potatoes onto her plate and absentmindedly handed him the bowl. One meal and he was raising her son? He was sure she'd have a lot to say about his thoughts on that.

They weren't seeing each other. They weren't a couple. He'd wandered into her bar broken and alone, and it was obvious by her mother's outpouring, that she was raised to take care of people. He was an idiot to think there was more to it.

"Can I have some of those?" Jason asked, and Mike snapped from his thought to see them all staring at him.

"Yeah, sorry. Guess I was thinking too hard." He smiled and handed the potatoes to Jason.

"What's on your mind?" Esther asked as she took a bite of meatloaf.

"My son, I guess."

"How old?"

"Nineteen," he said with an immediate smile forming on his lips.

"It shows you're proud of him."

"I am. Just as proud of him as she is of this one." He nodded toward Jason.

"Eh, she's not proud of me. I hate math," Jason protested.

He heard Chandra take the breath to argue, so he interrupted. "Math is hard."

"Yeah, it is. I hate it."

"Nah, you just don't like it."

Jason let out a huff. "That's what I said."

"No, you said you hated it. Hate is an ugly word. It's like a common four letter word. I'll bet when you put your mind to it you can do the math, you just don't like to."

Jason shrugged. "Yeah, I guess."

He could feel Chandra's eyes on him, and he turned to catch her stare. Silently she mouthed, thank you, and once again that feeling of warmth washed over him.

CHANDRA LISTENED TO HER MOTHER TALK ABOUT THE LINE AT THE grocery store earlier. Jason said something about throwing the football at lunch recess and everyone started to call him Peyton Manning. Then Mike's voice broke through her muddled mind.

"Your mom says you could help me on Saturday. I get all my stuff."

"What stuff?"

"My big moving container arrives."

Jason groaned. "You volunteered me to do that? I have an indoor soccer game."

Chandra nodded. "Right. I knew that."

"Bud, I have enough stuff it'll last till after soccer," he laughed. "Who do you play for?"

"YMCA. Nothing big. Just for fun. We can't afford a real league."

Chandra pointed her fork at him. "Hey, it's a good team."

Jason shrugged. "Yeah." He looked up at Mike. "You wanna come?"

"To your game?"

"Yeah. What else do you have to do?"

Mike laughed, and so did her mother. "I'd love to. I'll get the address from your mom and figure out my bus route."

"I could take you with me," she said without even thinking about it.

"Then yeah, I'll go."

What had she just done? She had to work. She couldn't take off. Then she listened to the conversation shift.

Oh, they were still talking soccer, but Jason's voice had a different tone. He was telling Mike all about the last game—

47

which she'd missed. He was on some kind of high. Was it because this man was going to watch him play? That was ridiculous. He didn't know Mike. She didn't know Mike. Why should it matter that he—she sucked in a hard breath. He was taking time out for Jason.

Suddenly the past two days became a jumbled mess in her head. How had she let herself be dragged in by this man? Now her family was involved.

Her mother had furnished his apartment and cooked him dinner. Her son was making plans with him and she—well, she didn't have anything to do with him, really.

This was nothing.

There was nothing to get worked up over.

He was a nice man who was lost in the world right at the moment. She'd offered a helping hand, and he'd repaid her. Story over.

Mike reached out and touched her hand. That zip of electricity ran up her arm and right to her chest.

"Are you okay?"

"Yep. I'm fine." She pulled her hand away. "I'm all good. I should check on the bar. I need to see what they are—yeah, they need me."

She pushed back from the table and left the apartment as fast as her short legs would allow.

She hadn't seen this coming she thought as she ran down the stairs. She liked him. More than just the flirting from the day before. Something had happened to her heart, and now she was at a loss for words or even how to feel. There were too many other important things happening in her life, and even involving a man in them—regardless of who he was or how nice he was— wasn't that important.

She kept people away from her family, so why had she brought Mike into it? She'd even asked him to tutor Jason.

Now thinking about how Jason reacted to him, maybe that would still be a good thing.

No! She pushed her way behind the bar and took the first order that printed up.

It had to end, right now. If Mike was going to live upstairs, then that's all he was going to do.

She knew enough people from the restaurant that had great businesses. Maybe she could help get him a job, something other than handyman work.

Chandra pulled out two bottles of import beers and flicked the tops off them. This, she thought, was where she belonged, behind the bar working and making plans in her head.

Calm began to take over again. She wasn't going to think about Mike for the rest of the night.

CHAPTER 6

*M*ike sat in the apartment watching Netflix on his computer since Chandra had kindly offered up the guest Wi-Fi password. In a few more days he'd have some of his own luxuries, but for now, he was grateful for all the things he had.

There was a lot of restaurant noise, but he didn't figure he'd ever mind that. It was another thing to be grateful for.

Esther and Jason had left only a half hour after Chandra had. He again had promised Jason he'd be at his game on Saturday and he'd in turn, perhaps under the slightest protest, agreed to help Mike unload his storage container.

Very cleverly, Mike had slid in the bit about helping with his math, and he'd been responsive. That was all he could ask for.

Mike looked at his watch. It was nine-thirty. On a week night, the restaurant closed at ten, but he knew that meant doors didn't lock until at least eleven-thirty. He wondered if there was anything he could help with. He'd certainly rather feel useful than alone.

Putting the key to the door in his pocket, he went down the

steps only to find that the door between the restaurant and the staircase had been closed and locked.

There was no denying that it was a disappointment, but that was how it was to be. He'd just go through the kitchen.

Mike let himself out of the door that lead to the alley and then back in through the open kitchen door.

The staff was busy cleaning the stoves and the dishes. Another man was mopping the floors and another taking inventory of the cooler.

It was fun to see the other side of businesses.

Chandra was still behind the bar. She had her head down studying that clipboard she'd had in her hands when the rep had arrived earlier that morning. He watched her make notes, check another area, and make more notes.

"Looks like you'll get home early tonight."

She lifted her head, but her eyes weren't as warm as he'd grown accustomed to. "What do you need?"

He realized very quickly it had been a mistake to wander downstairs. Now he was just in the way.

"Just thought I'd offer to help out if there was anything you guys needed a hand with."

"We do this every single night. This night is no different," she spat out the words then went back to work on her list.

"Got it. If anything comes up…" He stopped as she lifted her eyes to meet his. "You know where I'm at."

Something had changed since she'd offered to have his apartment furnished and dinner made for him. Mike turned and headed for the front door this time.

"Wait," Chandra called after him, and he turned back to her. "I'm sorry. Thank you for the offer. It was very kind of you."

"Sure. Offer always stands," he said making sure to attach his best smile—hoping it didn't look like a dopey dog or something.

"I should ask you if you need anything."

"Me? I think you set me up very well. I can't imagine I'd ever need anything."

"The door at the end of the stairs is secure. No one should bother you."

"I noticed. Nothing will bother me. I'll just head back up to watch some Netflix and do a little more job hunting."

"Any luck yet?"

"Few leads I think I'll follow up on in the morning."

He watched as she worried her lip. "I'll be here around nine-thirty if you want to come down for some coffee," she offered.

Now he knew the smile on his face was genuine. "I'd like that. I'll see you in the morning."

This time he left the restaurant, through the front door, walked around the building, and back up to his apartment. The thought crossed his mind as he walked toward the windows and looked down at the street, which still had people out walking in the snow in the dark now, who watched her leave each night? It was silly to think that she'd be alone going to her car, but it bothered him.

Certainly, there was a process. And even more, she'd probably done it for years.

So why should he worry?

But he did.

There was no way he'd get any sleep until he knew she was in her car and safely driving home.

~

CHANDRA HAD SEEN MIKE'S CURTAINS MOVE AS SHE PULLED OUT OF the alley and drove down the street. There should be some comfort in someone keeping an eye out for her, but she wasn't used to it, and she wasn't sure she liked it much.

This was all her fault. She'd worked very hard for the past ten years to keep men out of her life. Who would have thought one would waltz right in?

Again, she'd done that to herself. There was nothing between her and Mike. He was a nice guy. He liked his ex-wife and loved his son. Things were just a bit sketchy for him right now, and she'd helped ease that pain a bit.

Why didn't she see if for what it was—a friendship.

Jason had taken to him, and so had her mom. Why wouldn't they? He was a nice guy. It seemed her attitude needed a check at the door.

Just because a man walked into her life, off the street, and when he smiled at her, her insides turned to goo, or if he brushed by her and a shot of electricity went through her, it didn't mean she was in love. All it meant was she didn't have to be on the defensive with him. Mike was just a nice guy, she considered again.

Her mind seemed to wrap around that explanation of her mood the best. She was just overworked, a little tired, and a whole lot of cranky. Then again, she was known for being just a bit cranky all the time.

As she parked her car, she noticed the kitchen light was still on. Seriously, why didn't anyone in her house go to bed?

Jason looked up at her as she opened the back door and walked into the kitchen.

"Before you say it, I know, I'm supposed to be in bed."

She set her bag on the kitchen chair in front of her. "Okay, I won't say it. So why are you up?"

"The game on Saturday is a big one. Do you think I'll score?"

She swallowed hard. He hadn't scored in nearly two seasons. "This could be the game."

"But I want to. I want to score so Mike can see it."

That stung a little, she thought. Didn't he want to score for her?

"I suppose you'll have to focus then. And I don't think he'll be disappointed if you don't score."

He nodded. "I know. I told him I'd let him help me with my math this weekend too."

And that was when she'd decided Mike was the master at parental manipulation. He'd convinced Jason that it was a favor to him. "I think that's a great plan. You have to help him move too."

Jason shrugged. "I'm strong enough for that." For a moment there was silence, but Chandra knew it was only because Jason had more on his mind. "He said you're not dating him."

Chandra gripped the back of the kitchen chair. "I never said I was."

"I know. You just don't introduce us to guys."

"None of them are as important as you."

He smiled at that. She was fairly sure he knew it to be true.

"I don't suppose I'll ever find a wife as awesome as you either, Mom." And the kid had a way with words. She kissed him atop his head.

"Thanks. Now go to bed. It's late."

Jason stood and pushed in his chair. "So that you know, if you want to date him, it's okay."

He'd stunned her into silence as he walked away.

What was she supposed to do with that?

She pulled out the chair next to her and sat down. Right now wasn't even the time to think about all of this. Maybe if Mike was still around after Gabe came back to work and if she decided that it was a good idea, then she'd think about Mike in that way. But since she'd just convinced herself that there was nothing between them, she wasn't about to let herself get worked up over what her kid thought.

She sat in the quiet of the house and closed her eyes. Every single part of her was tired. Maybe after Gabe came back to work, she could take a week off. Of course, she'd have to convince him to pay her for that week off, but maybe it would happen.

The thought humored her as she stood and walked to her bedroom to put another day behind her.

CHAPTER 7

*M*ike had been in town long enough to know that the city woke early. He'd never known a trash dumpster to be emptied at six o'clock in the morning, but the one behind the restaurant was.

It didn't matter much the time. He'd been awake since three. Lack of sleep could be blamed on the new living area. That fear that when you woke and you didn't know where you were. But he knew that wasn't it. Chandra had been on his mind.

No sleep had proven to be a benefit. He'd located four jobs he'd be sending his résumé in for and, it was hard to believe, but somewhere between ten o'clock the night before and three that morning, he'd had someone ask for an interview.

He'd mapped out his plan to get to the Denver Tech Center, which wasn't even close to where he was. Light rail could get him there, but he'd have to walk a bit to get to the building he needed. In the end, most of his day would be spent getting to this one interview, in the cold, and in the snow.

Was it worth it? He pondered that for a while. Yes. It was absolutely worth it.

Luckily the interview wasn't until two o'clock. That would give him the better part of the day to get there.

He was missing his coffee maker. At least it would arrive tomorrow, he hoped. For now, he decided to walk down the street for a cup of coffee. By the time he returned, Chandra should be at the restaurant. Maybe she'd have some helpful tips as to how to get to his interview.

~

CHANDRA SIGNED FOR THE BEER DELIVERY, WHICH WAS EARLY FOR A change. She started a pot of coffee and turned on the TV over the bar to watch the news. For some reason, this morning she needed the distraction.

It was nearly ten o'clock, and she was sure Mike would have been down to see her by now—not that it mattered.

Gabe had emailed her the list he'd made of things he wanted to be done to the apartment. She'd give it to Mike if he ever came down.

A moment later there was a knock at the front door. There he stood. His cheeks were red from the cold. She walked to the door, unlocked it, and let him in.

"You can come in the back door. You don't have to walk around."

He handed her a small bag. "Went to get coffee this morning. Had one of these muffins and thought you'd like one too. Have it later if you'd like."

He pulled off his coat and draped it over his arm.

She looked him over. "You're dressed nicely."

"I have an interview."

"Today? Where?"

"Denver Tech Center. Software development company."

"Tech Center? How are you getting there?"

He pulled a folded piece of paper out of his pocket and

opened it. "I figured this all out. If I catch the light rail from the station, I should get a direct train out. Now, I still will have nearly a mile to walk, but…"

"This is not a plan." Her voice shook just as it did when she disagreed with Jason or her mother.

His eyes were wide. "It's the first interview I've had. It's a plan."

"No. I mean you can't go walking a mile in dress shoes in the snow."

He chuckled. "Today, it's my option."

"You can use my car."

Now he narrowed his gaze on her. "That's very nice. I'll be just fine. I have to get around on my own and…"

"Use the damn car, would ya. I'm here until ten-thirty tonight anyway. It's not like you won't be back."

Mike ran his fingers over his chin and studied her. She didn't like it one bit.

"If you don't want to then fine. Walk in the cold," she said as she turned from him.

He caught her arm and stopped her. "Are you upset about something? Did I do something? You seemed mad at me last night too."

Oh, this wasn't happening. Some man holds her back and looks for answers.

"I'm just trying to be nice, damn it," she said pulling her arm from his hand. She looked at the keys in her hand and then began to slide the car key off the ring. "I know you know which car. You watched me drive away in it last night."

He winced. Yep, he'd been watching her just as she'd thought.

Mike took the key when she offered it. "I really appreciate this. What do you say to dinner upstairs again tonight? This time I will cook."

"Jason has soccer practice."

"Are you taking him?"

"No. My mother will take him. I'll be here."

"Then dinner for just the two of us. Let me do that for you. This is big for me."

She huffed out a breath as she walked back to the bar. "Fine. I can get away about eight."

"I'll have it ready."

Chandra pushed the printed paper with the email on it toward him. "This is Gabe's list for the apartment."

Mike took it and looked it over. "Seems reasonable. He gave me his number, so I'll give him a call and talk it over with him."

"Do that."

"I will." He smiled. Damn it, he smiled. "I'm going upstairs to replan my route. I'll be back down in about twenty minutes to fix the faucet on the sink in the kitchen."

"Who told you there was something wrong with it?"

"The guy using it. I have my own little list started." He winked this time before he walked away and disappeared into the kitchen.

MIKE WASN'T SURE WHY IT WAS SO REWARDING TO GET UNDER Chandra's skin, but it was. Perhaps because she seemed like the kind of woman who wouldn't let anyone get to her—and yet he did.

He climbed the steps to his apartment as his cell phone rang. It seemed like the day was getting even better. The moving company would be delivering his container in the morning. Things were almost normal again, he thought.

It only took him ten minutes to reroute his trip to the Tech Center and another twenty to plan out a menu for dinner. He'd never thought to ask if there was something she wouldn't, or couldn't eat. He'd ask when he went back down to fix the faucet.

Mike changed his clothes and headed down to the kitchen to fix the faucet.

The kitchen was bustling with everyone getting ready for the lunch rush. He was going to be in the way, but he knew if he got in and out, the rush would go smoother.

He settled in and got to work.

There was a multitude of different languages being spoken around him. He'd forgotten how much fun it could be to be mixed in with different people from all over the world. For years he'd been in his office and then downsized to a cubicle. It had been lonely. The people he worked with had big educations, but little personality, and yet here he was chasing that dream all over again.

Giving the wrench a turn, he thought about what his parents did while he was growing up. The bed and breakfast was always filled with different people. They traveled far and wide to visit the area. What an awesome thing to have when he was growing up. It was sad that he was now late into his forties and just figuring out how amazing it was to have had that.

His life then wasn't too different than Chandra's now, he supposed. People walked in and out every day from somewhere, and she'd greet them on their journey.

He finished the faucet and checked it before turning it back over to José who moved right back in and began prepping.

It felt good to be part of something that wasn't cold like coding. There was satisfaction in seeing José's face when the faucet worked again, and he could do his job. That wasn't something Mike had the pleasure of seeing when he developed software. In fact, the few times he'd been on call and received the angry words from an end user, there was no satisfaction in his career at that moment—or lack of career as the case might be.

Mike gathered his tools and walked them back up to the apartment. He then cleaned up and put back on his suit.

Chandra was knee-deep in orders when he walked back downstairs to the bar.

"I'm going to head out. Can I get anything for you on my way back?"

She shook her head so that the ponytail flipped from side to side. "I'm good. I'm busy."

"I see that. Any food allergies?"

She looked up at him as she mixed a drink with a bottle in each hand. "What?"

"For dinner tonight."

"Oh. That. I forgot. You don't have to do that."

"Already planned out. Just wanted to ask. You let me know if something comes up. Have a nice lunch rush." He winked as he swung on his coat and headed out to Chandra's car.

CHANDRA WATCHED HIM WALK OUT THE DOOR WITH THAT GRIN plastered on his face. It irritated her, but she knew that was her own irritation at play. She was only mad because, unlike everyone else in her life, when she switched to bitch mode, he hadn't seemed to be bothered by it.

Well, she was bothered by it, and that made it worse. The man was just trying to be nice and do the job she'd set him up to do.

He was off to interview for a job. Once he got it, then he wouldn't be under foot, and she wouldn't have to worry about him getting in her way. Yes, that's how it would be.

Dinner would be nice since she'd forget to eat if he didn't feed her. Some conversation that didn't have to do with running the restaurant would be nice too.

She turned to pull a beer from the draft, and take a deep breath. The man hadn't come into her life to try and take it over. He wasn't there to use Jason as a ploy to get her into bed. He had his own family to worry about.

Chandra looked up as the door opened and two familiar faces walked in.

Her mother smiled as she hugged the hostess and then moved

toward the bar. The woman with her, Tracy Briggs waved, her zillion bangle bracelets chiming as she did so.

"Hello, sweetheart." Her mother leaned in over the bar and hugged her.

"Mom, what are you guys doing here?"

Tracy leaned in and hugged her as well. "We thought it was time to meet for lunch. It's been awhile since we've done so."

The two women sat down.

"Can I have a Blue Moon?" her mother asked.

"You're going to drink?"

She narrowed her eyes at Chandra. "It's lunch time. I'm out with my friend. I don't have to pick up Jason until three. I promise only to have one. Now, bartender, may I have a Blue Moon?"

Chandra growled and turned her attention to Tracy.

"Hot water, honey."

Chandra nodded. That meant Tracy had some herbal tea concoction in her purse.

She poured the water for Tracy and placed the orange atop the glass for her mother's beer, then served them.

The two women at the bar were both in their fifties. There wasn't a speck of color on their faces or in their hair. Her mother's hair was pulled back. Silver and black strands weaved together to create a braid that traveled toward her waist. Under the leather jacket, she wore, was a Harley Davidson shirt Chandra had given her. It was from Sturgis, and a patron had brought it back for her.

Tracy, on the other hand, had jewelry on every finger and bracelets nearly all the way up her arm. Her earrings dangled and also chimed as she shook her head.

Her hair was just as long as Chandra's mother's, only it flowed freely with its own natural curl. She had on a flowy, cotton blouse, and a tie-dyed skirt. She was practical though. Unlike some of the women in the restaurant who still wore heels in the snow, Tracy had on a pair of big snow boots.

The two women had met when Gabe and Holly had their first baby. Tracy, who owned a textile company, was Holly's boss and surrogate mother—the kind that pampered and didn't belittle, as Holly's actual mother tended to do.

Chandra had always laughed. The biker chick and the hippie had become quick, and dear friends. And why not? They were two of the most down to earth, and lovely ladies anyone could ever meet.

She felt her bitterness ease as she leaned in to take their orders.

Chandra filled a few more orders and served a few more drinks before the food was brought out to her mother and Tracy.

Tracy reached for Chandra's hand as she refilled her hot water. "Your mom tells me there is a nice gentleman living upstairs now."

"Did she?"

Her mother grinned, and it warmed Chandra's heart to see her do so.

"Yeah, he's a nice guy. He's out on an interview right now, so hopefully, he'll be an employed man soon."

Tracy's eyes opened wide. "I thought he worked for Gabe."

"He's helping out. Seems to have gotten stranded here without a job."

"I heard Jason likes him," she said as she unrolled her silver-ware from the napkin and placed it on her lap.

Chandra looked at her mother, who kept her eyes and her smile diverted.

"Jason likes him just fine. Is there anything else I can get you ladies?"

Tracy reached out to her again and gave her hand a squeeze. "Have you found me a rich old man yet? I really want a rich old man to take care of me."

Now Chandra chuckled. "You've been asking that for the past two years. I seem to be falling short in that department."

Tracy eased back. "Maybe he doesn't have to be old. But he has to appreciate the Grateful Dead."

That had both Tracy and her mother laughing. Chandra shook her head with a smile and went back to work.

CHAPTER 8

$\mathcal{M}$ ike was no fool when it came to reading a map, but damn if he could find his way around the area they called the Denver Tech Center. He'd merged onto one highway, only to find himself on another, and then the sign read Colorado Springs.

He cursed as he turned off on another street to find a parking lot where he could recalculate his route.

With a call to the office where he was headed, he started back around, and a half hour later he found the location he'd been looking for—across the street.

One thing he'd always been taught was to be plenty early, especially if he didn't know where he was going. It seemed as though mom's words of wisdom were the savior for the day. That meant he'd better call her and let her know he was thinking of her.

He checked his appearance in the mirror and laughed wondering if Chandra ever did that. She didn't seem like the kind of woman to use the mirror for anything but backing up. Then again, she didn't need a mirror. She was naturally the most beautiful woman he'd ever met.

And with that thought, he shook his head. This was no time for daydreaming about the bartender. He had a job to land.

The campus of offices reminded him of back home where he'd become a number on a time card and a cubicle in a sea of nameless workers.

It should have felt like home, but it was quite depressing.

The reception area was filled with job applicants. And here he'd thought he held something special to get an invite. Obviously, they were thinning the heard, and at the moment he looked like the oldest applicant in the room.

Mike checked in with the receptionist who offered him a drink, which he turned down. No need to spill coffee on the only clean suit he had.

The younger applicants moved in and out of the office until he was the last one waiting. Perhaps he should have just walked out with them. This had disaster written all over it.

"Mr. Cavanagh?" The woman behind the desk said, and he raised his head from the copy of the *5280* magazine he'd picked up to read. "They're ready for you."

Mike laid the magazine back on the pile and followed the receptionist into a conference room just down the hall.

Finally, he thought, men who were his age.

"Mr. Cavanagh?" The first man stood to shake his hand. He was dressed casually in a pair of khakis and a polo shirt with the company's name on it. "Peter Roberts, CEO."

Mike shook his hand. "It's nice to meet you."

The other's shook his hand and introduced themselves. He knew he wouldn't remember names, but it was Peter Roberts that was important. He'd been through this process before.

The interview began with basic questions about his previous jobs and lead to the story of his being in Colorado looking for a job. The usual education questions and interests, and of course, "Why are you right for the job?"

Mike pondered the question and gave his very best answer, of course, suddenly, he wasn't sure he was the right guy for the job. His mind seemed to wander a lot during the interview back to fixing the faucet and the work he had to do in the apartment. It certainly wasn't the time to be distracted.

Once the interview was over, Peter Roberts walked him to the door and out the reception area, which Mike hadn't seen him do with anyone else.

"It was a real pleasure to meet you, Mike."

"Likewise. I look forward to hearing from you," he said with a firm handshake.

"Play golf?"

"Haven't had the clubs out in a while, but yeah, I've knocked a few balls around."

Peter laughed. "There's a great two story shooting range just a few miles from here. Maybe we could shoot a few rounds someday."

Mike hoped the smile was still firmly on his face and his mouth hadn't dropped wide open. "That would be great."

Peter gave him a nod and went back to the conference room, no doubt to weed him out with the other applicants.

Mike drove back toward town, exactly how Siri told him to. And once again, he ended up in a residential area that was on the outskirts of downtown. How was it that he couldn't find the center of this city?

As he maneuvered his way down one-way streets that crossed diagonally with others, he slowed down and took in the sights. There were some magnificent houses mixed in with the modern architecture. One specifically caught his eye, and he pulled over to take a look.

It was a Queen Anne style house with window crowns and undecorated masonry. The yard was overgrown, and one of the windows was broken. But it reminded him of the bed and break-fast his parents had owned when he was growing up.

Mike found a parking space a few blocks away and walked

back to the house. It didn't look occupied, but there was no sign on it.

Carefully, hoping that there wasn't some deranged homeowner with a gun inside, he walked up to the house and looked in the window.

It certainly had been abandoned. The inside hadn't been taken care of, which was a shame because the plaster molding and the woodwork had been exquisite at one time.

All this house needed to be was loved and it would be the most beautiful house on the block. People would come to stay here, he thought. They'd eat breakfast on the small patio above the front porch, which must have been accessed from a bedroom.

He looked at the trees. They could be shaped and groomed to block out the other neighbors, but leave a peaceful view of the city skyline.

His blood was pumping now, and he laughed at himself. Fixing up an old house wasn't in his plans. Neither was dreaming up his parents' old bed and breakfast. But he couldn't help but think of how fun it might be.

He took out his phone and took a picture of it before he walked back to Chandra's car only to find Jason looking inside of it.

"Hey, Jason," he called out, and the boy's eyes widened as if he might run. But he looked at him and eased back.

"This is my mom's car."

"She let me borrow it for a job interview. I saw an old house I wanted to look at, so I stopped." Mike looked around. "What are you doing here?"

"Just got off the bus. We only live about six blocks from here."

And that gave him a little more insight into Chandra, knowing where she lived.

Mike noticed a few kids on the other side of the street watching them. "Those your friends?"

Jason shrugged. "Not really. I usually try to walk on this side of the street and let them have the other."

That hurt him to the core to think that someone might cause his new friend pain.

"I could walk you home if you'd like. As long as I don't get lost walking back."

Jason laughed. "I suppose that would be okay."

And so they began to walk the neighborhood toward Chandra's house. "You ready for that game this Saturday?"

"Sure," Jason shrugged. "I mean we've never won against this team, but I'm ready."

"My son is a good soccer player. Played for years growing up. Was a goalie his first two years, but he wanted to be the guy who scored."

"I wanna be that guy too," Jason said with his voice soft.

As they turned the corner, Jason walked up the walk toward a house.

Mike was familiar with this architecture too. A basic foursquare house, he assumed it had been built at the turn of the last century.

"Thanks for walking me home," Jason said as he climbed the three steps to the front porch.

"My pleasure. If anyone ever gives you trouble, I could walk you home anytime. You let me know."

He laughed and opened the screen door, disappearing inside.

Mike tucked his hands into his pockets and started back to the car when he heard his name called from behind him.

He turned to see Esther in the doorway. "What are you doing here?" she asked.

"I went on a job interview. Jason saw Chandra's car since she lent it to me," he made sure Esther knew that. "He was walking home, and I offered to walk with him. I'm heading back to the restaurant now. After I make a trip to the store," he said suddenly remembering he was making dinner for Chandra.

"I have that plant I told you about. Would you like it?"

He wasn't sure this was the right time to go into their house and accept gifts, but then too, it would be rude not to.

With a smile, he walked up the front steps and into Chandra's house.

The inside of the house was simple. There was nothing for show in her home. Everything was practical.

Jason had discarded his backpack and his shoes just beyond the door and disappeared.

"The plant is in the kitchen. I just made some cookies. Would you like one?"

Mike breathed in the air, and that took him back. The scent of warm cookies. "I would love that."

His mother made fresh cookies every day for those staying with them, and that was the scent he came home to every day. His mother made sure that there were two cookies and a glass of milk waiting for him on the counter when he got off the bus.

He flashed a smile at Esther who was busy excusing the state of the house, though Mike saw nothing out of place.

Esther told him to have a seat at the table, and she hurried about the kitchen collecting a plate for the cookies and a glass of milk.

His heart might have exploded right then when she set them on the table and then joined him, just as his mother would every afternoon.

"So how did the job interview go?" she asked.

"The man thought we could play golf together some day. I'm going to take that as a positive sign, right?"

She laughed easily and sat back in her chair. "I would too. If you can work with Chandra, I assume you could work with anyone. She's fairly picky about the people she keeps around."

That was quite a compliment considering Chandra not only had him working with her, but had set up the opportunity for him to live that closely too.

He bit into the warm, soft cookie and had to remind himself to refrain from moaning, but that was hard. If anyone had nailed his mother's cookie recipe, it was Esther.

"It was funny," he said as he swallowed his bite and then sipped his milk. "As I was driving down to the interview I was thinking how depressing it was. I've worked corporate for twenty some years. Now here I am, new city, new opportunity, and I'm chasing that again? I'm not sure that's what I want."

"Yes, but will your handyman skills take you where you need them to?"

"That becomes the question." He took another bite of the cookie which still oozed chocolate from the melted chips. "There was a house around the corner that caught my eye."

"One you want to live in?"

He shrugged. "My parents used to own a bed and breakfast. It had that kind of charm."

"There are a few of those around here. Denver has a lot to offer a visitor. I don't see where another one would hurt."

"There are a lot of options," he pondered aloud. "It could even be an *Airbnb*."

Esther's brows drew together. "What is that?"

He chuckled. "You can now stay in someone's home—like renting a hotel."

"I wouldn't want to do that."

"Yes, but it wouldn't be my home, per say. It could be an investment."

She leaned in and rested her elbow on the table and her chin in her hand. "So you'd buy the house and rent it out like a hotel?"

"Yeah." The thought of it stirred in his head until there was a giddy surge that zipped through him. "You know what else would be fantastic? I could have a few bicycles for the people to use. Of course, that's not practical in the snow."

Esther laughed and sat back again. "This is Colorado. Have

you not seen the crazy people outside running in the snow? Bicycles don't have a season here."

Yes, he had seen that. Those college students had shorts on, and it had been snowing.

"I'll have to do some digging," he said dipping his cookie into the milk. "There was no sign on the house."

"You have money to invest?"

Suddenly the zip of excitement exited his body. "No. And that's where the stuffy job comes into play. Maybe in time, I will."

Esther patted his hand. "Don't give up the dream. It's a good one," she said with a warm smile.

It was a good one, he agreed. It would occupy his mind while he was stuck in some cubicle with no windows.

CHAPTER 9

*a*nother one of those skills Mike had learned from his parents' bed and breakfast, was the skill to set a nice table and cook a great meal.

He threw the dish towel, one of many that Esther had sent, over his shoulder and tasted his sauce. Letting out a moan, he decided that it was perfect.

Lifting the lid from the pan, he checked his chicken and gave himself an approving nod.

Esther had thought of everything he'd need for a few days. He had the table set with the paper plates she'd brought. Paper towel squares were folded under the two forks he had.

On his way out of the grocery store, he'd stopped by a little liquor store and bought a bottle of wine. It was a normal thing to do when planning a dinner. It wasn't until he got back to his apartment that he thought maybe that was a mistake. Chandra was only stopping by for dinner, not staying to linger. After all, she would have to go back to work.

When he'd passed through on his way home, they'd agreed on an eight o'clock dinner time. He'd have liked something a little earlier, but he wasn't the one with the demanding job.

He opened the oven and checked on the potatoes. Everything looked great. There were fifteen minutes before his guest would arrive. Just enough time to check his email.

Mike sat down on the sofa and opened his laptop on the coffee table. The email reader refreshed, and he scrolled through the many junk emails that cluttered his inbox. But then he saw the name he'd been looking for. There was an email from Peter Roberts.

His finger hovered over the touchpad on his laptop. Something kept him from clicking on the email. Perhaps a glass of wine would be nice to have in his hand before he opened it. Or, he could save it for after dinner, and then follow Chandra downstairs and have a beer. That was more his style.

Closing the laptop, he decided he'd wait until later to look at the email. He didn't want it to change his attitude. At the moment he was happy and content in his new home and expecting a lovely lady for dinner.

And at that moment there was a knock on the door. The lovely lady had arrived.

Mike moved to the door and pulled it open. Without a word, Chandra walked straight in, as if her mind were somewhere else.

"I only have a half hour," she said passing by him looking down at her phone.

"Everything is ready. Have a seat."

She lifted her head and looked at the table. "I thought you were doing something simple."

"This is simple. Paper plates. Paper towels. And Styrofoam cups." He chuckled.

"I'll admit I was expecting a bowl of spaghetti. What did you do? Chicken?"

"With garlic cream sauce and baby potatoes?"

Her eyes went wide. "Oh."

"It's all ready. We can have you back downstairs in a half hour.

Is it still busy?" he asked lifting the lid from the chicken and ladling the sauce over the top.

"Just down a few people. Snow becomes a freaking excuse for everyone," she growled.

"There's a salad and some dressing in the fridge if you want to pull that out," he said, trying to distract her mood.

She moved in behind him in the tiny kitchen and opened the refrigerator. "You bought wine? I thought this was just dinner. Not a date." Her tone had a bite.

"I just thought it would be a nice touch. But I don't have an opener until tomorrow. So it looks like I'll be saving it. Besides, I didn't consider your having to go back to work."

"For the record, I'd rather just stay up here and drink wine." She took out the container of salad and the bottle of dressing before nudging the door closed with her hip.

Mike transferred the potatoes to a bowl Esther had brought him and set it on the table. He picked up the paper plates and carried it to the stove. Carefully he loaded each plate with one of the chicken breasts and then realized he should have asked her to bring up a couple of plates. His nice dinner might just fall through the plate after all.

Managing to make it to the table, he let out a breath. "Glad you're not wearing that," he joked, but she was looking at her phone again.

"Is everything okay?" he asked as he sat down across from her.

"What? Oh, yeah." She tucked her phone in her back pocket. "Sorry. My phone seems to be blowing up. You went to my house?"

Her question caught him off guard as did the look of accusation which fired from her eyes.

"Yes, I did."

"Why? Are you stalking me? I don't need trouble. I thought you looked like a normal guy. I introduced you to my kid."

"Who is a fine young man," he interrupted.

"That's what worries me. What the hell were you doing with my family."

Mike sat back in his chair and took a moment to inventory what was happening. She was feeling threatened by him, but there was no reason for her to feel that way. But she was a protective mother and daughter. This would have to be an issue he trod lightly.

"I was driving back from my interview, and I got lost on the side streets. I came upon a house that was of interest to me, and I stopped to look at it. It just so happened to be the same route Jason was walking home on."

"What house? Why?"

Trying to remain casual, he served potatoes onto both plates and then opened the container of salad.

"It was a vacant house, and it made me think of my parents' B and B. So I stopped to look in the windows. It didn't have a for sale sign, but no one lives in it."

Lines formed between her brow. "You took my son into a vacant house?" Her voice rose.

"No." He kept his voice calm to balance the room. "When I turned around he was looking in the car. He knew it was yours. I'm fairly sure he thought I'd stolen it." The thought made him chuckle. "He told me he was walking home and saw the car. Then there were other kids on the other side of the street that I think he was trying to avoid. So I offered to walk him home."

The look on her face changed from accusation to worry, and he knew that look was reserved for Jason.

"I think those kids give him a hard time," she said.

"Well, they didn't today. I walked him home, and we talked about his game this weekend."

With a huff, she sat back in her chair. "That game. Why is it so important? He's an average player putting too much stock in a league game."

"We're guys," he humored, as he leaned in and cut his first bite of his chicken. "We will always want to be the biggest and baddest dudes around."

Finally, she laughed, but the seriousness crept back over her face as she leaned in to put salad on her plate. "I'm sorry I freaked out there."

"Don't be sorry for that. You have a lot on your mind, and part of that is the protection of your family. I suppose me showing up at your house seems a little creepy in hindsight. I think it took your mother by surprise too."

She nodded. "Considering your mantel has a new plant, she must have gotten over it."

"She fed me cookies too."

"Sounds like her." She cut a piece of her chicken and then stabbed it with a fork. He watched her drag it through the sauce deep in thought. "You'll really go to his game on Saturday?"

"I'll be there. I promised him."

"He's going to put a lot of stock in that."

"He should. A man promised him something, and that man should follow through."

Chandra bit down on her bottom lip. "You're a decent guy."

"Thanks."

"I mean it. You stepped in here and helped out. You thought to walk my kid home, so he wasn't picked on. And I think you'll actually follow through with your promise to be there."

"I will follow through."

She lifted her fork to her mouth, finally, and took her first bite of the chicken. He watched her savor it, and it gave him great pleasure to do so.

"This is good."

"I'm glad you liked it. I have about ten recipes I know by heart. This is one. You have nine more dinners before we repeat."

Now she laughed with ease and the tension she'd been holding in her shoulders released.

Dinner continued with the casual conversation. No big insights into her soul, but perhaps some soothing for his.

When they were done, they'd managed to spend forty-five minutes over dinner, and that set her into a panic.

"I'm sorry I have to run. I took longer than I anticipated," she said as she stood.

Mike rose. "I'll take that as a compliment."

"I can help you clean up."

He shook his head. "No. I've got it. If it's not too busy downstairs, I thought I'd come sit and have a beer. If that's okay."

"Sure. Sure." She moved toward him as if she were going to hug him, or perhaps kiss him. Then she awkwardly moved past him as if she needed to avoid him. "I'll see you down there."

He watched her walk out the door and then he sat back down. Something told him this new friendship was about to become complicated.

CHAPTER 10

*C*handra hurried down the stairs and out the door to the back of the building. She let the door close behind her and pressed her back to it.

What in the hell was that? She'd nearly moved in to hug the man when less than an hour ago she'd been convinced he was some stalker. Pressing her hands to her cheeks, she realized not only had she nearly hugged him she'd almost moved in to kiss him. Perhaps he hadn't noticed. That's all she could hope for. The last thing she needed in her life was a man. She had enough on her plate.

Chandra walked back into the restaurant from the back door. It was nearly nine o'clock, and the dining room was winding down. A man sat at the bar, and she welcomed the distraction from the man that would soon join her.

"How are you?" she asked the man as she dismissed the waiter who had been covering for her.

"Doing okay. This is a nice place."

"Thanks. Did they take care of you? I see you have a drink. Did you want to put in an order for dinner?"

"No, I was looking for someone, actually."

"Well if you're looking for the owner, he's on paternity leave."

The man's eyes widened and then he smiled. "Good for him. Boy or girl?"

"Don't know yet. She's ready to go at any moment."

"Exciting. No, I'm looking for Mike Cavanagh."

That took her by surprise. "He'll be down shortly. Who are you?"

The man held his hand out to her. "Peter Roberts."

"Chandra Chavez," she introduced herself as she shook the man's hand. "How do you know Mike?"

"He interviewed with me this morning."

"And you're here to give him a job?"

Peter rolled the glass between his palms. "No."

"No, he sent an email that said I was overqualified for the job," Mike's voice rang in her ears, and she noticed he'd walked up to the bar.

"Hey, Mike." Peter stood and shook his hand.

"I'm surprised to see you here."

"Yeah, not my usual process. Can I buy you a drink?"

"Sure," Mike agreed and sat down next to Peter as Chandra pulled him a beer and set it in front of him. Then she stepped back from the bar and began her nighttime ritual of closing down the bar, but keeping a keen ear focused on the men.

"I'm sorry about the job," Peter said.

"Hey, big world. Lots of competition out there. I understand."

"Well, you were my choice if it's any consolation."

Mike lifted his beer to his lips. "It is."

"The reason I stopped by, and this is between you and me," he made sure to make eye contact with Mike, who nodded in agreement. "I'm breaking away from the company, and I'll have a new startup going in a month. I'm putting together my team. My investors are in place."

"That's exciting."

"It is. And I want you to be part of it. There'll be a signing bonus if that helps to get your attention."

Mike laughed. "You had my attention, but now you have all of it."

Chandra listened as Peter explained the company and the role he wanted Mike to play in it. Most of the things he was talking about were over her head, but Mike had input and Peter seemed to appreciate it.

She watched as the last of the diners left, and the kitchen began to go through their closing process. When the clock above the bar said it was ten o'clock, she moved back in front of the men and laid her hands flat on the bar.

"Gentlemen, we are closing up."

Peter reached for his wallet and handed her his credit card. "I appreciate you letting us stick around and talk."

"Of course." She swiped the card and handed it back to him. "Anytime."

Peter turned to Mike and held his hand out to him again. "I'll call you tomorrow, and maybe this weekend we can go hit those golf balls."

"Sounds great."

Peter started for the door just as it flung open and Tracy burst in. "Her water broke!"

Chandra instinctively grabbed Mike's hand and squeezed. "They're going now?"

"Saint Joe's. I'll meet you there." She beamed and then noticed the man standing next to her. "Sorry. I'm in your way."

Peter smiled broadly as he pulled on his coat. "Not at all. I take it that the owner has now officially started his paternity leave?"

Tracy nodded as if he'd rendered her speechless, but it was quickly corrected. "I'm Tracy," she said offering her hand.

"Peter," he replied, taking her hand and kissing it.

Chandra was fairly sure she'd just seen the strong-willed Tracy swoon.

"Give them my best. Mike," he turned with a wave, "I'll call you tomorrow."

Peter walked out the door, and Tracy watched him disappear before she turned back toward the bar. "Him. I want him," she joked, and Chandra laughed.

"He fits your profile." She looked at Mike whose lips had curled into a warm smile, and she realized she was still holding onto his hand. "Tracy, this is Mike."

Tracy held out her hand with the million bracelets. "It's nice to meet you. I've heard wonderful things."

"Thank you."

Tracy stepped back and tapped her fingers together. "Okay, I'm headed to the hospital to meet my new faux-grandbaby. I'll meet you there."

When she had walked out the door, Mike turned to her. "Faux-grandbaby?"

"That's what she calls Holly and Gabe's daughter. Her faux-granddaughter. She doesn't have any children."

"She's a free spirit."

"Yes she is." She looked around at the staff wiping down tables and cleaning the floor. "I guess I'd better get a move on if I want to be there to see that baby."

"Tell me what to do. I'll help get everyone out of here for you. I know how important this is for you. Especially if you'll go in the middle of the night to the hospital to be there for them."

Her eyes met his as he made his generous offer. How could she have ever thought he wasn't a sincere man? It nearly oozed out of him.

"Will you go with me?"

"To the hospital?"

"You don't have to. I just thought the company..."

"I would love to. Give me a task. Let's get this place closed down."

THEY WALKED OUT OF THE DOOR AT ELEVEN. MIKE HAD ON HIS warmest coat, but he'd need to buy another. Chandra, on the other hand, had only a sweatshirt, and she seemed content.

Chandra opened the door and started the car. It sputtered to life under protest, but then hummed as it warmed. She pulled two ice scrapers from the back seat and tossed one to Mike.

"If we both have a go at it, it'll take less time."

He began to scrape the ice from the window, realizing he'd soon need a pair of gloves too. This certainly wasn't something he'd ever encountered in Southern California.

Once the glass was clear, they both climbed into the car, but the heater was taking its time to kick in.

"Sorry, it'll be a cold drive. By the time we get there, we might be warm."

"I'm warm enough," he said.

"You're probably running on adrenaline. That was quite an offer Peter brought to you. Did you expect that?"

"Not at all. I'll admit, I was a little saddened that I didn't get the job, but I was the old guy in the room."

"You're not old," she shifted a glance his way.

"No, just in my industry."

They drove the empty streets in silence. The hospital wasn't too far away, but he figured he'd seen nearly every economic variation of the downtown area.

The hospital looked to be fairly new. That didn't surprise him. Denver seemed to be one of those cities that was always updating and putting in new things.

Chandra parked the car and sat quietly for a moment. "I want to apologize to you again for jumping you for going to my house."

"Don't feel the need to do that. I'd have been suspicious too. You've got a great kid. If he were mine, I wouldn't want anything to ever happen to him."

"Thanks for staying up and coming with me."

"My pleasure. You're going to be beat tomorrow."

She chuckled. "Yeah. I might have to call in some help."

"Tell you what. We'll go inside, and you head to them, I'll get us some coffee. Does Tracy drink coffee?"

Now she laughed aloud. "No. But bring her a cup of hot water. She carries some homemade teas in her purse, and trust me when I say her taste isn't like anyone else's."

"Hot water then." He reached his hand to hers, and much like at the bar when she'd covered his hand, he gave hers a squeeze. "Gabe is lucky to have you."

Mike watched her as she took in his compliment. He was sure it was the way the streetlights shone through the window, otherwise, he might have thought her eyes had misted.

MIKE WENT ONE DIRECTION, AND CHANDRA WENT THE OTHER until she found Tracy seated in the waiting area.

"Anything yet?" she asked.

Tracy lifted her head. "Not yet. I was just texting Gabe's mom and Holly's dad. Her parents are with Madison."

Chandra sat down next to Tracy, who smelled of essential oils. "What's your bet? Boy or girl?"

"Oh, sweetheart, you know it's a girl. What would Gabe Maguire do without another woman?"

Both women laughed, but she knew Tracy was right. She figured that's why he'd always treated her so right. Gabe was surrounded by strong women in his life. Chandra didn't put him off.

"Ah, I found you," Mike walked through the door balancing three cups. "Tracy, yours is the one in front. It's just hot water."

She reached for it. "Thank you, sweetheart."

Chandra took the next one in his hands as he sat down right next to her. There was something comforting about having him so close, and it bothered her that she liked it.

Midnight quickly crept up on them, and the TV in the waiting area droned on. "Put your head on my shoulder and get some rest," Mike said as he slid down in his chair and rested his head against the wall.

"You don't have to stay here," she offered as she shifted to lay her head on his shoulder. "You have your own life."

He let out a tired sigh. "Oh, I don't have anything I need to tend to until tomorrow when my moving truck arrives. I'm happy to be here with you."

The sweet words he spoke buzzed in her head as she relaxed against him. He smelled nice. Had she noticed that before? She liked it she thought as she let the sounds around her drift away.

CHAPTER 11

*I*t had been a long time since he'd felt the comfort of a woman's body pressed to him, even if it were just her arm against him and her head on his shoulder.

Mike rested his head against hers and breathed in deeply the smell of her shampoo. He felt the rise and fall of her breath and the warmth of her skin next to his.

The first moment he'd looked at her a few days ago, he never could have imagined he'd be where he was. The tattooed woman with a heart of gold had saved him from himself. He'd easily have fallen into a depression from the failures in his life had he not wandered into Maguire's for that beer.

Brushing a strand of her hair from her forehead, he looked down at her sleeping peacefully. She was a hard worker. He'd meant it when he'd said Gabe was a lucky man. Who else would put her life on hold for someone whom they weren't in love with or related to? But Mike was a good judge of character. He knew Gabe appreciated her as much as she appreciated him.

Mike looked at the clock. It was nearly two in the morning. It could still be hours until baby Maguire made it into the world. Perhaps he should wake her and offer to drive her home.

That was when a weary Gabe walked through the door. "They're both out cold, huh?" he asked looking at Chandra and Tracy.

Mike smiled. "Yeah. A few hours now. They wouldn't have wanted to miss this for the world."

Gabe reached down and rubbed Chandra's arm. "Sweetheart, wake up," he said softly and Chandra's eyes opened slowly, then she sat up, nearly fully alert.

"Well?"

Tracy stirred at the conversation and quickly stood. "Well?"

Gabe smiled at both of them and then pulled Tracy to him in a grand embrace. "We have another little princess," he said with genuine pride oozing from his words.

Chandra stood and hugged him, her arms wrapped tightly around Gabe's neck. "I knew you'd have another girl."

Gabe laughed. "It's my fate."

Mike stood and held out his hand. "That's fantastic. Congratulations."

"Thanks. Madison will be very happy. Before we left, she said she wanted a sister. When I asked her what she would think if we brought home a brother, she said she'd take him back."

He chuckled. "Everyone will be happy then."

Gabe stepped back. "You guys want to see her and Holly? They're both in the room."

Tracy and Chandra both nodded and followed Gabe. When Mike didn't move, Chandra turned to him. "Aren't you coming."

"I've never met Holly. This probably isn't the time she wants to meet new people. I have no doubt I'll get my chance to see them both. You go ahead and take all the time you need. I'll be right here."

She smiled, and his heart melted in his chest. Would anyone look at that woman and think that she was a softy? He wouldn't have pegged her for one, but he was glad he was getting the opportunity to see that side of her.

Gabe walked with Chandra and Tracy back to the room. Tracy walked ahead of them and in to see Holly, but Gabe pulled Chandra back.

"So what's up with you and our handyman?" he asked with a grin on his lips, which she hadn't seen in nearly two years.

"Nothing. Why?"

"Nothing? You're certainly comfortable with him."

Chandra crossed her arms in front of her. "He's a nice guy. Can't I have a nice guy in my life?"

"Don't get defensive," he said, still grinning. "You're easy around him. You let your guard down. C'mon, you were sleeping on his shoulder."

"I'm tired."

"And usually you'd rather sleep on the hard floor," he challenged.

Chandra kept her eyes on Gabe, whose stupid smile was about to irritate her into an irrational argument with the man. "Listen, he's a nice guy. Jason likes him and so does my mom. He's nice to have around, have dinner with, and…"

Gabe stepped in closer. "Have dinner with? You guys went out on a date?"

"No, he cooked me dinner tonight."

"And you're not seeing him?"

"No." She felt the aggravation shake in her voice. "Gabe, he's alone. I guess I'm his friend."

He nodded, but still, that irritating smile was on his lips. "He seems like he'll be a nice friend to keep around."

With a growl, she pushed past Gabe and walked into the hospital room, where Tracy had already scooped up the baby.

"Hey, Chandra," Holly said, her voice soft and tired.

"How are you?"

"Much better now."

Chandra walked across the room to where Tracy sat with the baby. "Isn't she precious?"

"She is," she said looking down at the tiny pink bundle. "What's her name?" she asked Holly.

"Jessica."

"Beautiful."

Tracy looked up at her. "Do you want to hold her?"

She shook her head. "Not now. When they're that little, they scare me."

Holly's eyes shifted to Gabe. "Did you get a hold of everyone?"

He bent to kiss Holly's head. "Yes. Mom will be on a plane tomorrow, and Madison said she's glad we're not bringing her a brother."

Chandra rubbed her eyes. "I'd better get going, so I can take Mike back and get a few hours of sleep."

"Mike?" Holly's brows drew together. "Who's that?"

Gabe sat down on the edge of the bed next to his wife. "Remember the guy who's doing handyman stuff for us and renting the apartment."

"Oh, right. You told me about him." She looked up at Chandra. "He came with you?"

"Yeah, he was at the bar when Tracy came in. He came to keep me company, I guess."

"You're dating him?"

Gabe laughed, and Chandra shook her head. "I'll let him explain. I'm leaving. Congratulations, guys," she said as she headed toward the door.

Gabe stood and hurried toward her. He pulled her in and gave her a hug. "Thank you for everything. Without you, I couldn't have been with her all week."

"Well, my rules stand. I don't want to see you for the next three weeks."

"At least two."

"Don't make me walk out on you."

He kissed her forehead, which was something he'd never done. "I promise you a paid vacation when I get back."

"You'd better," she agreed and walked out of the room.

◈

MIKE LAY IN BED LOOKING AT THE LIGHTS THAT DANCED ON THE ceiling from the cars passing in the early morning. Chandra had dropped him off at home around four o'clock, and he had yet to fall asleep. Now his six o'clock alarm was minutes from going off, and he didn't have it in him to get up and get ready. It was going to be a long day with his storage unit arriving. He'd need to find some energy to carry all of his belongings up the stairs. Jason wouldn't be any help until after school, but at this rate, he might just have to wait him out.

He thought about their drive home, and how silent Chandra had been. Of course, he wrote it off to being tired, but there was something deeper. He could only imagine there was a jealous side to her. Was it over Gabe or the baby?

She didn't seem to have feelings for Gabe, but Esther had said Gabe and Holly were a one-night-stand gone right, which was the first time he'd heard of something like that. But had that shifted his attention from Chandra? He wasn't sure about that hypothesis. Perhaps it was that her son was now ten. He knew that women got sentimental when other women had babies. It was a thing with them that he'd never understand. His son was nineteen and babies didn't make him go all crazy.

On the other hand, he thought as he rolled to his side and pounded the pillow into place, ten-year-old boys made him miss those simpler times with Dane. Those were times filled with big dreams, such as making a professional soccer team or playing in the Olympics. It was fishing on the weekends and bike rides down the coast.

His heart began to ache a bit, and now he understood a woman holding a newborn baby.

He rolled onto his back again and tucked his hands under his head. Perhaps getting stuck in Denver was how it was meant to be. Maybe he was supposed to fill some greater need. Why else would it just work out to have a woman with a son, who didn't have a dad around, enter his life? And, add that they had nothing in common, but damn if he didn't want to spend every moment with her.

Now the bed was becoming more uncomfortable, and he swung his feet to the side and rested his head in his hands. Was this the moment when he was supposed to admit to himself that he was attracted to Chandra? Well, of course, he was attracted to her. No man in his right mind wouldn't be. That long dark hair, those well-toned muscles, and that air of confidence that tugged at a man. Hadn't he, in the past week, nearly memorized every tattoo visible on her arms?

Mike got to his feet and went into the bathroom. He turned on the water and splashed his face with it. Turning it off, he looked into the mirror.

There had to be at least ten years between them. To Chandra, he was probably just some old guy she was friending to be nice. Sure, that was it.

He finished in the bathroom and went to the kitchen to make coffee, only to have that reality hit him too. The coffee maker was in the storage unit he was waiting for. Well, he might as well get up and walk down the street to get some coffee. The brisk walk would do him some good.

By six-fifteen, he was standing in line at the Starbuck's. Didn't people have coffee makers at home? Wasn't that the norm?

He placed his order and moved down the line to wait it out. That's when a hand came to his shoulder, and he turned to see Peter Roberts standing there.

"Hey, you're hitting the juice early, huh?" Robert joked.

"Sure," Mike laughed and shook his hand. "It was a long night."

"So what did they have? Boy or girl?"

"A little girl," he said smiling as they called his name for his drink. "We got home around four. I'm running on black magic."

Peter laughed with a nod. "Yeah, I'm headed over to meet with an investor before trekking to the tech center. So what about golf this weekend? Saturday?"

Mike took a breath to accept, but then stopped, thinking of his prior commitment. "Saturday is busy. Chandra's son has an important soccer game I promised to be at."

He saw the shift of humor in Peter's expression. "You can't back down from a kid. How old?"

"Ten."

"My son is twelve. And if you make a promise, you'd better follow through with it, or you'll hear about it for life. Let's plan another day. I'll call you this week, and we can talk some more about the job."

"Sounds great," he said, shaking the man's hand again.

Mike took the walk back slowly. The air was crisp but fresh. The mountains with their caps of snow gave the perfect backdrop to the orange hues of the sunrise which reflected off them.

He sipped his coffee and thought about his life a week ago. He'd been packing and finalizing his move. Everything had gone so wrong, but somehow it was turning out to be so right.

As he walked past the front of Maguire's, he looked inside at the stillness. There was peace there in the hours they were closed. No wonder Chandra went to work early, he thought, and at that moment he saw the light in the back hall.

He moved closer to the window and pressed his face to it. It was not even seven o'clock, and Chandra was standing at the bar pouring herself a cup of coffee.

Without any thought, he tapped on the window, and she snapped her head up. She studied him in the window, and when she realized who he was, she started toward him. However, the look on her face wasn't one of welcome, and he suddenly was rethinking having knocked.

"What do you want?" She scowled as she flung open the door.

"Just to say hi. I saw you and instinctively knocked."

"What are you doing walking around this early? I could have made you a cup of coffee for free," she said looking at the cup in his hand.

"I didn't know you were going to be here this early."

"I never left."

He narrowed his gaze on her. "What do you mean you never left?"

"It was so late I just stayed in the office. I slept on the couch. No need to wake up my family just to turn right back around and come back."

The thought that they'd slept, or not, under the same roof seemed to give him a little jolt. He hoped to God it didn't show on his face.

"Have you had breakfast?" he asked.

"Are you kidding me? I just got off the couch. I'm going to drink my breakfast and try and clean up for my shift."

"You could use my shower."

She shifted her stance and crossed her arms in front of her. "You're very forward today. I didn't say I wanted to shower with you, did I?"

He held up his hand in protest and couldn't help but laugh. "I didn't say that. I said you could use my shower." He watched that process in her tired brain, and her expression eased. "I'll go pick us up some breakfast." He pulled his keys from his pocket. "I know you have a set, but this is just as easy. Get ready, and I'll be back in a little bit. We're both dead tired, so we'll need some fuel."

Chandra took the keys, looked at them, and then back up at him. "Sorry."

"It's okay. In a few weeks, you'll get some time off. Maybe you can take a vacation for Jason's spring break."

She nodded. "That would be something. It's been a very, very long time since I had a vacation."

"I don't know anyone who deserves it more."

The compliment hung in the air. Neither of them walked away. Nor did either of them move.

Mike felt his fingers twitch to reach out and touch her. Her tired eyes looking up at him made him want to pull her to him and hold her against him. He told himself it was for her comfort, but he wasn't sure about that.

Finally, he took a step back. "I'll come back through the back and meet you upstairs."

CHANDRA WATCHED HIM WALK AWAY AS SHE LOCKED THE DOOR AND lingered there. She wasn't one to worry about having made an ass of herself in front of people. So why did it matter, at that moment, that she'd thought he was making a move on her? Perhaps because she'd hoped he might.

She threw her hands in the air, in silent protest. She was stupid. With all the things going on in the world, and she was looking for a little ego boost. Letting out a growl, she crossed the restaurant and walked to the door that would lead up the steps to Mike's apartment.

Letting herself in, she took a moment to look around. Last night she hadn't noticed how homey it was. Mike only had what her mother had brought him, but somehow, just with him in it, it felt warm.

Walking toward the fireplace, she noticed he'd added a photo to the mantel. Chandra reached for it and pulled it down. It was a picture of him and his son. His son looked just like him. Oh, and the smile on Mike's face said just how proud he was of him.

She replaced the photo and looked at the picture which Gabe had left there when he moved. This one she was familiar with.

It was a picture of him and his first wife on a ski trip. They looked so happy. But she'd been killed in a car accident, and moving to Colorado and taking over his uncle's bar had been Gabe's salvation. He'd mended his broken heart right there in that apartment.

She looked around and smiled. Maybe it was a good place for new beginnings she thought as she replaced Gabe's photo.

Chandra decided if she didn't stop messing around, Mike would be back and she'd still be standing there. She continued to the bedroom and stopped.

His bed was rumpled, and that brought a smile to her face. She would have taken him for a neat freak when it came to making beds. But the twisted sheets and the unfluffed pillow made her feel a bit more at home.

Chandra walked into the bathroom and closed the door. The set up there made her think back to him being more of a neat freak. Everything was lined up just so, and the towel wasn't just wadded up on the bar, it was neatly placed.

Well, for a moment she'd thought he was in her league, and she laughed as she turned on the water.

CHAPTER 12

*T*he lingering scent of warm water and soap filled his apartment and made his stomach knot just a bit. Just in the next room, Chandra was naked in his bathroom.

Mike could feel his cheeks fill with heat. Well, all that meant was he was a healthy functioning man. She was a looker, and it was perfectly normal to think of her then, he decided.

He pulled out a few paper plates and a couple of forks. He'd found a small diner a few blocks away and ordered them a few different things. It would be a private buffet of sorts, he humored himself with the thought.

When his bedroom door opened, he couldn't help but quickly look up. Chandra moved through the doorway. She had on her regular uniform, but he supposed the perk was that there were clean ones downstairs. Her hair was damp and laid over her shoulder. He'd never seen her with her hair down. It gave her a softer look.

It took his breath away.

"You can stop gawking," she said as she walked toward him. "I'm not naked."

"You know any normal man would wish the woman in the

other room would come out naked. I'm just normal," he said lightly, hoping she'd find humor in it.

She smiled, and he decided that was a win.

"Okay, so I have us a little buffet. Pancakes, eggs, bacon, hash browns, biscuits and gravy, toast, and an orange juice we could share."

The corner of her mouth lifted into a slight smile. Ah, he'd melted the frigid off her.

"I'm starving," she said. "I think I want a little of everything."

That brought a smile to his face. He'd never much cared for his ex-wife's lack of eating. Oh, he knew she binged when he wasn't around. But after twenty years of marriage, he'd have thought she'd have gotten over not eating in front of him. He hadn't been only in love with her body. How shallow had she thought he was?

He tensed when he realized he'd suddenly been bothered by it. That was then, he thought. Now he had a new start. There was no reason to dwell on the past.

Chandra pulled out her chair and sat down. She immediately dove into the carryout containers and filled herself a plate.

She looked up at him watching her as she bit down on a piece of bacon.

"Are you just going to stand there?" she asked and he smiled.

"No." He pulled out his chair and sat down across from her. "It's nice to have breakfast with you again," he said.

"Yeah." She bit off another bite of bacon. "You're the only guy I've eaten breakfast with more than once and haven't slept with," she said with a snort, and then horror took over her face. Her eyes grew wide and she began to cough from choking on the bacon.

He pushed her orange juice toward her.

She waved her hand in the air as she drank. "I didn't mean that. I mean, yes I meant it, but not like that. Oh, shit, you must think I'm some crazy slut."

Mike lifted his cup to his lips to sip his tepid coffee, and perhaps hide his grin. "You don't have to apologize for anything you say around me."

"Well, that was out of line." She cleared her throat. "I don't just sleep around." She snorted out another laugh. "I guess that was pathetic too. All I do is work."

"You've been pretty busy raising a great kid too."

That eased the tense look on her face. "Yeah, he's great." She finished her piece of bacon and then took in after the scrambled eggs with her fork. "So that job offer you got last night. Are you going to take it?"

He smiled as he took a bite of the biscuits and gravy. "Thinking about it. It's an opportunity, that's for sure."

"You don't seem convinced."

"No, it's just something your mom said to me."

She lowered her fork and looked at him. "My mom?"

"Yeah, yesterday when I was at your house. She invited me in, gave me a plant, and offered me cookies."

"Right, you told me that."

"But I was telling about the house that I had seen. It would make a nice B and B."

"Like what your parents had?"

"Yeah." He took another bite. "It's just a dream. Not very practical. But she said not to give up on my dream."

Chandra nodded. "That sounds like her."

He sat back. "It's only been a few days that I've been here. I haven't even gotten out of downtown. Maybe I don't want to be locked into another office. Maybe I want something new."

Their conversation was interrupted by his cell phone ringing. The storage unit company was on their way. "Looks like I'll have my own coffee pot tomorrow."

She lowered her fork. "Yeah. Kinda disappointing."

"How's that?"

"This was nice."

"Tomorrow, I'll have coffee too. I'd still love to have you for breakfast."

Her cheeks pinkened. "Until Gabe gets back, I'd take you up on that offer."

"Consider it a date then."

She lifted her glass of orange juice. "Considered and accepted."

Maybe downtown life would be just right, he thought.

~

THE CONTAINER DELIVERY HAPPENED AT THE SAME TIME AS Chandra's produce delivery arrived. Somehow they managed to make it work, and finally, everything Mike owned was in his possession.

He unlocked the container and looked inside. He'd moved out of a house, and now was moving into a one-bedroom, furnished apartment. What in the hell was he going to do with all of his stuff?

The unfortunate part was, he would have to move it all out to find all the things he needed.

He supposed he could rent a storage facility, especially since he wasn't paying rent on his apartment. It sure was becoming more difficult to enjoy having his things there.

Mike heard the door behind him open, and he turned to see Chandra standing there looking at the storage unit with a bit of horror.

"What are you going to do with all of that?" she asked and he chuckled.

"I was just thinking the same thing. I don't need the bed or the furniture. Some of these personal items don't need to be dragged out if I'm only going to be living upstairs for six months."

"Are those your terms?"

He shrugged. "Gabe thought we'd be caught up by then and

then could discuss it. I don't think it'll take me that long. And it's suited for someone just getting their footing. I'd like to think I'd have mine by then."

"Can you fix sprinklers?"

Now he laughed. "It's thirty degrees, and you need your sprinkler fixed?"

"No," she huffed and stuck her hands in her back pockets. "My sprinkler at home needs to be redone. It hasn't worked for years, and I haven't shelled out the money to fix it. But I do have a two car garage that you could store your stuff in if you fix my sprinkler."

He nodded thoughtfully. "You've saved my ass a lot this week."

"Yeah, well, I guess you're rubbing off on me."

There was a compelling need to move to her. Somewhere between him walking into that bar four days ago and now, they'd forged some kind of friendship. Not just acquaintances, but a deep friendship.

He stood there, not quite a foot taller, looking down at the woman who at perhaps five foot carried a lot of confidence and attitude. Her eyes grew wide, and she crossed her arms in front of her, but she didn't back away.

"You'll let me store my things at your house?"

She shrugged. "What's the big deal? You're going to help me out."

"You've known me four days."

"Yeah, so? And in four days you've managed to get yourself a job here, an apartment, and a job offer with a startup. My kid likes you. So does my mom and my boss. You must be okay, huh?"

"I must be," he said inching even closer.

She narrowed her eyes on him, and he actually thought she might punch him if she had to. "When does Jason get home from school?"

"Three."

"I'll sharpen my math skills and offer up dinner for the family. Is he still coming to help me move in?"

"Yes."

Now he moved and pulled her into a hug, her arms still in front of her pressed into him. "You are a great friend. Thank you."

When he let go, she rocked back to get her balance. "You're a softy."

He smiled. "I am. I'm a big ole softy, and I can't help it."

"I'm not soft."

"I won't argue, but quietly I'll disagree."

The corner of her mouth turned up into a slight smile. "How old are you?"

Mike laughed. "You think we're good enough friends you can ask?" She raised her brows and waited for an answer.

"Forty-seven," he replied

Her lips pursed and she turned and disappeared back into the kitchen.

Perhaps she was disappointed in his age. But he laughed it off and went back to digging through the container in front of him.

ike spent most of the day weeding out what he needed and what he didn't need in the storage container. He was grateful, as well, for the use of the restaurant's dumpster to throw away the things he'd held on to. He shook his head as he dug through yet another box of items he should have thrown away when he'd packed them. What possessed him to keep recipe cards that he'd never used? If he wanted something he looked it up online. He grunted as he threw another stack of items in the dumpster.

When the door to the restaurant opened, it was Esther with a large travel mug of coffee. "Chandra said you'd been out here all day. You must be frozen."

"Well, don't want to pay more for this unit than I need to. Might as well get it done."

He pulled off the gloves he'd borrowed from Gabe's office and held the cup between his hands. "Can I offer you a seat?" He motioned to the sofa, inside the container, and Esther laughed.

"Don't mind if I do."

They sat together in the storage container and Esther looked around.

"What all do you have in here?" she asked.

"I've come to the conclusion, nothing."

Esther laughed. "Nothing important, huh?"

"Not a bit of it. You know you spend all that time wrapping things that you later think you should have just gotten rid of. So why the hell keep it?"

"I know what you're talking about. When I moved in with Chandra, I purged most of my life. And it was worth it. It was time to start over and think fresh."

"Yeah, that's what I think I'm going to do."

"She said you're storing some of it in the garage for a bit."

"Until I get a place. Then I'll need the bed, and sofa, and table."

"Jason will be happy not to have to help carry that all upstairs. At least dumping it into the garage will be easier."

"Sure, once we put it in a truck and take it back out."

Esther laughed again. "We won't tell him that part." She stood. "He's inside with his mom. She had a plate of something made for him for a snack. I hear we're having dinner at your place."

"You are if you'll come."

"Oh, if I'm not cooking, I'm there."

"I figured with moving and tutoring we might have to go simple. You don't mind pizza delivery do you?"

"I'll bring a six-pack."

"Sounds like a plan. Thanks for delivering my helper."

"Anything to get him off that video game for a few hours." She waved and went back into the restaurant.

Mike sipped his coffee again. He hadn't realized just how cold he was until the coffee warmed him. Well, he'd be done with this task soon enough, and then he could move on to the next great thing.

CHANDRA WIPED DOWN THE BAR AND FILLED ANOTHER ORDER while Jason picked at the plate of fruits and vegetables she'd had prepared for him. She hadn't expected anything less, but he'd survive.

Her mother walked back into the restaurant from the kitchen. "Mike's making progress," she said placing her hand on Jason's back. "But you get to eating so you can help him."

"That doesn't sound like fun."

"Well, you'll be happy to know he doesn't plan on moving the big stuff upstairs."

Jason's head popped up. "Good."

"Yep, and he's ordering pizza for dinner."

"Perfect!" Now he was smiling.

"I knew you'd be okay with that." Esther kissed him on the head and looked toward Chandra. "Need anything on my way back?"

"I think I'll be fine."

Esther walked behind the bar and hugged her daughter. "Want me to bring you some clothes for tonight?"

Chandra pulled back and narrowed her gaze on her mother. "What is that supposed to mean?"

Esther smiled. "You didn't come home last night. I'm just putting two and two together."

"Right, and I texted you and told you that Gabe and Holly had their baby in the middle of the night."

She nodded. "So you were at the hospital all night?"

"No."

"You showered and got ready today," she said taking a handful of Chandra's hair, which hadn't been pulled up, and tossing it over her shoulder.

"I used Mike's."

"And I'm not supposed to think something has happened?"

"I slept in Gabe's office," Chandra said turning her back to Jason. "Mom, why would you think like that?"

Her mother kissed her cheek. "Maybe I was just hopeful."

She walked back around the bar and kissed Jason again, who shrugged her off. Then with a wave, she left the restaurant.

Chandra stood there, deflated. Her mother was putting way too much stock into something she knew nothing about.

"Are you almost done playing with your food?" she snapped at Jason.

"Yeah."

"Get your gloves on and go out back and help Mike."

"I have to?"

"You promised."

He jumped down from his stool. "No, you promised. This sucks," he said as he walked out of the restaurant and through the kitchen.

Chandra rested her hands flat on the bar. She needed to wrap her head around all of this Mike stuff. She could admit, she moved too fast in giving him a job. It was Gabe's fault he lived upstairs. And what was with that hug earlier?

The printer to her side began to print. Thank goodness someone needed a drink. She knew she sure did.

MIKE LAUGHED EVERY TIME JASON PICKED UP A BOX AND GROANED. He couldn't blame him. The feeling was mutual.

"How much more do we have to do?" Jason asked as they trudged up the stairs for the hundredth time.

"Just a few more. I'll put the rest of the storage container in your garage."

He turned and looked at him. "You're putting it in our garage?"

"Your mom offered."

"Did she say I had to help?"

"She might have mentioned it."

"Ug," he growled as he carried the box into the apartment.

"Maybe you should just marry my mom, and then you won't make me move you again."

Mike dropped the box he was carrying at the suggestion. "Wow, so that you don't have to help me again? You're selling out your mom?"

Jason put the box he carried into the pile of boxes that line the back wall. "I'm just saying. She likes you. You like her. I like you. I don't ever want to do this again. You might as well get married."

It would be rude to laugh, he thought, especially since Jason seemed to be completely serious. "I've only known your mom four days. She might want more time to think about it."

"She only knew my dad for a week before she got pregnant with me. I guess you're ahead of the game."

And just like that, Mike was at a loss for words.

"I'm going to go down and lock up the container," he said to Jason. "You alright up here?"

"Sure. I won't touch anything."

"You know my TV is hooked up to the satellite in the bar. You could watch something if you want. I'll ask your mom for something to drink, and then we'll work on math."

Jason fell on the couch and groaned. "See, you're just like a dad. Do this. Do that. Let's work on math. Why stop?"

The air in Mike's lungs whooshed out. Things were about to get very complicated.

CHANDRA WATCHED MIKE WALK THROUGH THE KITCHEN AND TALK to everyone as he passed through. He was certainly a fixture there now. She caught herself smiling, and turned it off.

"Where's Jason?"

"Upstairs watching TV. I told him I'd come and get us some drinks. What can we have, Mom?" He grinned, and her stomach tightened.

"I'll get some juice. What do you want?"

"Whatever he's having. Fair is fair."

She pulled the apple juice container out of the refrigerator under the bar and poured two glasses as Mike pulled his wallet from his pocket. "What are you doing?"

"Buying us some drinks," he said very matter-of-factly. "I'm not here for the freebies. You've already extended enough of them to me."

"For work."

"Sure, but..."

She pushed the glasses toward him. "No buts. You're not paying for these."

"Well, we thank you," he said tucking his wallet back in his pocket. "Can I tell you that I like your hair down, without you thinking I'm coming on to you?"

Chandra narrowed her gaze on him. "My mother is already convinced that's the case. You might as well."

"Oh, I'm missing something good here. What did she say?"

"She wanted to know if she could bring me back some clean clothes since I slept here and all."

"You did," he confirmed as he took a sip from one of the glasses.

"That's not what she's assuming. She thinks I slept with you."

Mike coughed on the juice. "Wow. We must have something hot going on, and we're not privy to it. Jason would like me to marry you."

"What?" She nearly dropped the glass she'd picked up to fill. "What in the hell did you tell him?"

"No, no. You have it wrong. He thinks that I sound like a dad. Do this. Do that. Let's do math." She chuckled, and he continued. "He also would like to not move my stuff again, and he figures if we get married we only have to move it one time, and not upstairs and to your garage, and then somewhere else."

Chandra snorted out a laugh. "He's lazy and selling me out."

"That's what I said. He says you like me. I like you. And he likes me. Really, I do sound like quite a catch," he laughed and picked up both glasses from the bar. "I guess you should give it some consideration." His grin was wider now, and she set the glass down as her hands had begun to shake. She watched him retrace his entrance and disappear to his apartment where her son awaited him—a father figure.

CHAPTER 14

*C*handra had received the text that pizza had been delivered, but she was right in the middle of a strange early Thursday rush.

Be up when I can, she replied.

She filled seven more drink orders, handled the hostess station while the hostess moved her car off the street for the third time, and delivered a meal that had been returned two times. Sometimes, all it took was someone with authority to approach the table and then things were fine.

When she finally climbed the stairs, she could hear laughter coming from the apartment. At least her family was having a fun night she thought as she knocked on the door.

Mike answered with a huge grin. "You don't have to knock."

"I most certainly do. This is your home."

"Come in. Meet my son."

Panic shot right into Chandra's chest. "He's here?"

"Skype."

Chandra stepped into the apartment and watched as her son juggled the soccer ball with his feet and the boy on the computer screen, balanced on the mantel, encouraged him.

"Little dude, you've got moves," the guy on the computer said as Mike walked into view.

"One more for you to meet. This is Chandra," he said pulling her in front of him and resting his hands on her shoulders.

She tensed under his touch but smiled.

"Chandra, this is my son Dane," Mike continued the introduction.

"Nice to meet you. Your father talks about you a lot," she greeted him and wondered what he must be thinking about Mike touching her as he was. It was completely out of the norm for them. Then again, in four days, did two people have a norm?

"Hey, Chandra. Nice to meet you too. Dad talks about you too," he said with a grin and a nod.

She could feel the heat rise in her cheeks and running away to escape the awkwardness of the moment crossed her mind.

Mike removed his hands and walked toward his computer, picking it up from the mantel, he walked toward the kitchen.

"I'll let you go so we can eat this overpriced pizza," he said with a laugh. "Email me your tentative schedule for spring break. I'll do some research on ski rental."

"Okay, Dad. I love you."

"I love you too, kiddo," Mike said before he closed his computer.

Jason began serving himself a piece of pizza and slapping it onto a paper plate. Chandra was quick to throw a napkin his direction.

"Did you guys work on some math?"

"Uh-huh," Jason grunted as he bit into his pizza.

Mike dished a piece out to Chandra and her mother before taking a piece for himself and sitting down.

"I tell ya," Mike began. "The math he's doing in fifth grade was what I was doing in seventh or eighth. Were we dumb or are they trying to cram these kids with a serious amount of information."

Esther held a finger up as she chewed her bite. "It's all that common core crap. Seriously, there was a good method in place. Why ruin it?"

Chandra shook her head. "Things change, Mom."

Her mother let out a snort and went on to eat her slice.

"So your son is coming out for spring break?" she asked Mike, suddenly not too hungry.

"He's thinking about it. He's worried about me and doesn't want to spend it with his mom and her new boyfriend."

"How's he dealing with that?"

Mike shrugged. "Better than I am I think," he admitted, and that seemed to put an ache in Chandra's chest. Shouldn't he be okay with it? What would it matter? A divorce meant that people moved on and went their own ways and saw other people. He had a problem, she decided, and it was reason enough to squelch any of those little feelings that seemed to be creeping in on her. Mike Cavanagh was the guy living upstairs. She didn't need to be more—perhaps considering him as a friend was causing her too much unnecessary pain.

Mike bit into his slice and looked up at Chandra. "Are you sure you're okay with me storing my stuff in your garage for a little bit? Jason and I got the important stuff up here, but the rest, well, it's just not that important."

Chandra nodded. She supposed there wasn't any getting away from the guy.

Esther sipped her drink and then threw up a hand. "I forgot, Mike. I had Jason take me by that house you were looking at yesterday."

"Oh, yeah? What'd ya think?"

"It was a looker," she laughed. "I think it would be a great investment."

"I suppose it would be."

"I did a little digging too. Not a whole bunch, but it's owned by an investment company. You know, buys up real estate. It is for sale."

Chandra watched Mike's eyes light, but the shimmer dimmed quickly. "I'm sure it'll be gone before I can even formally accept the offer on that new job."

Esther sat back in her chair and folded her arms in front of her. "You need a partner."

"Mom…" Chandra said in warning, but her mother leaned in toward Mike without care.

"You and I should sit down and discuss it. I need an investment. You need some capital and some roots. Let it sink in for a spell. That house ain't going nowhere," she accentuated her offer with a nod.

Mike's eyes were wide now. "I'll give it some thought."

Chandra could feel a tension headache forming behind her eyes. Her mother was one who studied someone's character very carefully before she fully trusted them. How come Mike was someone she was so willing to give everything to?

He was going to get a very late night visit she decided as she finished her pizza. They had some boundaries to discuss when it came to her family.

～

WHEN EVERYONE HAD LEFT FOR THE EVENING, MIKE CHANGED into his favorite lounge pants, which were now in his possession. He turned on ESPN and enjoyed watching a vintage hockey game. Things had changed, he thought as he watched. The sticks were much more sophisticated now, and he wondered why anyone would ever want to play the sport without a helmet.

He'd asked Esther for the address to the house, and now he was doing his own investigation.

After nearly an hour of looking at his computer screen, Mike closed his laptop and walked toward his window. It was just past ten, and the restaurant had been quiet for the past two hours. He was sure it wouldn't be long before Chandra drove away.

He'd considered going down and having a beer an hour ago, but after her mother had proposed the partnership with him, Chandra had grown a bit distant. He didn't think he needed to egg on any animosity she was brewing with him.

Mike stood in the window for a few minutes and saw the others leave and drive away. Chandra would be driving by any moment, he thought, and that's why when there was a knock at his door it startled the hell out of him.

He walked across the room and pulled open the door. There was no doubt who was on the other side. No need to look through the peephole.

"I want to talk to you," Chandra moved by him and walked into the apartment.

Mike closed the door and turned to see her standing in front of the mantel, looking at his photos.

"You look moved in," she said.

"Those were there a few hours ago when you were here."

"I wasn't looking then." She picked up one of the frames which had his ex-wife and son in it. "How long ago was this?"

He moved to her and looked at the picture. "Hawaii, ten years ago."

"You look happy together."

"We were then," he remembered. "I can't say we were ever horribly unhappy. Just not compatible."

She replaced the frame and turned to him. Her hair had been pulled back in the past few hours, and he noticed the dark circles under her eyes.

"I think you and I need to talk."

"Okay. Have a seat. We can talk," he offered. "Can I get you anything?"

"No. I'm fine." She took a deep breath. "I'm worried about you with my family. They don't know you, and they're buying a lot of stock in you."

"We're getting to know each other. All of us."

"Yeah, well, it bothers me that Jason says things like if you married my mom. Or my mom wanting to go into a business venture with you."

"Chandra, hold up a moment."

"No. You need to know where I stand on all of this. I mean you walk into the restaurant all sad, and in four days you have a handyman job, an apartment, my son counts on you being at his game, my mom wants to be your partner..." She tugged at her ponytail and tightened it. "It's a lot."

Mike took a step closer to her. "And none of this would have happened had you not believed in me from the moment I followed you up those stairs to fix that sink." He pointed toward the kitchen.

"Right... well..."

He inched in even closer, and she stepped back until her back was to the wall.

"What are you really afraid of?" he asked keeping his eyes on hers.

"I don't need this. I have a full plate. I'm a single mom. I'm doing all I can until Gabe gets back. I'm..."

"Afraid that in the past four days something has sparked between us, and you can't figure out what it is."

She fisted her hands on her hips. "There is nothing."

"Really? Your son said you don't introduce them to many men."

"No. I don't."

"I met them the next day."

Her shoulders dropped, but he was sure she hadn't realized she'd let down her guard as her eyes were still focused.

"It was by chance."

"No," he said moving even closer to her and resting his hand on the wall next to her so that he was leaned in over her. "You had to place the call to get me a house full of stuff and dinner that night. Why would you have done that if you didn't feel something."

"I'm a nice person, damn it."

"Yes, you are. You're absolutely beautiful too."

Her eyes went wide. "What?"

"You heard me," he said lifting his hand up to her hair and twirling her ponytail around his finger. "You think you're tough, and you are. But your heart is soft, and that scares you."

Chandra moved out from beneath him. "You don't know anything. I came here to tell you… well, I think you…"

He folded his arms in front of him. "You want me to keep away from your family."

"Yes. No." A crease formed between her brows. "I don't want you to lead them astray. You made promises…"

"Which I will keep whether you drive me there or not," he confirmed. "I promised a young boy I'd watch him score against the other team, and I'll damn well be there."

"My mom. She doesn't throw her money around."

"She's a sensible woman. Just like her daughter. I would never lead her astray either. I would only consider her offer if I thought there was nothing to lose."

"There's always something to lose."

"You're right," he agreed as he moved to the kitchen and rested his hands on the back of one of the chairs. "Are we done here?"

From the look on her face, he'd turned the tables, and she hadn't been prepared for that.

Chandra licked her lips and looked at the floor as if she were gathering more fuel for a fight. But when she looked up, she looked lost, and that's what he'd been hoping for.

"Mike, I…"

He was done talking.

He walked around the table and swiftly pulled her to him with one arm around her waist, and a hand pressed to her cheek.

Her hands came to his chest, and she gasped, but she didn't pull away.

Mike kept his eyes locked with hers. "I don't want to stay away, and I will never let you down on purpose," he said clearly before covering her mouth with his.

CHAPTER 15

*C*olors swirled behind her eyelids, which Chandra had instinctively closed when Mike's mouth came down on hers. It would have made more sense to have pushed him away, but for some reason, that hadn't even come to mind at the moment he began to kiss her.

Her body had gone against what her mind should have told her. Everything went soft the instant he'd yanked her to him.

Mike hadn't lifted his head. His hand still caressed her cheek and his lips—soft, yet strong—still covered hers and she was lost.

Oh, it had been a long time since she'd been kissed, and she wasn't sure she'd ever been kissed this well.

His tongue pressed through her lips and tangled with her own, and now her breath became thick and hard to push through her lungs. All she could do was wrap her arms around him and hold on tight because he was taking her under and the sheer pleasure of him was making her unable to think.

As the kiss heated, her hands moved to his hair, and they began to move backward until her leg hit the arm of the couch and they both tumbled back on it.

Now his body was pressed on hers, and her legs came around

him to keep him close. His lips moved from hers and traveled down her throat. Every part of her body throbbed with need as she pulled him back to her mouth and kissed him again.

When she thought her mind might go numb from the kiss he'd presented her with, he pulled back so that his forehead was pressed against hers.

"You're right, there is always something to lose, but at this moment, I'd like to think that all my misfortune found me something worth keeping."

Her heart pounded in her chest. "Mike, this isn't smart."

"It's not supposed to be. What are you worried about? No one is going to see us."

She took a moment and collected her thoughts, before she pushed him off her, rolled off the couch, and stood. "I'm not good at this stuff. I mean it's been a very long time since a man kissed me like that."

"That's too bad. You're very good at it."

She let out a slight laugh. "Jason…"

"Will be fine with me if you're honest."

"You're not doing this because of what he said are you?"

Mike shook his head and moved to her, wrapping his arm around her again, keeping her close. "No, I've pretty much wanted to do that since I sat down at your bar the first day. You take my breath away."

"No, I think you just did that to me."

"I mean it. I won't let you down on purpose if you keep me in your life. And, now you know where I stand."

She stared up at him, enjoying the feel of his arms around her and his breath against her cheek. Chandra bit down on her bottom lip and wondered how long something like this could last. It hadn't been a lie. She was horrible at relationships. They usually didn't last a month. But she couldn't help but want to see what Mike had to offer.

Gazing into those crystal blue eyes, she saw something more.

There was a gracious heart in this family man, and he wanted to be with her. Or did he really?

She pushed back and broke from his embrace. Wrapping her arms around herself, she looked out the window, down to the dark street below.

"Why did you do that?"

"Kiss you?"

"Yes," she said as she turned to him. "What does a man want when he kisses a woman only a few days after meeting her?"

When his eyes went wide, she figured she'd crossed a line, but she held strong and continued, "I've been in this business a long time. This isn't the first place I've tended bar. Men come to drink their sorrows away and get laid."

"And you think that's what I'm doing?"

"You're a man," her answer was direct and blunt.

He nodded and ran his hand over the new growth of whiskers on his chin. "Well then, I guess you know where I stand and I know where you stand." Mike walked to the door and pulled it open. "Well, Ms. Chavez, I guess this is goodnight. If you wouldn't mind texting me the address of the soccer game for Saturday, I'd appreciate it."

Chandra stood there at a loss for words. She was supposed to have told him how she felt and walked out. Now she was being escorted out.

As she walked toward the door, she took a breath to say something, but then she wasn't sure what to say, and that was when Mike closed the door between them.

CHANDRA'S DRIVE HOME SEEMED LONGER THAN USUAL, AND SHE only lived a few miles away. But she'd found herself driving slowly, watching the snow fall and catch the street lights. Somehow she managed to drive down the streets Jason walked every day from school, and she saw the house Mike had been telling her about.

She stopped in the middle of the street and watched the moon shine against it as the snow collected in its yard. For the first time in her life, she could see the potential in something dark and ugly, just as she assumed Mike had seen.

Chandra continued on home and parked her car out front. She usually parked in back, but tonight she needed to appreciate it as a home. For a moment after she turned off the engine, she sat there and watched the snow glisten in the light from her porch. Many memories had been made in that house. It had always been hers and Jason's. She'd bought it with her inheritance from her father, and shortly after her mother moved in to help her. What would Chandra have done if she hadn't stepped up and taken on that role that a husband or a present father might have?

Tears came to Chandra's eyes, and she quickly wiped them away. She'd long ago given up even thinking of a husband for her or a father figure for her son. Gabe wasn't the only one who fell into a child. Only his story had a happy ending.

Oh, who was she kidding? Her story was just as happy. She had the world's greatest son, what did it matter that his father didn't care?

He'd come around every few years, stayed a day, confused her son, and left after making empty promises. After a while, it stopped being important to her to have a man around. Jason was just fine without one.

Panic rose in her chest. What if Mike's promises were empty too? What if he didn't show up to that game tomorrow? What if he didn't help him again with his math, or talk to him anymore? Would that be her fault? He'd pushed her out of his apartment after kissing her senseless.

It wasn't worth the commitment and the disappointment to get involved, she decided as she opened her door and stepped out into the fresh snow. Jason would get over him, and soon he'd just be the man living upstairs.

Chandra walked around the side of the house and let herself into the dark kitchen. Even the light over the stove wasn't on for her tonight. On the table was a covered plate, and she moved in to partake in whatever her mother had baked.

On top there was a note; For Mike, Don't Eat!

She gritted her teeth and moved on to her room. All these years she'd been working to support her family, and some man comes along and steals their hearts. Enough was enough.

Shutting her door, she gave it a quiet kick. How depressing was it that she couldn't even throw a good fit in her own house if she wanted to.

Pulling the band from her ponytail, she let her hair fall to her shoulders. She could smell his shampoo in her hair, and even that infuriated her.

Four days. She'd known him for four days. There was no reason to get so worked up about a man she—and then she stopped internally berating herself and plopped down on her bed.

It was if it all made sense.

None of this had anything to do with Mike and everything to do with her.

She batted her eyes against tears that fought to surface. There was no reason for tears. Only one man had ever made her forget her senses before in such a short amount of time. She wasn't about to do it again.

It had been a moment of weakness that caused her to fall in love with Austin. He'd been a smooth talker and oh, what a looker.

Just that fast she'd fallen in love and fallen in bed—only to get pregnant and watch him walk away three months later.

She probably could move on from it. After all, it had been ten years. However, every time the man decided to make an appearance in his son's life, she fell all over again. And every time it ended with him leaving her—and Jason.

She couldn't afford to do it again. Jason was right. They didn't meet the men she dated because she didn't date. And if she went out with anyone, she left it as a date and moved on. There was no reason to give her son false hopes and have a relationship with a man.

Chandra wiped her eyes. She was just a lonely woman and a man, whom she found herself attracted to—oddly enough—had shown interest in her. Flattery was all it was. He'd swept her off her feet for just a moment—and she'd enjoyed every breathtaking moment.

Now she could move on. The kiss was just a kiss between two lonely people. Tomorrow she'd go to work, and he'd attend to his remodeling. If he bothered to show up to the game, well, then she'd see him there too. And of course she'd give him the address, but she was under no obligation to see him to the game. He was a grown man.

Satisfied with her decisions, she began to undress. Until Gabe returned to work, sleep was the only time she had at home. She might as well try to get some.

But as she laid her head back on her pillow the tingle of the kiss with Mike tickled her senses. What were the chances he'd ever try that again?

~

BECAUSE SHE WAS IN NEED OF SOME, CHANDRA STOPPED FOR coffee. And in fact, she was a foofy creamer kind of girl on this particular Saturday morning. Not only that, she felt like a breakfast sandwich would be well deserved since she had to open the restaurant in the fresh snow.

Of course, she wasn't an unkind person, so she ordered two of everything, just in case Mike might be standing at the door ready to apologize for kicking her out of his apartment or kissing her in the first place.

But much to her dismay, he wasn't standing there. When the first of her staff arrived, she walked up to his door and knocked, but he didn't answer.

Where could he have possibly gone, she wondered. Was he inside and ignoring her? That was just rude.

She left the coffee and the sandwich on the floor. He'd know it was from her. He'd have to come and thank her for it. Chandra was sure that then he'd issue his apology.

Eventually, the lunch rush came and occupied her mind, but then again so did he. He'd never shown up. When her phone buzzed in her pocket, she quickly pulled it out to see that her mother was calling.

"Hi, Mom."

"Are you coming to this game?" she asked, and Chandra felt her heart sink into her stomach.

"I'll be there in ten."

Damn it. She'd been so preoccupied with worrying about Mike she hadn't kept track of her time. Ernest was at the restaurant,, and he was taking her place for a few hours. That should have signaled to her that she was supposed to be somewhere else.

She grabbed her bag out of the office and headed for the door. Then she remembered she'd never texted Mike the address. Oh, she wasn't going to let him off the hook for this.

She unlocked the door between the restaurant and the stairs and ran up them. Sitting at his door was the coffee and the sandwich she'd laid there that morning.

Now she was furious with the man. Where had he stayed all night? If he hadn't left his apartment all day, chances were he'd never been in it in the first place.

Anger boiled inside her, and that man was going to get an earful when she saw him. Because now, he was poised to disappoint her son, and she wasn't going to have that.

CHAPTER 16

*M*ike paced next to the field, chewing on his thumb as Jason lined up. He'd given him the pep talk he'd always given his son, and he'd seen the glimmer in Jason's eyes that he'd once seen in Dane's.

It was silly really, to pray and wish for a miracle goal for a kid he barely knew, but he was doing it. In fact, it was making him a little sick inside. The worry. The look in a young boy's eyes when he'd been defeated. Did he have it in him to talk him back up?

Seriously, it was too much pressure he thought as he bit on his thumb.

"You should come sit," Esther yelled down to him from her seat in the bleachers. "You can see better up here."

He laughed. "I will in a bit. I guess this is ritual. I used to do it with my son."

Her smile changed tone, from humored to heartfelt. She gave him a nod and eased back against the stadium seat cushion she'd carried in with her.

The whistle blew, and the game began. Mike looked down at his watch and then up in the stands. Where in the hell could

Chandra be? She hadn't texted him the address. He'd had to ask Esther for that. She hadn't called him—not that he'd expected her to be pleasant if she had. He was quite sure she'd be mad at him for kicking her out of his apartment last night, but hey, his ego had been crumbled, he had every right to ask her to leave, he'd decided.

"Where have you been?" He heard her voice, and when he turned, she was hurrying toward him.

"I've been here," he quickly snapped and then turned his attention to the game.

"Since seven o'clock this morning?"

"Checking up on me, Ms. Chavez? Didn't see it in the lease where I had to leave my schedule."

He kept his eye on the game, but he could see her nostrils flare and her eyes grow wider.

"You're right. It's none of my business."

"Nope."

"You don't have to be an ass about it."

"I don't think that's in my lease either. I can be an ass if I want to. You don't seem to like it when I'm genuine about my feelings, so…"

"You're throwing that in my face?"

He shifted her a quick glance. "No, I'm stating a fact. I thought the kiss was decent. Maybe not my best work, but hey, I enjoyed it. You seemed put out and not interested. I moved on."

"Moved on? Since last night, you've moved on? Is that why you didn't sleep in your own bed last night?"

Now he turned to her fully. "Excuse me?"

He saw her cheeks fill with color, but her eyes remained dark. "Since seven o'clock this morning, you haven't been home."

"You're right. I haven't."

"So where were you?"

"Is that part of my lease, because I'm missing the part where I have to check in with you."

Her body tensed, but at that moment his phone rang. Thank goodness for his son's timing, he thought as he accepted the face-time call.

"Sorry I'm late, Dad. Did I miss the game?"

"Just got started. He looks good. He's number 7," he said as he turned his phone toward the field so Dane could partake in the game.

CHANDRA STOOD THERE AND WATCHED MIKE TALK TO HIS SON, while his son watched her son play soccer from California. Seriously, he'd invited his son to watch too? Who was this man?

Her attention turned to the field when the whistle blew, and she watched Mike turn the phone and look at his son.

Did he know his face lit up when he looked at him? She knew hers did the same when she looked at Jason. Everyone told her that.

"Say hi to Chandra," Mike said as he turned the phone and she was then face to face Dane.

She smiled, hoping it looked genuine. "Hey, Dane."

"Hey. Thanks for inviting Dad to the game. This is fun. I miss playing league."

"Can you see it okay?" Her voice shook.

"Yeah, yeah. I'll be out for spring break. Maybe we can kick a ball around when I'm there if he's interested."

Her throat tightened, and she pushed down emotions she didn't want to surface. "I'm sure he'd love that."

"Game on," Mike said as he turned the phone back around.

Though she didn't know what to expect, she decided to let her guard down, and she stepped up next to Mike. He turned to look at her, so she offered a smile. Any man who made sure to be at a game for a boy he promised, even though she'd neglected to give him the address, and then facetimed his own son to watch— he was a keeper. Maybe romance wasn't right for them. They really were two lost souls, but he couldn't be that bad for her right now.

She turned to look up at her mother and noticed that she looked away when Chandra made eye contact, but there was a smile there.

It had been a long time since she'd let her heart try something new. Maybe it was time.

"He's got the ball. He's got the ball!" Mike's voice shook her from her thoughts.

Dane's voice rang out from the phone. "Go! Go! Go!"

She looked out onto the field and watched as her son took possession of the ball, and he maneuvered it down the field. He was fast. He was accurate, and no one was catching him.

Her heart pounded in her chest, and she pressed her hands to the glass.

Jason took the ball to the end of the field, and both teams were now running in his direction. It was between him and the goalie.

Chandra heard Mike yelling, and Dane too. Her mother's voice stood out from the crowd behind her. She lifted her hands to her eyes. She couldn't see this. She couldn't watch. What if he missed?

"He's got it. He's got it," Mike repeated as she looked between her fingers as her son took the kick he'd been talking about for weeks.

It went toward the goal, and the goalie moved in its path. As the ball rose toward the net, the goalie jumped, but only managed to deflect the ball back to Jason who then gave it another solid kick, and it flew into the net.

The team rushed Jason and pulled him in. She couldn't even see him anymore. A moment later Mike's arm came around her and pulled her close.

Her breath caught as he cheered Jason, and then swiftly pulled her in and kissed her hard on the mouth.

It was a reaction she knew because he then went back to cheering with his son. But when she looked for her son, he stood there watching. There certainly was an air of confusion on his face having just witnessed Mike kiss her, but then it turned into a wide, accepting smile before he gave Mike a thumbs up and ran back to the sideline.

As Jason walked to the sidelines and the next line of players moved into position, Mike took his phone and walked out of earshot.

She stood there alone, the heat of the kiss still surging through her. She turned to look up at her mother, who seemed to be intently watching the game, but the smile on her face surely gave away the fact that she'd seen what Mike had done.

Perhaps it was time to face it. Chandra started up the bleachers and sat down next to her mother.

"He did it," her mother said as the whistle blew and the game continued.

"He sure did."

"I think Mike had a lot to do with that."

"I think Jason did that on his own," Chandra argued. "He's had it in him the whole time."

"Yeah, but as a parent, you can tell them they're the best at everything, and they don't believe you. But bring in just the right person, and they suddenly do believe it."

"I don't want him to think that everything in his life will be good just because of Mike."

Her mother shrugged. "You seem happier." The smile was back, and Chandra shook her head.

"Don't read into that. He was just excited."

"Excited enough to kiss you. And kiss you very well."

"We're too different for anything to work between us."

Her mother turned her attention from the game. "What's happened between you?"

"Nothing. He kissed me last night and then kicked me out of his apartment."

Her mother nodded slowly, but Chandra would have felt better had she found it appalling that he'd dismissed her. "I assume he kicked you out because of this negative attitude you have."

"Look at him." She shifted her attention to where he stood talking to his son on the phone. "He's not like us."

"I spent my whole life tearing down stereotypes, and now my daughter believes in them?"

"You know what I mean," Chandra argued.

Her mother folded her hands in her lap. "No, I don't think I do know what you're talking about. I assume that since you have tattoos and he doesn't, that's a deal breaker. Your mom and dad drove trucks to feed you, and his parents had a nice B and B, that's a problem. You tend a bar. He's got a good job offer now for a startup that could become something. You think that you're less than him?"

She wanted to argue that her mother had it all wrong, but she wasn't sure she did.

"I'm not good at relationships. He deserves someone better than me."

"Your taste in men just sucks. You're stuck in the mindset that they have to be like you. Maybe different is better. Same hasn't worked out for you, has it?"

Dealing with the disappointment from Jason over missing his soccer game would have been easier than listening to her mother point out her grand flaws.

"I understand same," Chandra crossed her arms in front of her. "Same has a way of finding me."

"Oh, my God," her mother said, and her eyes had gone wide.

"What?"

"It has a way of finding you, alright. When you least expect it and need it."

"What are you talking about?" she asked as she followed her mother's line of sight. "Oh, my God!"

~

MIKE TOLD HIS SON HE LOVED HIM AND HUNG UP THE PHONE. TWO more weeks and he'd be coming for a visit. He couldn't remember when he'd been happier. Not having his son close by had been the only downfall to moving to Colorado, but he continued to convince himself that it was for the best. It gave Dane a chance to be an adult without his father hovering over him. And it gave Mike an opportunity to move on.

He hadn't seen the detour coming that was for sure. Who would have thought he'd stumble into the restaurant that would now become his whole existence? And of course, then there was the feisty tattooed bartender that seemed to have all of his attention.

It was going to take some time to win her over, he decided. But since the moment he'd kissed her last night, he knew he wanted to.

Jason jogged across the field and high-fived the glass, waiting for Mike to return his gesture. Ah, one of the perks to indoor soccer, Mike thought, as he returned the high five.

Then he noticed Jason's expression change as he looked up toward his mother. The enthusiasm was gone. He hurried to the center of the field, but the same energy wasn't there.

Mike tucked his phone into his pocket and turned to see a man standing with Chandra. His hair was long, nearly as long as hers, and jet black, pulled back in a ponytail that also matched hers. He had on a heavy leather jacket, but Mike could clearly see the tattoos on his neck and hands.

He sported a full goatee and a few earrings. No one needed to tell Mike who the man was. No one needed to explain why

Chandra had been so put off by his affection either. Mike wasn't her type of man, that sure as hell was obvious.

The man put his arm around her shoulders and pulled her in tight to him.

Mike was out of place. Perhaps it was time to head out. Jason and Chandra looked as though they'd have plans later, and he had a job to do. That apartment wasn't going to refurbish itself while he stood at a soccer arena feeling sorry for himself.

CHAPTER 17

*J*ason's expression had been as loud in her head as if he'd screamed at her, Chandra thought, as he'd gone back out to play. He hadn't expected to see his dad, and by the way he was playing now, he wasn't too keen on it.

She'd kept her eyes on where Mike had been standing, but he'd disappeared. He showed up for his glory, just as he'd promised he would, and then took off. What was it about men deciding it was better just to leave?

Austin hollered at the referee when he blew the whistle, and the players looked up in the stands. Chandra could feel the heat fill her cheeks, and Jason had walked off the field.

Chandra sat down, and eventually, Austin followed suit.

"What are you doing here?" she asked.

"Came to see you and the kid."

She hated when he called him that. "You should have told us you were coming."

He shrugged. "Things just work out, ya know? I had some time." He winked, and she knew exactly what that meant.

"You're out of a job, huh?"

"Freaking idiots who run casinos. Laid off a handful of us. You know, we don't fit the bill."

Oh, she'd heard that excuse from him for years. But what he was really saying was he couldn't pay the few dollars in child support she sometimes got, and he was going to be looking to sleep on her couch.

Her mother squirmed next to her. She hadn't even acknowledged Austin and vice versa.

"Where are you staying?" She had to ask. Might as well get the obvious out of the way.

"Oh, babe, I was going to stay and visit for a while. You know. Spend some time with you and the kid."

"Jason."

"I know his name," he argued, then flashed her that smile that used to turn her into a pile of goo.

She watched as Jason took the field again. When he looked her way, there was sadness in his eyes. The day certainly wasn't going the way she'd wanted.

Jason ran down the field. He was open for the pass, but when the ball was kicked in his direction, it was swiftly intercepted by the other team.

"Damn!" Austin shook his head. "He's not very good, is he?"

Chandra watched her mother close her eyes and take in a deep breath. Then she began to gather her things and stood to collapse her stadium seat. "I'm going to head out to the lobby and get something to drink," she said, carrying her bag and seat with her.

Chandra wasn't a fool. The woman wasn't coming back to sit and listen to her grandson's father criticize him.

When her mother was gone, Chandra sat down, and Austin followed. "You know he scored earlier. The first point of the game."

"No kidding? Wide open net, huh?" He laughed at his own joke.

There wasn't even any reason to go on, she thought. She looked again to where Mike had stood, but he hadn't returned. She'd focus on giving him a piece of her mind when she got back to work. The last thing she wanted was him letting Jason down.

~

MIKE HAD GOTTEN AS FAR AS THE DOOR BEFORE HE'D TURNED BACK around and stood off to the corner of the lobby to watch the rest of the game. He rested his arms on the counter and watched as Jason let the ball slip away from between his feet.

"You hiding too?" Esther's voice had him turning his head.

"Was under the impression I was going to be in the way," he said.

Esther plopped her bag up on the counter. "For the next week to a month, we'll all be in the way."

"I take it that's Jason's dad?"

"Can you really even call him that?" She huffed out a breath. "Dads are interactive. Dads care. Dads… well you know. You're a good dad."

He smiled. "Thanks."

"Jason deserves more than that," she nodded in Austin's direction. "Shows up when he needs something, and that girl of mine seems to forget everything when he's around. Gets her heart broken every time."

"How does Jason deal with it?"

"See how he's playing?" Mike winced when she said it. "Yep, you know what I'm talking about. He takes it in stride. Enjoys the attention for the few minutes he gets it, and then he gets heartbroken too. There's a cycle."

"That's not fair to either of them."

"Never is. So I've already texted Tracy and asked to stay with her for the week."

"You have a system?"

"Boy do I." She turned to him and rested her arm on the counter. "Still looking into that house?"

He folded his hands in front of him. "Keeps crossing my mind. Peter offered me a signing bonus, thought that could go a ways. I have the apartment until I'm done renovating it. Then I could live in the house. But I just can't commit yet. Besides, it still doesn't have a for sale sign."

Esther puckered her lips. "I'm nosy. I poked around. The investment company that owns it is just holding it. They're willing to sell."

"Really?" His voice rose. "You're a good sleuth."

"I have nothing to do when Jason's at school." She laughed. "Offer is still on the table. I'd like to be part of it if you move ahead with it."

"Chandra's afraid I'll steal your money."

She laughed again. "I'm not."

He leaned over and kissed her on the cheek. "Let's have lunch next week and lay out some plans. Then we can look into moving forward."

"I think that sounds lovely."

～

CHANDRA PLACED THE CALL TO THE RESTAURANT TO CHECK ON Ernest, as they walked out of the soccer arena. Austin had momentarily won Jason's attention as they hurried toward her car.

Ernest convinced her that he was fine in charge and she should take the afternoon off. He'd be there until close anyway.

She hated to turn over her responsibilities, especially since she was covering for Gabe. But it seemed as though she was going to have no choice.

Once they got home, she and Austin were going to have a long talk. She didn't want to keep going through this on again off again relationship when it was convenient to him. She didn't want it for Jason either. They both deserved better than a man who dropped in every two or three years and made a mess before he left again.

She unlocked the car and Jason threw his stuff into the backseat. "Where's grandma?"

"She texted and said Tracy came by and picked her up," she said through grit teeth.

"Did she watch my game?"

"All of it."

"And Mike?"

Austin climbed into the front seat and turned to look at Jason. "Who's Mike?"

Chandra quickly started the engine. "He's a friend. He lives above the restaurant where Gabe used to live."

His brows drew in, and she knew he'd been gone a long time.

Putting the car into drive, she pulled out of the parking lot. "Gabe is the nephew of the man who owned the restaurant where I work. He lived upstairs until he got married. He's on paternity leave, and I'm managing the restaurant."

She saw the grin on his face from the corner of her eye. "You're the woman in charge, huh? Making the big bucks?"

She thought she might be sick just listening to him talk. "I'm in charge. No big bucks."

"And the guy upstairs?"

"He's a handyman who helps out and is renovating the apartment."

"Handyman?" He clucked his tongue. "My son worries about the handyman?"

She gripped the steering wheel tightly. "They've become friends," she said as she looked in the mirror at Jason, who simply looked out the window. He might be mad at her, but at least he didn't dive into anything that would lead Austin to believe there might be something between them because until

Austin arrived, there might have been that thought. "How long are you staying?"

"I'm back, baby," he said, just as he always did when he came around. "Thought I'd teach the kid how to play soccer for real."

She glanced back again, but Jason still stared out the window.

Somewhere inside of her, a piece got lost when Austin would show up. She could escort the biggest, drunkest men out of a bar, but she couldn't stand up to the weasel that showed up every few years. Jason didn't even carry his last name, so why did she worry that she couldn't just dump him on the side of the road?

Glancing at him, she remembered why. She'd fallen for the bad boy image. He was tattooed from his neck to his knee, and she loved the mystery in that. When she was younger, she'd admit, she loved him for the danger he brought on the back of his bike and the sensations he gave her in bed. But the heartbreaks he'd dished out over and over didn't make up for it.

A little piece of her disappeared each time he came back, and there was no doubt in her mind she'd fall into his charm, his arms, and into bed with the man before he disappeared into the night again.

Her mind wandered back to Mike kissing her in his apartment and then escorting her out. Why hadn't she let that kiss linger longer instead of turning on him? Perhaps if she thought Mike could love her, she wouldn't already be considering the eventual fall she'd be having over Austin.

It hurt so much she rubbed her palm between her breasts to numb the pain.

She had a type. Looking at Austin, she realized he was exactly it. Bad boy, tattooed, and damn it—unemployed.

Wouldn't it be nice if a decent man, one who was employable and kind to her son, wanted her too?

As she waited for the light to turn green, she bit down hard on her finger.

"Oh, you're nervous. What's up, sweet cheeks?"

She watched the light turn green, and she gripped the steering wheel and gunned the car through the intersection.

"Don't call me that."

"Chill."

"I need to get back to work."

"That's cool. I'll hang with the kid at the house."

She gritted her teeth and took a breath to combat the idea when Jason spoke, "It's okay, Mom. We'll be okay."

She cringed as Austin turned and held up his hand for a high-five. Jason returned the gesture, and Austin sat with a satisfied smug grin.

This wasn't going to happen, she promised herself as she pulled up in front of her house. He wasn't going to weasel his way into their lives. He didn't belong there, and he'd never wanted to be there.

But for a few days, she'd give him the gift of their son's attention. And as they climbed out of the car, she thought she'd head back to work and give Mike a piece of her mind.

CHAPTER 18

*M*ike stood a few feet back from the wall and studied the two paint samples he'd painted. He'd give it a few days to decide which shade to go with. His mother had always taught him to look at it in the dark, the light, bright sunlight, and dim as well. Let it grow on you, she'd say.

As much as he wanted to get a move on the apartment—and perhaps get out, he knew his mother's advice was still good.

He picked up the notebook from the kitchen table and his tape measure. As soon as he painted, he would hang new blinds. If he measured for them and ordered them, they'd be ready just in time. There were three windows in the living room and one in the bedroom. It wasn't going to be a huge cost, so he thought he'd opt for something a little better than what was there.

Later he'd set up a time to have Gabe come up to the apartment, and they could discuss the kitchen, bathroom, and the bedroom. He had some storage ideas to make the bedroom a more effective use of space.

The thought caught him and made him laugh. Bedrooms were used effectively enough, if one was lucky, he amused himself as he heard the knock on his door.

Setting the notebook on the table, he hurried to the door and pulled it open.

Esther and Tracy both stood in the hallway with grins adorning their faces.

"Well, this is a fantastic surprise. Come on in."

"We hate to bother you," Tracy said, dropping her woven bag on the table. "I brought tea. Can I interest you in some?"

Mike shut the door. "I think I have a teapot. I'll start some water. Have a seat."

"Do you mind if we sit at the table? We have some things we want to go over with you."

Mike opened the cupboard and looked around. He'd been right. There was a teapot up on the top shelf. He pulled it down, filled it, and set it on the stove.

"What could you ladies want to discuss with me?"

Esther took her jacket off and hung it on the back of the chair before sitting down. "I was telling Tracy about your thoughts on investing in that property."

"Oh, and what do you think?" he posed the question to Tracy.

"Well, I have to admit, I thought it was something I'd like to get in on. Now that I'm up here," she whistled, "I'm convinced I was right. You do wonders to dark, desolate spaces." She looked back at him after scanning a glance over the updated room. "I want in," she offered as she clapped her hands together and the arm full of bangle bracelets jingled loudly.

Mike chuckled. "Really? You both want a piece of this?"

"We do. We can finance a great deal of it. But it would be your manpower and know how that gets it going in the right direction."

He could feel the permagrin on his face tugging at his cheeks. "I can't think of two more enthusiastic partners. I have to admit. I was still on the fence about it, but looking at you two, it's hard to say no."

Esther smiled and Tracy pulled a notebook from her bag.

"We've looked up some information online and ran some preliminary numbers. Give them a look."

She pushed the notebook in his direction, and he picked it up. "You did find a lot of information online."

"I can help with the interior design," Tracy offered.

"And Jason can put in a few hours of labor after school, if you think you could use him," Esther also offered.

"He'd be a great asset if his mother is okay with it."

Esther huffed out a breath and shook her head. "She'll be fine with it when she gets her head out of her ass."

Mike was glad that the teapot began to scream at him at that moment. He turned and pulled it from the stovetop.

Opening the cupboard, he turned back to the women. "I only have two mugs."

"Oh, you two enjoy," Esther said with her lips pursing. "I'm fine."

Mike took down the mugs, filled them with water, and set them on the table. Tracy opened her bag again, and pulled out two homemade tea bags and set them in the water.

"They need about ten minutes," she said. "Sit down with us."

Mike pulled out the chair and took a seat.

It had only been a few hours since he'd talked to Esther, but in that short amount of time, she and Tracy had managed pages and pages of notes and information. It was quite fascinating.

They had facts on the neighborhood, and on the house itself. Information on who built it, and who lived in it, filled the pages of the notebook.

They'd brainstormed on marketing, and that included becoming members of the Chamber of Commerce.

Tracy, he assumed, had even thrown in a few pieces of fabric. He wasn't sure what those were for, but he liked her thinking.

"So if we get it listed with the historical society, we might be able to get a grant?" he asked after looking at the notes.

"Never hurts to look into it. It was one of the original houses in that area," Tracy said. "And you know how that goes. The historical society wants to preserve everything."

She rose from the table, walked to the cupboard, and pulled down a plate. Setting it on the table, she took her seat and pulled a mug toward her.

With her fingers, she pulled out the bag, and set it on the plate. Mike watched, and then followed suit.

Tracy picked up her mug and sniffed the aroma, and then she sipped satisfied.

Mike picked his up, sniffed as well, and forced his face not to contort into some pathetic scene. He couldn't help but notice Esther's slight grin—he'd been set up.

He took his first sip of Tracy's tea, and he hoped his skin hadn't gotten noticeable goosebumps. Swallowing the concoction Tracy had considered tea, he set his mug down and picked back up the notebook.

"I have a meeting with Peter on Monday morning about his job offer. I'll see what he's thinking, and what his terms on the signing bonus are."

Tracy looked at both of them. "Peter? Was that the man I met the night Holly and Gabe had their baby?"

Mike thought for a moment. "Yes. That was the night he'd offered me the job too."

She sat back and fanned herself. "I always tell Chandra to find me a nice looking, older man, who is rich." She leaned in over the table. "What do you know about him?"

Mike laughed. "Nothing really. I'll see what I can find out."

She grinned and brushed her hands over her skirt, which sent her bracelets into song when her arms moved. "You do that. He was a looker."

Just as Mike lifted his cup to take another obligatory sip, there was another knock at the door. He'd never been so grateful for a visitor.

This time when he pulled open the door Chandra stood there,

her hands on her hips, hair pulled back, and her lips pursed so hard they creased.

"I want to talk to you," she said as she pushed through the door and came to a quick halt when she saw her mother and Tracy sitting at his table.

"Oh, Chandra, hello," Tracy greeted. "I heard that boy of yours scored in the game today. I'm so happy for him. Let him know for me, okay?"

She nodded. "Yeah, I will."

Tracy and Esther exchanged glances. "Mike, we'll leave you with our notes," Esther said as she stood and put her jacket on.

Tracy quickly stood as well and gathered her bag. "It was lovely to see you, Chandra. Mike, thanks for letting us stop by."

Both women hurried out of the apartment as quickly as they could, causing Mike to laugh as he closed the door.

He turned to see Chandra in a defensive stance with one hand on her hip, while she bit on her other thumb. It kind of took the edge off of her mad he thought as he watched what must have been a nervous tell.

"I have a nearly untouched cup of tea if you'd like some." He pointed to his cup on the table.

"Tracy's blend?"

"Yep."

"Oh, hell no," she said, and that had him burst into laughter as he picked up the cups and poured their contents down the sink. Then, with some thought, he poured some soap down the drain and started the garbage disposal. He wanted to be sure that the tea didn't grow back.

When he turned off the disposal and the water, he turned, leaned against the counter, and crossed his arms in front of him. "So to what do I owe the honor?"

"You left Jason's game," she bit out the words harshly.

"Yep. The moment it was over, I left the game. I managed to

get over to the sidelines and give him a high-five first, but I did leave the game."

Her mouth opened and he could have sworn she even squeaked as if she were going to say something, but nothing came out.

"Is that all? I'm in the middle of getting some measurements for the new blinds."

She turned her head and looked at the windows, and then the mismatched colors he'd painted on the wall seemed to catch her eye, and she walked toward them and studied them.

"I like the lighter brown one," she said softly enough he had to move from his position against the counter to hear her.

"Which?"

"Lighter brown. I think it would open the room up."

"I'm leaning that way," he admitted. "Not sold yet. My mom would say to give it some time."

She agreed with a nod and turned to face him. This was when he decided he'd move back toward the kitchen, a few steps away, and separate them with the table between them at least.

"I didn't know you stayed to watch the whole game. Here I've been mad for hours and…"

"And you were ready to let me have it, huh? Well, I promised him I'd be there to see him score, and I was. Even my son watched him score, so I think I should earn some bonus points for that."

"Right." She looked at the floor, chewed on her lip, then shifted her gaze to him. "Why did you leave?"

Mike gripped the back of the chair, just as he had the last time they'd started arguing with each other. Only this time, he wasn't going to be kissing her when it was over.

"At one point I'd turned around and saw a man cuddling up to you. There's one thing for sure, Jason looks like his father, doesn't he?"

"I didn't know he was going to be there."

"You didn't seem to mind having him so close.

"Mike, you have no idea…"

"You're right. I don't," he said moving to the door and gripping the handle. "I know I laid things out and told you I was interested. You, on the other hand, let me know that wasn't an option. I kissed you today out of sheer excitement at the moment Jason scored. I'm sorry for that."

"I didn't ask him to come."

"But did you ask him to leave?" he asked as he twisted the knob.

"No."

"Where is he?"

"At home with Jason."

Mike pulled open the door. "I'll fix anything you need to be fixed, but I'm not the kind of man who likes to be left just waiting as a second option. I'll get the apartment fixed, and then I can move on. It seems I have a few business partners who are interested in my B and B now."

Chandra stomped toward him. "You're going to go into business with my mother?"

"Her and Tracy."

"Tracy? How did you get her involved?"

"I didn't. They came to me, and I'll tell you, I wasn't sold completely, but I am now. I'd be honored to have those two women finance me. You've got an incredible support system with those two, do you know that?"

"Of course I know that."

He pulled the door open fully so she could walk through. "Well, then, don't keep old baggage around too long if you want your mother back at your house or she just might find permanent residence on Tracy's couch."

"She told you that?"

"Goodbye, Chandra. Call if you need something fixed."

Her eyes had gone sad, but he had to let her go. He didn't

want to be the man that was just around if she needed him. He wanted to be more than just needed for leaky faucets, but if that was all she could handle, then that was all he'd offer.

She passed by him, and he was careful not to inhale, making sure not to catch her scent. When she stopped in the hallway and looked up at him, he waved and closed the door.

CHAPTER 19

Somehow Mike managed to avoid Chandra for two days. That stupid storage unit was still outside, and he needed to decide if he was going to carry his belongings up the stairs or rent a storage unit. Right now, trekking to Chandra's house to use her garage wasn't the option he was most excited about.

He made himself sparse around the restaurant and worked hard all night on the remodeling of the apartment.

He'd agreed with her paint choice and nearly had all the walls done when he had to clean up for his meeting with Peter to discuss the job offer.

Esther had called and asked him to dinner. He couldn't think of any reason not to enjoy a meal with her and Tracy, so he'd agreed.

At noon, he sat at a brewery in LoDo watching the men and women filter in and out in their suits and skirts. Was he really considering going back into the corporate world? He hadn't worn a tie since his interview, and he was quite enjoying that.

Glancing at his watch again, he noted that Peter was nearly

twenty minutes late. Maybe that was a sign, he thought, just as the man rushed through the door.

"God, Mike, I'm so sorry. Today has taken its toll already," Peter said as he pulled off his coat and hung it on the back of his chair before extending his hand to shake Mike's.

"Had a few days like that recently myself," Mike admitted as he shook his hand and watched Peter sit across from him. "Can I order you a beer? Or are you strictly a water guy during business hours?"

He watched Peter's expression change, and suddenly he knew this meeting wasn't going to go the way he'd intended.

"You know, I'll take that beer," Peter said as Mike motioned for a waitress.

A few minutes later she returned with their drinks and took their order.

Mike watched as Peter wrapped his hands around the glass and stared at it, deep in thought.

"So, bad day?" he finally asked as if to bring the subject back up again.

"What's wrong with this world?" Peter groaned. "I've had my job for fifteen years. Someone got word about the startup, which I thought was common knowledge, and suddenly I'm on my ass out of a job."

"They let you go?"

Peter picked up his glass and took a long sip. "Yep. Just like that."

Mike laughed, though he hadn't meant to. He lifted his glass to Peter's. "To new opportunities that come your way when you least expect it."

He watched as the expression on Peter's face lightened. "You know exactly how that goes, don't you?"

"I do. Sold my car, my house, and gave away my dog. Moved here and got laid off. Seriously thought that was the end."

"But you're not doing what you came to do yet. You're a handyman."

Mike nodded, but he knew there was a wide smile on his lips. "I am, and I'm loving it. I'm renovating the apartment I'm living in in exchange for rent. Can't beat that. I'm constantly busy at the restaurant fixing things. And it looks like I have my own group of investors in a real estate buy."

"You're buying a house?"

"An old house just outside of downtown. We're going to look into purchasing it and turning it into a B and B. I grew up in one. It'll be just like home."

"You might be too busy for my startup," Peter finally relaxed in his seat.

"I'm still on board."

"Well, at least I'm a saver. Ex-wife didn't take off with my savings. I live in a condo I've had paid off for years, and I own my car."

"Then look at it as this was just the new door opening."

Peter nodded as he saluted Mike with his glass. "I like your thinking. Now all I need is a woman who thinks I'm the king of the world."

Immediately Mike thought of Tracy. "How do you feel about hippies?"

Peter grinned. "I used to be one."

"Well, then, I might know a gal."

CHANDRA WATCHED THE FRONT DOOR, AND THE KITCHEN DOOR, disappointed that every person who walked through wasn't Mike. The thought had crossed her mind to go up to his place and make sure he wasn't dead. It had been Saturday since she'd talked to him. Of course, her mother had let her know that he was fine when she'd called to say goodnight. They'd had dinner

BERNADETTE MARIE

together, and Mike had told her all about the work he'd been doing in the apartment.

It chapped her backside to think her mother hadn't come back home yet, and she was having meals with Mike. This wasn't how things were supposed to be working.

To top it off, she'd already had a phone call from the school regarding Jason's behavior. That, she knew was a direct correlation to his father being in the house. Hell, if Gabe were there, he'd be sending her home too, since her mood was so sour.

She'd already snapped at three waitresses, a busser, and maybe a gentleman who was looking for the restroom. And that, she knew, was also a direct correlation to Austin being in her house.

Since he'd shown up on Saturday, she'd washed his clothes, lent him money, watched him slam through two six packs, and pour at least three shots of whiskey. It had been a non-stop X-box party, and of course, Jason was still awake when she returned home.

This wasn't what she signed up for, but for some reason, she grew weak around the man, and it broke her heart.

When the door to the kitchen pushed open, she looked up, waiting for Mike. This time, however, it was Gabe, and he wasn't looking to happy.

"What are you doing here?" She greeted him before he could say anything. "We had a deal."

"Yeah, well the deal didn't include my mother-in-law. I'm getting out of the house, and there is nothing you can say to me, or I'll fire you." He winked, and she realized the grim look on his face had been the knowledge that she would jump him for being in his own restaurant, just as she had.

"Why don't you sit down and take it easy then and I'll get you something to drink. Want some food too?"

He laughed and gave her a kiss on the cheek. "You spoil me."

"I do."

"Where's Mike?" he asked as he pulled himself a beer from the tap.

Chandra felt her jaw tighten. "Haven't seen him."

"I was going to see if he wanted to watch the game while I was here." He set his beer down by the register. "I'll be right back. I'm going to ask him. Why don't you put in an order of nachos for us."

She watched as he disappeared down the hallway and through the door to the staircase that led to Mike's apartment.

The way her heart began to hammer in her chest, she would have thought a celebrity was going to walk through the door. Why was she so nervous to see him? Wasn't it what she'd been looking forward to?

Chandra picked up the rag she'd been wiping down the bar with when she noticed her hands had begun to shake. It was just Mike. She'd even consider him a friend, so there seriously was no reason to get worked up over seeing him.

When she looked up, Gabe was walking toward the bar alone.

"No need for the nacho order?" she asked as he picked up his beer and took a sip.

"Have you been upstairs? It looks fantastic," he said as he set his glass down. "He's finishing up some trim. He'll be down in about fifteen minutes. So I'll take those nachos. And you will take the night off."

Her hand curled around the rag, and she felt her jaw tighten. "You're not supposed to be here," she reminded him.

"And you're still going to take the night off. You've been a life saver, Chandra. I love that I've been home with my wife and my girls. But tonight, I want to be here where I'm equally at home. I want to serve the bar and watch the game with my friend. Go home to Jason and have a nice night. I insist."

She looked toward the stairs again, but Mike hadn't come down them.

She was torn. Part of her wanted to take the offer and run. The other part wanted to see his face—hear his voice.

Giving into Gabe's request, she set the rag down and walked to the computer to put in his nacho order.

When the order had been sent she looked around the full dining room. Any other time she'd have taken his offer and run. Why was she even considering hanging around?

"You're sure?" she asked before she left her post.

"Very sure. I don't want to be home with my mother-in-law, but she insists on helping. I guess she's had a change of heart since she's become a grandmother."

"It happens. Okay, I guess I'll go then. Call me if anything comes up. I can be right back."

Gabe chuckled. "I'm fairly sure I'll be just fine."

She gave him a nod and headed to the office to collect her things.

Chandra swung on her coat and scarf, then picked up her bag and headed out of the office. Just as she closed the door, she saw Mike descend the stairs and stop.

His eyes lingered on her for a moment, and a smile came to his lips.

"Hi." His voice was soft, and it fell on her like a warm blanket.

"Hi. Coming down for the game?"

"Gabe was looking for some company. Headed out?"

She bit down on her lip and nodded. "He gave me the night off since he's here. I tried to argue, but…"

"You need a night with your family," he agreed, and she could see the vein in his temple pulse as he did.

She wanted to argue that Jason was her family. Her mother was her family. But she surely didn't want him thinking that Austin was her family—not anymore.

Mike gave her a little smile and turned toward the restaurant.

Something inside of her didn't want to see him walk away, so she called after him. "Gabe says the apartment is coming along nicely."

He smiled as he turned back toward her. "It is. I'm happy with it."

"That's fantastic."

"Would you like to come up tomorrow and see it?"

Chandra swallowed hard. "I would love that."

"I'll let you know when I'm home. Have a nice night," he said and left her standing there alone in the hallway.

It ached, and she didn't like that it did. But what she wouldn't have given, at that moment, for a goodbye kiss.

Peeking around the doorway, she watched as Mike sat down next to Gabe and they laughed as two men enjoying a moment might. At that very moment, she felt lonely. Her mother had Tracy, Gabe had Mike, and she had no one she could call and sort out her feelings with. No, instead, she'd been released from duty to return home to her son—whom was her salvation—and his father—her nemesis.

CHANDRA OPENED THE BACK DOOR TO THE HOUSE AND immediately heard the sounds of her son and his father as they commented on the same game she'd left Gabe and Mike watching.

Hanging her bag and coat on the peg by the back door, she looked around at the mess of chip bags and Dr. Pepper bottles that littered the counters. A half-eaten pizza sat on the kitchen table. What had happened to walking into the clean kitchen and the smell of freshly baked cookies?

Chandra walked into the living room where Jason lay sprawled out on the couch and Austin, in only a pair of boxers, reclined in a chair.

"Hey, honey. What are you doing here?" Austin lifted his beer to his lips and took a long pull.

"I live here. Or did you forget?" Irritation filled her voice. "Jason, do you have homework?"

"I'll do it in the morning," he argued without looking at her.

She clenched her jaw, turning her attention back to Austin. "Where did you get the money for the pizza?"

"Your bra drawer," he admitted with a chuckle. "You haven't changed much. There's some left. Have a slice and grab a beer. Grab me one too," he ordered, as he turned his attention back to the game.

This was a moment she should take control of, she thought to herself. So why was she turning to simply head to her bedroom and fall into bed? It was early. Any other day she would have cherished the extra hours she'd get with her son, but now she was hell bent on hiding from him.

She heard Austin call after her when she didn't return with his beverage, but she wasn't about to start serving him in her own home.

CHAPTER 20

*M*ike fell onto the couch with the remote in his hand and a satisfied sigh. It had been a nice evening watching the game at the bar with Gabe and getting to know him.

The man had quite a story to tell. He'd lost his first wife in a car accident and had taken over the restaurant from his uncle as a method of healing. His wife Holly had been someone he'd met at the restaurant, and they'd had a one-night thing, which was uncharacteristic for both of them, and she'd ended up pregnant.

Now they were happily married with two kids, and Mike knew a smitten man when he saw one. Gabe Maguire was one of them.

They'd called Peter and invited him to join them. That too had been interesting. He had a story too. A fast rise in the corporate world with lucrative stock options. Then his wife runs off with another man.

Mike was genuinely glad the two men had happened into his life, though. It made him feel as though he had solid footing in this new life he was carving out for himself.

Pressing the channel button on the remote, he stopped at an

early season of NCIS, back when Kate and Tony were still trying to figure each other out. He'd be the first to admit he didn't mind when she'd left the show. He rather enjoyed Ziva. She was an exotic mystery.

Then the realization of that very thought hit him, and he set the remote down next to him on the couch.

When he was hanging out with the guys, there hadn't been too much to tell about his ex-wife. Sure, she was dating again, but aside from the initial shock of it, he wasn't bothered by it. And she hadn't been unfaithful. That hadn't been what drove them apart.

They just hadn't been the right fit for each other.

Their relationship had always been friendly but certainly hadn't had any heat to it. Life goals between them were similar. Job promotion was important and even having that one kid that they could dote on was equally agreed on.

But one day, it wasn't enough.

That's when his life changed, and he'd ended up in Colorado —and then there was the exotic beauty that was out of his league.

Mike hadn't been prepared for the woman who happened to be behind the bar that sorrowful day he'd walked into Maguire's. He'd gone inside simply to get warm and have a beer. Never would he have thought his entire life would change at that moment.

The thought of her face and that long dark hair flooded his mind. The tattoos that covered her arms fascinated him, and the few times he'd pressed his lips to her—well that could fill nights of wonder for him.

Mike sunk in the couch, kicking his feet up on the coffee table. The disappointment of Austin returning hit him solidly in the gut.

To look at the man, he'd easily be convinced that Chandra and Austin were equals. He and Chandra shared a common look, which simply said don't mess with me. He could see where they'd found easy attraction in one another.

And he was back and in their lives. He was living in her house, and being a father to Jason. There was no room for competition there.

It was a sad reality, he decided as he reached for the remote and turned off the TV. There just wasn't enough room in Chandra's life for him.

Mike stood and turned off the lamps on his way to the bedroom. Thoughts of kissing Chandra filled his head, and he certainly needed to shake them free.

Deciding to take a late night shower, he turned on the water and let the small bathroom steam up around him, and he undressed.

It wasn't going to be very easy to avoid Chandra now, he thought as he stepped in under the water. He and her mother, and her mother's friend had all become business partners.

Like marriage, his partnership with her mother signified that Chandra would always be in his life—and likewise Austin.

It wasn't as if they had a relationship. He was simply a middle-aged, smitten man. Of course, that sounded creepy even in his head, and it had him laughing to himself.

It was time to move forward he decided as he lathered the soap between his hands.

The apartment was coming along nicely. If things went well, he'd be able to secure the house in the next month or so. Part of having a B and B was that he'd live there too. No more small apartments above restaurants, or hotel rooms for him.

The bonus would be that Jason would still be around and he couldn't wait for Dane to get to know him.

And he and Chandra would still be friends.

The loneliness of the evening began to wash away.

Perhaps tomorrow he'd borrow Gabe's truck and get the rest of his stuff out of that storage and over to Chandra's garage.

Mike rinsed and turned the shower off. His mind had eased as he dried off and then climbed into bed.

But as he closed his eyes the thought of the kiss he'd shared with Chandra in his living room filled his mind. Maybe he was going to have a harder time letting the thought of her go.

~

LAUGHTER RESONATED FROM THE OTHER ROOM, AND IT BROKE HER heart. What she wouldn't have given for Jason to have a father he could have been proud of. One that would go to his soccer games every week and cheer him on. But she'd fallen hard and fast for Austin, and she always did when he returned.

She should have been enjoying her son's sounds of enjoyment, but she wasn't. She didn't want to think about what it all meant for him to get so comfortable with his father around, only to know he'd leave again.

But he wasn't leaving.

That had Chandra turning in her bed, bundling the quilt around her, and over her head to dull the noise. Just when she thought she'd met a nice man she could trust, Austin walked back in.

Who was she fooling? Mike was just that—a nice man. An interested nice man, she had to remind herself. And now her mother's business partner. There was no getting away from him, but did she want to?

What she wanted was a warm set of arms to hold her when she was feeling low, just as she was right now. She wanted an attentive ear when she had a story to tell. An easy glance her way that spoke of affection and appreciation would be nice too.

The laughter in the other room died down, and soon she heard footsteps and closing doors. Then there was a tap at her door.

Without invitation, the door opened, and Austin stood with the light from the hallway illuminating him from behind.

"Hey, you seemed mad about the pizza."

Chandra sat up and studied his figure in the doorway. Once upon a time, those tattoos told stories, and she'd fallen for each and every one of them. That hair, which now fell around his shoulders, was an instant attraction to her, and so were his dark eyes.

Why couldn't he have lived up to her expectations?

"I am mad about the pizza. You can't just steal my money."

He stepped into her room further. "I'll pay you back. It was a spur of the moment thing, and we were having fun."

"It's fine."

Austin moved in further, closing the door behind him. "You know, usually when I come home, you're a lot happier to see me."

She let out a snort. "Home? This isn't your home. It never was your home."

"Home is with you two."

"You've never felt that way," she reminded him as she tucked her legs under her and pulled the quilt around her.

"Things are different now. I'm thinking I need some stability. You know, a real job, time with my kid, and my woman."

That was a knife in her gut. "I'm not your woman."

Now he moved to the bed, sat down, and took her hand in his. "I'm not kidding, Chandra. This is what I want."

The smell of alcohol on his breath and cigarettes smoke on his clothes was a familiar memory. Why couldn't it be a bad one, she wondered as he stroked his thumb over her knuckles.

"Austin, this isn't a good idea."

He reached behind her and pulled the band that held her hair in its braid. "I like your hair down," he said as he pulled the strands until it fell over her shoulders. "I'm not going to let you down, sweetheart. You can trust me," he said as he stroked his hand up her throat.

His fingers offered her that contact—that connection she'd been dreaming of. She closed her eyes and let his touch warm there on her skin. "I'm afraid I can't trust you," she admitted, her voice full of air, her eyes closed.

Because he was predictable, she knew his lips would come to her neck, and they did. They would trail kisses from her ear to her collarbone—but in her desperation, it was welcomed.

Austin eased her back on the bed, still trailing kisses over her skin. She was going to regret this in the morning she thought as she felt his hand on the bare skin of her stomach. But it had been a very long time since a man had touched her or kissed her—except for Mike.

Squeezing her eyes shut, she soaked in the feel of Austin's touch. It was only one night, she promised herself. Only one night.

CHAPTER 21

The blinds had been pulled, and the room was still dark when Chandra forced open her eyes. Her bed was empty, and she pulled all of the covers over her naked body.

She closed her eyes again until the reality of the voices outside her door shook her into full alertness. Grabbing for her phone on the nightstand, she turned it on to realize she'd overslept. Dear God, this was only one reason not to sleep with a man she swore she would never have anything to do with again. Now she was late for work.

Pulling on the pair of pants she'd thrown to the floor, she hobbled to the closet to find a Maguire's polo. Luckily she had two left. Now the reality of needing to do laundry hit her too.

When she opened the bedroom door, she could hear Austin and Jason in the kitchen.

"Hurry. You're going to miss your bus," she shouted over their talking.

"Mom, Dad is taking me to school. I'm fine."

She turned her attention to the man who was wearing boxer shorts and one of her mother's aprons.

"You're taking him to school on your motorcycle? It's February."

"It's Colorado," he said as he flipped a pancake which was much more batter than cake. When he turned to look at her, he lifted a brow and wrinkled his nose. "You're going to work like that? You're a mess."

Chandra gritted her teeth. Never a warm word. Never a compliment. It was never going to change.

"Jason, get your stuff and get in the car. I'm taking you to school," she demanded as she gathered her coat and her bag for work. "And you," she turned and directed her anger at Austin. "You'd better have this all cleaned up when I get home. This is a freaking mess."

"You're just pissed cuz your mom moved out and isn't cleaning up after you." He flipped another pancake and batter splattered on the wall behind the stove. "It'll be fine, and I can still take him to school."

"I'll take him. He's worked too hard to keep his grades at passing and his attendance in good standing. I'm afraid you might forget to go to school, and they'll be calling looking for him. I'm not sure my heart can take a phone call like that."

"You worry too much," he accused as he ladled more batter onto the griddle.

For the first time since he arrived, he was right. She did worry too much—and thank goodness for that. If she didn't worry if she didn't care or have a concern, who knows where her little family might be. Had she not, at one time, had some sense about her, Austin would probably have been a permanent fixture in their lives. As it was now, he dropped in and left when he was done with normal.

But as she flung her bag over her shoulder she realized this was perfectly normal. He came. He caused chaos. He fell into her bed. He left. What did it matter what he promised this time? It would all be over soon, and she'd go back to worrying too much without him in the picture.

Jason's snappy moves as he flung his backpack around and stomped his feet into his shoes as he tried to put them on without untying them, brought her back to the moment. Sure, he never wanted to go to school, but he was usually very diligent about getting ready and getting on the bus. But watching his mood sour as it was, she couldn't help but blame Austin for the disruption to their lives.

Once they were in the car, and Jason had thrown his backpack at his feet, he crossed his arms in front of him and kept a narrowed gaze out the window.

"Something wrong?" she asked as she pulled the car out into traffic and headed to the school.

"I'm fine."

"Hmmm. This doesn't look like fine to me."

"What would you know? You're working all the time now."

Seriously? This was going to be her fault?

"You knew that I'd be gone the whole time Gabe was at home with his new baby. Trust me. Holly needs him home more than I need him at work."

"But you're gone all day."

"It's almost over. He'll be back by spring break and then we can have a nice week doing fun things."

"Whatever. Even Grandma doesn't want to be around me."

That was the last straw she thought as she pulled the car over to the curb a few blocks from the school. Turning toward him, she rested her hand on his folded arms.

"That's not true and you know it."

He shrugged, keeping his eyes forward. "Feels like it."

"She doesn't want to be in the way with your dad here."

"She's not in the way."

"I know that, but…"

He let out a huff. "It's not like he's going to be here for long anyway. C'mon, Mom. He can't stand to be a family. We know that. This is just a game to him."

Chandra was sure her mouth had fallen open, so she mindfully shut it. So this was the new wise age?

"He says he wants to stay," she reminded him. "He's going to get a job and stay with us."

Jason rolled his eyes, and his head, toward her. "And you believe him?"

No, she really didn't. "I don't know."

"For spring break do you think we can spend it together? Doing stuff?"

She chuckled. "Yes."

"Dane is coming to visit Mike for spring break. Maybe we can do something with them."

Chandra swallowed hard. "Maybe."

"I like him, Mom. He's a good guy. I'm glad he'll be around." He sat up and looked out the window. "My bus is pulling up. I'll walk from here." He lifted from his seat and kissed her cheek. "I love you. Tell Mike hi."

Opening the door, Jason climbed from the car and walked toward the school while she watched. It seemed as though he'd grown so much in the past few weeks. He was turning into a wise young man.

Traffic heading into downtown slowed Chandra's progress. She was now twenty minutes late. Hopefully, the kitchen manager had his key.

She hated being late. Catching a glimpse of her reflection in the mirror, she cringed. Perhaps she'd get the chance to see the remodel on Mike's apartment after all. It looked as though she might need that shower she'd missed if she was going to make it until close at ten.

Now nearly a full half hour late, Chandra pulled up behind the restaurant to see Gabe's truck parked there.

Slamming the car into park, she ripped the keys from the ignition and grabbed her bag. Of all mornings for him to break his promise of staying away. She didn't know if she should be grateful, or if she should kill him.

Chandra plowed through the back door. The few kitchen employees who saw her stopped and watched her rush through.

She marched right to his office, only to find it locked.

With a huff, she walked out to the restaurant where others were setting tables and stocking the bar. But Gabe was nowhere.

The only other place he might be is visiting with Mike, and even that seemed a little too close for her.

The door to the stairwell was locked. She fetched her keys from her jacket pocket and opened the door. Quickly she ascended the stairs and pushed open the apartment door.

Mike stood in the small kitchen, over the stove stirring something in a pan with one hand and holding a cup of coffee in the other. He was shirtless, barefooted, and his lounge pants rode low on his hips. He must have been freshly showered, as his hair was still wet and looked as though a towel had been run over it.

Chandra swallowed hard as she held up a finger. "Where is he?"

Mike cast a look around the apartment. "Good morning," he said first. "Where is who?"

"Gabe and I have an arrangement. He kicked me out yesterday, and he's not going to do it again. I have two more weeks, and then he can give me a goddamned vacation."

Mike pulled the pan from the burner and set it on another. "Did you eat breakfast? I have bacon and eggs. Take your coat off and sit down."

It was then she finally smelled what he was cooking. "I'm fine. I want to know where Gabe is."

Mike pulled two plates from the cupboard, filled them with eggs, and set a slice of bacon on each. He carried them to the table, set them down, then retrieved another cup of coffee and two forks.

"Sit," he demanded as he moved by her to close the door to the apartment. "I'm going to go put on a shirt."

He disappeared into the bedroom, and when he reemerged he had on a University of Southern California shirt, a pair of socks, and his hair had been combed.

Mike retrieved his cup of coffee, warmed it from the pot, and sat down. Looking up at her, he motioned with his eyes for her to sit, so she finally did.

"Gabe isn't here. And he's not downstairs as far as I know," Mike offered as he scooped up a forkful of eggs and put it in his mouth.

"His truck is here."

She watched the humor slide over Mike's face as he hid his smile behind his coffee mug. After taking a sip, he lowered the mug to the table. "Someone offered me storage space in the garage," he said narrowing his gaze on her. "I needed his truck to make that happen. Then they can come get the storage unit and restore the parking lot to normal use."

"You have his truck?" she asked, then looked at the eggs as her stomach growled.

"Yes. Later I'm going to load my stuff into it. Peter is coming to help me, and then we'll take it to your house. Your mom is going to meet me there. If the sale on the other house goes through then I'll move it there."

Unable to resist, Chandra loaded her fork with a bite of eggs. As she tasted them, she was sure she'd closed her eyes and let out a sigh. How was it the man could whip up eggs that tasted like heaven?

Swallowing, she looked up at him and noticed he was watching her, still smiling.

She washed them down with a sip of coffee. "So you're going through with buying the house?"

"Yep. Your mom and Tracey have done nearly all the early footwork. The physical stuff will be all me. It's going to be great," he said promisingly.

She took another bite of her eggs. "Well, I'm glad Gabe isn't here. That was going to piss me off."

"I gathered that by you busting through the door."

She winced. "I'm sorry about that. You should have it locked."

"Couple of your employees were looking for you bright and early before your kitchen manager got here. I guess they thought they'd look up here. I went down the stairs to answer when I heard them knocking."

"I'm sorry. Did they wake you?"

He laughed and sat back in his chair. "No. I was painting the bedroom. I woke up about three and couldn't go back to sleep."

"I don't smell paint."

"Good. I've been using some new stuff I learned about that doesn't have paint smell. I thought it would be best, especially with the restaurant." He watched her for a moment. "Your mom picked out the color. Would you like to see it?"

Chandra gripped the fork tightly. "My mother was in your bedroom?"

He chuckled. "No. I said she picked the paint."

She felt small for saying that. Setting her fork down, she pushed back from the table. "Yes. I'd like that."

They both stood and started for the bedroom, nearly running into one another. Mike stepped back and motioned for her to go through first.

When she stepped through the doorway, she certainly saw her mother's approval painted on the walls. They were a rich, creamy color and they warmed the space. The blinds were new and she noticed he'd even put some kind of storage system in the closet.

His bed was covered with a tarp, but she imagined if he were to have a dark bed set, it would compliment the room perfectly.

"This looks beautiful, Mike."

"It looks clean. He'll be able to up his rent when I'm done."

She turned to him now and pushed a strand of hair that had fallen in front of her eyes away.

"I'm sorry I barged in here like I did. That was uncalled for."

"Forgiven. I wish I had someone who looked after me the way you did Gabe. He's a lucky man to have a fantastic wife and a caretaker."

"I'm not his caretaker." She winced at the thought. "We took care of each other for a time, and now things are different, but we're still here for each other."

"I meant it as a compliment," he clarified. "C'mon, our eggs are going to get cold."

Mike walked back to the table and sat down. Chandra followed suit. "Would you mind if I came back up in a few hours and used your new and improved bathroom? I overslept, and I could use a shower." She'd felt the heat in her cheeks when she'd admitted to oversleeping. Or perhaps it was the understanding in his eyes, without her having to say why she'd overslept that filled her with dread and embarrassment.

"Sure. I can go down and get your inventory started. See to the delivery. You can get ready after you eat."

Because he'd mentioned eating, she forced herself another bite, though she'd lost her appetite thinking about what she'd done the night before.

"If you're sure."

"Positive. I'll just change real fast. I don't think this looks official enough." He took his plate to the sink and rinsed it off. "How's Jason? Getting excited for spring break?"

"Yeah, he mentioned it this morning. Actually, he told me to tell you hi."

It warmed her when Mike smiled. "Tell him I say hi. Dane will be here in two weeks, too. Already have us a place booked in Breckenridge. I think the runs will still be good enough to get some good skiing in."

"You'll have a good time."

Mike leaned a hip against the counter. "You and Jason wouldn't be interested in joining us would you?"

A nervous excitement filled her stomach, and she felt the smile form on her lips, but then just as quickly she released it. "Austin doesn't ski."

She watched the disappointment shadow his face. "Right. Maybe while Dane is here, he and Jason could kick around the soccer ball a bit. I know Dane wants to meet him."

"He'd like that."

"Right." He cleared his throat. "So, clean towels on the shelf in the bathroom. I'll change quickly, and then the place is yours."

She thanked him, watched him scurry around, then quickly leave. Chandra sat alone in his apartment with the breakfast he'd made for her—or shared with her.

She thought of the invitation and how much Jason would like to go with Mike and Dane. Resting her elbows on the table and then her face in her hands, she thought about Austin being part of their lives again. Would it bring any of them joy—including Austin?

She looked around the apartment which Mike had made feel homey and warm. Would he have that same touch with the house that he was buying with her mother and Tracy?

Of course he would. She couldn't help but wonder why a woman ever would have left him, and then that thought hit her harder. Why would she choose Austin over him if there was a choice?

The thought had to go. She stood, took her plate to the sink and rinsed it. A few minutes later she started the shower and stepped inside. His scent surrounded her. His soaps. His shampoos.

Jason wasn't the only person who liked the man enough to want him around. She wanted that too. But with Austin in the picture, she couldn't move forward at all.

Chandra tipped her head back into the stream of warm water. She lingered there hoping the water would wash all the uncertainty away. But it seemed to do the opposite.

The more the scents of him surrounded her, the more she wished she'd given into his kisses and his interests. Her mother always said she deserved better than what she got. Mike was better.

He was kind and decent. There was great vision in a man who would buy a house to make it something bigger—better. She turned off the water, stepped out, and wrapped in a towel. She looked around the small bathroom and realized even in this space he had vision. So why had he had an interest in her?

Chandra wiped the steam from the mirror and looked at herself. The tattoos on her arms usually scared men, but he didn't seem put off. Her hair was just hair. She wore it tied back, but rarely ever curled it or wore it down. Perhaps she didn't think enough of herself to take the time to do that. That was a crock. She thought a lot of herself. She was strong and brave. She was a freaking single mom who rocked the title she reminded herself.

Austin was the ass that came and went and found no pleasure in family. That wasn't her.

Mike found pleasure in family. She'd seen his eyes light up when Dane was mentioned. The joy in him only intensified when Dane called.

Last night, she'd sold herself short. Trying to recapture something that was never there—well, it was a waste of time.

Chandra took the comb off the sink and ran it through her hair. It was all new, and it needed some time. Interest was one thing. Seriousness was another. Mike was building a foundation for himself. She was building one for herself and Jason. Right now that included Austin. With Mike being business partners with her mother and Tracy, it wasn't as if he'd be going anywhere. All of this pent up frustration just needed some time to ease. She was overworked right now and full of stress. Yes, that was it.

Pulling her hair back to put it up, she looked at herself again and let her hair fall. Maybe today she'd let the process of foundation building look different. It was okay to ease up a bit.

CHAPTER 22

S he'd taken longer showering than she thought she had. Chandra was surprised at the number of people already in the restaurant and kitchen when she finally emerged from Mike's apartment.

Her food rep was in the kitchen talking to the kitchen manager, and the bakery rep was taking inventory.

She could hear Mike's voice when she ducked into Gabe's office to gather the clipboard with orders and inventory numbers. With her newfound enthusiasm about taking control and feeling out the interest Mike said he had for her, it seemed to send a jolt of excitement through her.

Mike was talking with the alcohol rep, and both men were fully engaged in their conversation and didn't notice her until she came to stand behind the bar next to Mike.

"Hey, Chandra. I thought you'd taken the day off," Keith said as he typed information into his tablet.

"Two more weeks and I'm out of here."

"Oh, yeah? Gabe's paternity leave is over huh?"

"Spring break, too," she said shifting a look toward Mike who was pouring a cup of coffee.

"Yeah, my kids are out too. They of course wanted to go to Disneyland, no, Disney World." He looked up at her. "That's in Florida right?"

Chandra nodded.

"Yeah, well, this job don't pay for a trip like that. I'm thinking a day at the movies and maybe some play time in that play area at Cherry Creek Mall, which is the only reason I'd go there."

"Jason used to like that place too."

"Okay," he said swiping his finger across the screen of his tablet. "I'm done here. You two have a fine day."

Mike lifted his mug toward Keith. "He's a friendly one," he said as Keith walked out the door.

"He is." She took a mug and filled it with coffee. "Thanks for covering for me. And thanks for the shower."

Mike gave her a nod and moved to the patron side of the bar.

She couldn't be sure, but it seemed as if he were avoiding conversation.

He finished his coffee at the bar as the staff came to her for answers to this and that. Of all days, the mundane annoyed her.

When Mike's phone chimed, he pulled it from his pocket and read the text. "Peter is on his way. I'm going to go up and get ready to load all of that stuff into Gabe's truck."

Picking up his mug, he stood, and walked back around the bar. He rinsed the mug and slid it into the small dishwasher under the counter. Without another word, he went out through the kitchen.

MIKE HAD THE FEW THINGS HE COULD LOAD INTO THE EXTENDED cab of the pickup truck when Peter pulled up.

"Tell me you did all the hard work," Peter joked as he climbed from his car and locked it.

"I've more than once considered having them haul this thing off and starting all over."

Peter laughed. "Well, I'm yours all day. Tell me where to start."

The men unloaded as much of the storage unit as they could, and then headed toward Chandra's house.

They'd made it to the first stop light at the end of the street when Peter turned toward him. "Tell me what's going on with you and the bartender."

Mike coughed out a laugh. "And why do you ask?"

"It's just the way you say her name when you talk about her mom, her kid, her house. I know we haven't known each other long, but I know when a guy has a thing for a gal."

"A thing, huh?"

"Yeah. Or do you have a thing for her mom?"

Now he laughed hard. "No, it's not for the mom, though she's a catch. Strong. Wise. Just like her daughter."

"See, you nearly sighed."

At the stoplight, Mike ran his hand over his head and caught the grin on his face. "I've told her I'm interested in her. Kissed her a few times. She seems to think it's not a good idea. Oh, and her ex-husband has come back into the picture and is living at her house."

"Ouch."

"Yeah." He shrugged and then eased through the light when it changed. "But she's a good friend, and her mother is one of my partners in the house, so I need to be okay with her not being interested since she'll be in my life."

"The ex-husband. Is he good material? Not all ex-husbands are dicks. I mean you and I are still catches for other women."

Mike laughed again. "We are catches, aren't we? I mean, who wouldn't want some of us."

Now Peter laughed too. "Right? We just picked wrong the first time. Or just need to remember to stay interesting. I don't know really what to think there."

"In my case, we were just wrong for each other from the beginning. We liked each other. We just never loved each other fully as we should have. It's clear in hindsight. We did make one excellent kid, though. For that I'm grateful."

"Nicely put."

"As for Chandra's ex, he made one great kid too."

Peter let out a hum. "But he's...?"

"Oh, I think he's a tool." He grinned. "But that's because I have a thing for his ex-wife."

"A tool it is then," Peter agreed as Mike turned the truck down an alley and parked next to a garage where a woman waited. "Is this her mom?"

"That's her."

Peter scanned a look over her before reaching for the door handle. "She looks like a hard woman."

Mike could understand that. Her long gray braid hung over her shoulder, and leather jacket with a chain of some kind. "I suppose if you messed with her, she'd mess with you."

They both stepped out of the truck.

"I thought I had some extra help for you," she said. "Austin was here until five minutes ago. I'm pretty sure he took off so I wouldn't ask him to help."

Mike pulled her in for a hug. "All the better. Esther, this is Peter."

She held out her gloved hand and shook Peter's. "Nice to meet you. You're the one with the startup business?"

"That's me."

"You've got a good one with this guy. Mark my word."

Mike smiled. "She likes me."

Esther opened the garage door, and Mike and Peter went to work unloading the few items in the back of the truck. They'd loaded boxes on top of the sofa, and had managed to get in a dresser.

"I'll be back in forty-five minutes with another load," he told Esther.

"I don't see why I'm here for this." She took the key from the keyring in her hand. "You can give it to Chandra when you're done. I'm not moving back here."

"Things are that bad, huh?"

Esther jammed her hands into her coat pockets. "That ass-hat of an ex-husband sat here telling me all about them sleeping together and how he's going to change their world. I don't imagine she's buying that crap. And I sure hope Jason's not. He's done nothing but let that boy down. It would be best if he just disappeared in the middle of the night, just like he's known to do." She huffed out a breath and it carried on the cold air. "Actually, I'm perfectly happy with Tracy at her place. It's nice not to have to worry about anything. Not that it was a big deal when it was just Chandra, Jason, and I. But now it's better."

She looked at the two men who both stood there in the cold, their mouths partially open. "Is there room in that truck for one more body?"

Mike nodded. "Whole backseat."

"Why don't I ride back with you both? I'll treat you to lunch at the restaurant and come back with you when you bring the next load."

"You don't have to buy us lunch," Mike said.

"I might be pissed at my daughter, but this is my opportunity to see her, and she can't argue with me," she said as she let out a laugh. "Let me just make sure the jerk locked the house up before he drove off."

CHAPTER 23

*C*handra watched as her mother walked through the kitchen door and straight to the bar.

"There are three of us for lunch. The bar okay, or do you want us at a table?"

Chandra couldn't help but stare at her. She knew her mother could be curt, but she wasn't usually that way with her. "You can sit here. I'll get you some menus."

"Three beers too."

A moment later she watched as Mike and Peter emerged from the kitchen and headed to the bar. They both sat down next to her mother, hanging their coats on the back of the high-backed stools.

She set the beers down in front of them. "Do you want something different to drink?"

Peter shook his head. "This is great. Thanks."

"It'll be fine," Mike answered every bit as curtly as her mother, and then directed his eyes down.

They ordered their meals, and she could hear her mother and Peter making small talk as if they were getting to know one another. Mike, however, nursed his beer and when his food came, he picked at it, but he hardly joined in the conversation.

When they were finished, he asked for a box to take the leftovers. "I can keep them in the fridge right here for you if you don't want to go upstairs."

He nodded. "Thanks. I'll get them when I get back. We're taking the final load over, and then I'll take Gabe his truck back."

He packed up his leftover lunch and handed her the box. "I could meet you over there in the morning and give you a ride back on my way to work," she offered.

He studied her for a moment, and she was sure he was contemplating any other way around it. "Sure. That'd be great. I'll see you later," he said and swung on his coat, before heading back to load up the truck one more time.

Peter finished off his beer, pulled money from his wallet, and handed it to her mother.

"Oh, no you don't. I said I was buying you lunch. Put that away," Esther scolded.

Peter smiled, laid a few bills on the bar, and tucked the rest away. He slipped on his coat and then kissed Esther on the cheek. "Thank you. I owe you one."

Her mother laughed easily with him, just as she did with Mike, Chandra noticed.

Peter gave Chandra a smile as well. "Thank you. That was delicious."

"I'll let them know in the back. And thanks for helping Mike."

He gave her a nod as he slipped away through the back.

As she picked up his discarded plate, she noticed her mother's quizzical stare.

"What?"

"You had to thank him for helping Mike? That's what friends do for one another, Chandra. They help each other out."

"Yeah."

"You act like his mother," she said sipping her beer. "I'll hold your food, so you don't have to walk up a flight of stairs. I'll meet you in the morning and drive you, so you don't have to make arrangements. You thank his friends for helping him." She snorted out a laugh. "You're smothering."

Chandra let the plate slide into the bussing tub, perhaps a little to zealously. "Smothering? He's a grown man. He has a lot on his plate right at the moment. I thought I was helping him out."

"If that's what you think."

Grabbing the rag, Chandra began to wipe down the bar. "I don't know how you think I'm smothering when you jumped right in and became business partners with the man after furnishing his apartment."

Her mother gave her a thoughtful nod. "You're right. I did all that. I taught you how to smother."

Chandra couldn't help but let the laugh escape. "I can't decide if I'm supposed to laugh at that, or be mad over it."

"It's better to laugh," her mother said as she climbed off her stool. "You're already mad at everyone."

She studied her mother as she pulled on her coat and hat. "What does that mean?"

"Just an observation. Mike's a great guy," she said laying money on the bar to cover their bill. "He's interested in you. That seems to piss you off. You're in a mood because you've been working too hard. You're in a mood because Austin showed back up. And damn it, Chandra, sleeping with him isn't going to make him a better husband or father."

She felt her cheeks heat. "Why did you say that?"

"He told me." Her mother waved her hands in front of her as if to ward off the thought. "I didn't ask. I didn't pry. He just thought I should know."

Chandra felt the churning in her stomach. "I'm sorry."

Her mother reached across the bar and rested a hand on hers. "It's no secret. I don't like him. He uses you, and he uses Jason.

This one," she said looking toward the kitchen where Mike had exited, "he's just a good guy. Now I can't say he's a keeper, but I put my money on him—literally. He's going to do great things with that house we're buying. His plans for a B and B are fantastic. He's laying down roots. Real roots that are going to stick. He takes time for your kid and his. He's a catch, and he's cast a line your way. But it isn't going to stay that way, honey. Bigger fish in the ocean if he can't get you to bite."

"Fishing metaphors?"

"Seemed to work in the moment." She pulled her hand back. "Austin did want me to tell you that he'd be stopping in sometime tonight with Jason for dinner. He didn't want to have to cook."

She felt the sting of her mother's words, from her speech to the message from Austin. "It's not so easy, Mom," she said referring to making Austin leave.

"Easier than you think," she said as she walked out of the restaurant.

THEY WERE WELL INTO THE DINNER RUSH WHEN AUSTIN WALKED past the hostess and sat himself at a table near the bar with Jason. Jason waved to get his mother's attention. She signaled to the hostess that they were fine where they were, and walked to the table with two glasses of water.

Setting the glasses on the table, she turned and kissed Jason on the head. "One more week and I'll have a normal schedule again," she said ruffling up his hair with her fingers.

"Good. I want a hamburger and a Coke."

She shook her head. "No soda. Water."

Austin leaned back in his chair and looked up a her. "I want something fancy. Whatcha got?"

Chandra bit down on the inside of her cheek to keep from saying what she truly wanted to say. "Fancy has a big price tag."

"And you run the joint. It ain't like you have to pay. I want a beer too."

"You're driving."

He dismissed her with snort. "One beer, Mom. I'm fine. Get me that prime rib sandwich. Yeah, that's what I want."

Why couldn't she tell him that he needed to leave? Why couldn't she push him out of her life? He'd done it to her plenty of times, but she saw the smile form on Jason's face as he handed her his menu. He was happy to be there having a hamburger with his father. She couldn't deny him that.

Though she was usually good at knowing when they would be busy, and when they wouldn't, there was always the odd Wednesday night that surprised her. The hostess had a waiting list going, the bar was full, and there sat her ex-husband looking at his smart phone, eating a free-to-him meal, and not even talking to their son.

"Where can I help you?" Mike's voice came from behind her. She hadn't even realized he'd come back to the restaurant.

"Cammie is behind on drink service. She's working the most tables. This tray goes to table eight. That tray goes to table thirteen," she said pointing to the other tray on the bar.

He picked up the first tray and moved on as if he'd worked there for years. When he returned, he placed the tray on the stack and reached for the other.

"Austin and Jason are having dinner huh?"

She growled. "Jason is. Austin seems to be very occupied. He hasn't said a word to him in ten minutes."

"What time is bedtime?"

She slid a look of irritation his way. "What does that mean?"

"I mean, what time does Jason have to be home and in bed?"

"Nine."

"I have a wall that needs another coat of paint, and I know his teacher puts his math assignments online. We could get his math done too. Then I can use Gabe's truck to take him home when we're done."

Her heart hitched. He was willing to step in and do the fatherly thing when Jason's own father wasn't. She should be giving that opportunity to Austin, but she was over it. Jason needed this kind of attention, and damn it, she was going to take it.

"I'll even give him a few bucks," Mike offered as he hoisted up the tray to balance it on his hand. "I know you're thinking I shouldn't, but a guy should have the opportunity to earn a few bucks here and there doing manual labor."

Now she realized she was staring at him. Hadn't she prayed for years for a good and decent man to come into her life? Here he was. It should have been a sign, the way he was stranded and opportunity had him staying.

He was interested, she reminded herself. Mike was interested in not only her but in her family, her son, her life. She swallowed hard.

"Thank you." The words were soft, and she was never soft. "He deserves someone like you in his life."

The comment must have taken him off guard just a bit. His cheeks had filled with color, and a small smile curled up on his mouth. "I'll always be here for him, Chandra. For you too."

He took off with the tray.

She watched him deliver drinks, bus tables, and make small talk when a couple stopped him, asking if he owned the place. She'd heard him tell them he was helping out since the owner was helping him out too. When they'd heard that Gabe was on paternity leave, the woman dabbed at her eyes. Why did that make people so soft inside, she wondered? Every man deserved time with their newborn, just as a woman did. And every woman deserved to have the father of her child there while she recovered.

She shook the thought from her head as she looked back at

Austin, who eased back in his chair, still looking at his phone. If she thought that was acceptable for everyone, why wasn't it acceptable for her? Why did she belittle herself like that?

Chandra grabbed up an empty tray and headed toward their table.

She began to bus the dishes, and Austin set his chair back on all four legs.

"What's the rush?"

She narrowed her stare on him. "I have a waiting list for seats. You're done eating." She turned to Jason. "Mike would like to have you stay here and help him with some painting upstairs. He'll pay you."

His eyes grew wide. "Far out."

"I could use some cash," Austin said, as he looked back down at his phone again.

"Then you can get your ass a job," she said as she carried off the tray.

It took all the control she could muster not to throw the dishes into the bin. She watched as Austin and Jason gathered their coats. Jason found Mike, and they headed up to his apartment eagerly talking about something. Austin walked out the front door without even leaving a tip for the waitress, saying thank you, or goodbye.

Chandra pressed her fingers to her eyes before pulling a few dollars from her pocket. "Cammie," she called to the waitress. "This is for you from table eight."

"That was your kid, right?" she asked as she took the money.

"Yeah."

"Sweet kid. Who was with him?"

Chandra forced a smile. "His dad."

"Not your husband, right?"

"No."

Cammie laughed. "I thought you had better taste than that.

What an ass." She strode away, but Chandra stewed in that. She did have better taste than that.

Suddenly she felt the prickly feeling of guilt and disgust cover her body. She'd given in to him. She'd let him kiss her, touch her, have her. But even that wasn't the worst part. Giving him leeway to use her again only spoke of her weakness, and hadn't she always fought to be such a strong woman?

The printer to her side kicked up four more orders. The night wasn't over yet, she thought. At least Mike had taken Jason with him, and he'd give him some attention. That's what she wanted. That was what was important.

If she could let down the shield she had put up to protect her heart, just a bit, perhaps she could manage to give Mike the appropriate thank you without being a brutal bitch. He didn't deserve that.

CHAPTER 24

*M*ike watched as Jason used the paint roller just as he'd shown him to do. He slowly moved it in a V pattern, careful not to go too fast and spatter paint. He felt himself becoming very sentimental over the process. Dane had helped him paint for the first time when he was Jason's age. They'd painted his bedroom from the blue, which his ex-wife had painted it when they found out they were expecting, to a bright green, which had been Dane's favorite color at the time.

They'd talked about soccer, school, Emily Watson who was Dane's obsession at the time, and Mike chuckled to himself even now for remembering her name.

He looked over at Jason who loaded up the roller again. "I told your mom I could help you with your math again. I know your teacher has your assignments online."

"That'd be great. I'll get an extra recess if I ace the test on Monday."

Mike gave him a nod. "You can't beat an extra recess."

"I'm captain of the blue soccer team in gym. I mean, it's just the P.E. teacher letting us choose teams and use her equipment at lunch time, but I get to pick my own team."

"That's exciting."

"I try not to be the guy that only picks good players. I mean, I like to win. But there are a couple of kids who don't play all the time, competitively," he explained. "That doesn't mean they shouldn't be on my team."

Mike thought his heart might have melted just a bit. "That's really big of you."

"Jake always picks the same guys. And they all play soccer in a real soccer club. We've beaten them a few times," he said with a smile as he rolled the paint on the wall. "It's not that we're better. But when they start to lose or argue between each other, they start playing bad. We just keep playing."

Yeah, Mike thought, his heart had turned to mush.

"Dane comes soon," he said as he loaded his roller. "He's looking forward to seeing you play in person. He'll be here for a little over a week. We're going to go skiing too, but he thought it would be fun if you two could kick around the ball."

Jason turned to him, his eyes wide. "Really? He'd want to do that?"

"He would."

"I'd like that. I'd love to go skiing too. I've never been."

"Maybe I can talk to your mom about it. Gabe will be back by then."

"That'll make me happy too. She's been working really hard. He should be with his baby, though," he said sincerely as he loaded his roller again. "Every dad should be with the mom and the baby."

"Did your dad do that when you were born?" he asked knowing it was a cheap shot to get information on Austin.

Jason shook his head. "No. They weren't together when I was born. He'd left Mom after she found out she was pregnant. I was about a year-old when he came back, and they got married. He came and went, just like he does, for a few years. Then she divorced him three years ago, and my grandma moved in."

He felt the anger brewing inside of him, but this wasn't his fight, he reminded himself.

"He's back now, though, right? So that's good."

Jason shrugged. "He'll be gone soon. He doesn't stick around long. I think Mom hasn't kicked him out yet only because she wants me to have him in my life." He inspected his painted wall and moved over to paint a different section. "I'm okay when he's gone too, though. Mom does a good job. Gabe lets her be anywhere I need her to be. Grandma is there when I get home and makes me dinner." His brows drew together, and he looked at Mike. "Well, she was until she moved out."

Mike nodded. "I'm sure if things were to change she'd move back in."

"I think I'm old enough to handle myself. I'd be a little scared at home alone, but don't tell my mom that."

Mike set his roller in the tray. "You know your grandma, Tracy, and I are buying an old house."

"That one you were looking at that day you walked me home?"

"Yeah, that's it. I'm going to have a lot of work to do on it. You wouldn't be willing to help out, would you? After school, maybe till your mom gets home, or your Grandma is free for the evening? I'll pay you."

"Heck yeah. I want a new skateboard really bad." His enthusiasm was contagious.

He wanted to ask what kind, but he knew it would be well over his head anyway. "I'll talk to your mom. We close on the house in another week. I'll almost be done with this job by then."

"Then you'll move into the house?"

"When it's ready to be lived in. I guess I'll stay here until then."

"I like that you're here," Jason said looking up at him. "I worry about my mom working late. I shouldn't, but I do. I know you'll take care of her cuz you like her."

Mike coughed and then cleared his throat. "I do like her."

"I saw you kiss her at the soccer game," he said looking down at the floor. "When I scored."

Mike felt the smile tugging at the corners of his mouth. "I was pretty excited for you."

Jason lifted his eyes back to meet Mike's. "I'm okay if you kiss her."

And wasn't this kid just about the greatest kid in the world?

When the wall had been painted, Mike pulled out his laptop and brought up the website Jason's teacher used for assignments and events. Mike fished a pencil out of the drawer, and a spiral notebook from the counter.

"You know what we need?" he asked as Jason sat down at the table. "Provisions. I'm going to go down and see if your mom will allow a snack."

Jason's brows lifted. "She's not going to let you."

Mike shrugged. "Worth the asking, right? I have a pencil that needs sharpening too. Gabe has a sharpener in his office. Lock the door. I'll knock and use my key to get in."

With a simple nod, Jason went right to work on writing down the homework problems from the computer.

Mike pulled the door shut and headed down the stairs. Leaving him in the apartment was a small test, he'd decided. There was no doubt he'd be okay at home alone after school for a few hours. There wouldn't be a need for it if he had anything to do with it. But, a boy should know he could handle it.

The dinner crowd had thinned out, and Chandra filled a table order of drinks at an empty bar.

"Where's Jason?" she asked immediately when she saw Mike standing there, alone.

"Doing some homework. I thought I'd give him five minutes alone. He mentioned that he thought he could be at home alone, he doesn't realize I've left him."

"You didn't tell him?"

"I told him. He just doesn't realize I did it so he could under-stand it. I'll be praising him in five minutes."

She wiped her hands on a towel and then leaned against the counter. "Dane is lucky to have you as a dad," she said softly enough he leaned in to catch the compliment.

"And Jason is lucky to have you. He was telling me how you do a great job."

She lifted her eyes to his and seemed to have braced her hands on the bar. "He did?"

Mike slid onto an empty bar stool and leaned in over the bar. "He's proud of how hard you work. He says you do a great job being a mom."

He watched as she batted her eyes, no doubt holding back tears that threatened.

"I got lucky," she said. "I have a good kid."

"That's not luck." He reached his hand across the bar and covered hers. "You did that. It's called respect, and it's something that is taught to children."

She caught the first tear that slid down her cheek with the back of her hand. "I still have three hours to work. Don't make me cry. I only cry over my kid."

Mike patted the hand he'd covered. "I'll get out of your hair." He stood and retracted his hand to his pocket. "I only came to get some provisions if you have some. You can't do math homework without a snack."

At least she laughed, he thought. Then wiping her eyes one more time, she let out a breath. "I'll even deliver them."

Mike gave her a nod then turned to head back upstairs after he sharpened the pencil.

"Mike," she called out, and he turned. "Thank you. You're a good friend to both of us."

He smiled, then went on his way.

He'd be a good friend to her as long as she'd have him, he thought. But at that very moment, it killed him not to be more.

There was a great need brewing in him to kiss her, just as Jason said he could. But not yet, not now. She knew where he stood, and it hadn't changed. He was still interested, but when he was the only one. Mike had never had much patience with women who played the field. They took what he had to offer, and made a commitment, or he walked off into the sunset.

Of course, no one he'd ever fallen in love with had a family before. This was a first for that. There were many layers to it now, he thought as he walked into the office, sharpened the pencil, and then closed the door as he left.

He'd also built relationships with Chandra's mother, son, and boss. There was no walking away when she chose Austin over him.

The moment of enlightenment darkened.

Mike climbed the stairs back up to his apartment trying to wrap his head around the rise and fall of emotion he'd just had. When he'd moved to Denver, he hadn't considered a woman at all. It was all about the job and the opportunity. Chandra was a gift, he decided as he took his keys from his pocket. Even her friendship was important.

So, he concluded, as he knocked on the door and put the key into the lock, that he'd have to get used to hanging on, even if he wanted to walk away. They might not be romantically involved, but they had a relationship, and it too had layers.

He could hold on.

He wanted to hold on.

And maybe in time, he could take that permission he was given, and kiss her again. Perhaps then, it would be the right time, and he wouldn't have to keep starting over.

CHAPTER 25

*W*hen Mike pushed open the door, he heard Jason talking to someone. That wasn't settling well with leaving him alone, he thought, until he heard his son's voice.

"Your Skype rang while I was on the website. I saw it was Dane so I answered," Jason said shifting the computer so that Mike could see his son's face.

"Hey, Dad! Still doing math homework?" Dane joked.

"I must love it. I'm helping my friend out here," he said as he ruffled Jason's hair. "I could go watch TV and leave you two to it."

"Sounds awesome, but I'm finishing up this essay I had to write. I have to include pictures with it. That's why I was calling. I wanted to get a screen shot of your face."

"You can't find a better picture than that?"

"Dad, it has to be current. I'm writing about people who change lives for others."

Mike sat in the chair next to Jason, not moving the computer to make the conversation private. If Dane wanted that, he'd call back.

"So what do you need my picture for?" Mike scrunched up his face.

"You and mom changed my life. You might not have stayed together, but you worked it out together. You taught me how to play soccer, and you did my homework with me, just like you are with Jason. Oh!" He moved out of the line of sight and grabbed a pen and an index card. "Look, you're still doing it."

"Doing what?"

"Changing lives. You go to Jason's games, and help him with his homework," he said, and Jason lowered his head as if to hide the smile.

"Jason and I are pals. I'm not changing anyone's life."

Jason picked up his head and inched in toward the screen. "What about my grandma and Tracy. He's changing their lives by buying that old house. They're all partners now."

"Right," Dane said as he wrote that down. "Dad, you're just an awesome man about town."

Mike laughed. "You're going to fail out of college writing about me."

"Worth it. So we have our plane tickets in hand. Me, Doug, and James will be out there in a week."

He felt his chest nearly burst at hearing that. "I can't wait. It'll be a little cramped, but it'll be a great time."

"Hey, Jay." He nodded toward Jason. "Are you going to get to go skiing with us? It'll be great."

"I'd like to."

Mike tapped the pencil to his chin. "We'll talk to his mother."

"Perfect. And we'll get a game on with these guys I'm bringing out. They suck at soccer, so we're going to win."

The glow from Jason's expression could have lit the room. "Yeah, man. That's great."

"Okay, I'll talk to you both later. Love ya, Dad."

"I love you too, kiddo."

The screen went dark, and they both stared at it.

"Do you think he got your picture?" Jason asked.

"I don't know," Mike said chuckling and clicking back to the math homework at hand. "He's a crazy kid."

"I like that you say you love him all the time. Mom says that to me. Dad's don't usually get mushy like that."

"You think that's mushy?"

Jason shrugged. "I don't know. Sorta."

"Maybe it is. But he knows how I feel."

CHANDRA KNOCKED AT THE DOOR. SHE COULD HEAR LAUGHTER from the other side, and she smiled. When the door opened, Jason stood in front of her with two pencils shoved up each nostril.

"What are you doing?"

He laughed. "We heard you coming. I thought it would be funny."

It took her a moment to not scold or turn unnecessary anger toward Mike. It was funny, so she laughed.

"Disgusting. Don't erase anything with those erasers," she warned.

Jason stepped back to let her in. "You actually brought snacks?"

"You thought I'd let you down? You need fuel, right?"

"And it's not food scraps." Jason moved in to inspect the tray as she shifted a look to Mike, who held his hands up in defense.

"He came up with that on his own," he said looking at the tray with the pretzel appetizer and fresh veggies with ranch dip.

"Gabe had some Gatorade in his fridge. I borrowed them." She winked at Jason.

"Thanks. Hey, Dane and his friends are coming next week to go skiing. He said we could all play a game of soccer. I'd be on his team, and he says the other guys suck." He laughed as he took one of the Gatorades and opened it.

"Sounds like a good time." She exchanged a look with Mike. "Could I talk to you for a moment in the hallway?"

"Sure."

"Get that math going," she said as she walked through the door. "You're super smart."

"I know, I know, in the mouth," he replied as he had to their joke a million times before.

Mike followed her to the hallway, and she pulled the door closed. "I'm in a bind. Can he stay with you until I'm done? We're not too busy, so we think we can close up early."

"He's always welcome. What happened to me taking him home?"

"Austin called. He and some buddies went to a strip club," she said, and had to clear her throat to get the words out. "He thought since Jason was in good hands…" The words trailed off as the tears that stung surfaced in her eyes. Then they spilled over, and she spat out a curse as she wiped them away.

"Hey, hey." Mike took her arms and studied her. "What's going on?"

"I told you. I only cry over Jason."

"So why are you crying over Austin?"

She opened her mouth to speak, to argue, and then realized that was exactly what she was doing. Quickly, she wiped away the rest of the tears.

"Jason doesn't deserve him," she whispered. "He deserves someone who cares about every part of his day."

"Then why is he here?"

"I don't know." She winced, gritted her teeth, and squeezed her eyes shut. When she'd bit back the anger, she opened her eyes and looked up at him. "You're good to him. You're good for him."

"He's a good kid. I'm glad we're friends. Dane can't wait to meet him in person."

She'd brushed him off when he'd kissed her and told her he

was interested. Why had she done that? Couldn't she have pursued that and let Austin visit?

"Listen," he took her hands in his. "Jason can stay as long as you need him to. If it gets late, he can fall asleep on the couch. I'll be up."

"You're too good to us."

"That's what friends are for," he said, and it sharply reminded her that that was what she'd made them be—friends.

He still held her hands in his. A warmly regarded friendship, she decided. But that wasn't what she wanted anymore, was it?

Chandra lifted her eyes to meet his. They were warm, oh so warm, looking back at her. He looked at her as if he could see her soul, the very essence of who she was.

No one had ever looked at her like that—especially Austin.

Her heart sank a bit as his thumb brushed over her knuckles. She'd worked so diligently on the hard exterior she showed everyone, but this man was making it crumble.

"Go back to work. Jason is fine here until you're ready to go home. I'll make sure he gets some rest."

Mike gave her hand a squeeze then turned back for his door.

She should have let it go at that. She should have let him go back into that apartment without another word. Things would be left just as they were and everything would be normal, but she couldn't do that.

"Mike," she said with her voice full of heat and air.

When he turned, she lunged at him, pushing him up against the wall as she encircled her arms around his neck and took quick possession of his mouth.

There was no argument from him. He pulled her close to him, his hands pressing possessively at the small of her back as he accepted the kiss she had sprung on him.

Heat and passion collided. Need and desire swam between them.

His mouth opened to hers as his hand moved up her back and

pulled her in even closer, which she hadn't even realized there was room between them.

The breath in her lungs grew heavier, and the temperature of her body warmed.

She'd been an idiot to take Austin back into her life. His touches, his kisses, everything dimmed when she thought of Mike. And oh, God! It paled in every way to the touch of his hand on her clothed body or his mouth on hers.

They broke from one another when they heard stirring in his apartment.

She backed from him just as the door opened. "Are you guys okay out here? You're taking forever. And I've eaten most of the pretzels," Jason said causing Mike to laugh.

"Figures," he said and then looked at her with that same infatuated gaze. "I have math homework to do."

"Yeah, get to that," she managed before she hurried down the stairs.

She'd avoided eye contact with Jason, and she wondered what he thought. On second thought, she didn't want to know. For one moment she only wanted to live in the bliss of that kiss that seemed to have rocked her world.

As she closed the door between the stairs and the restaurant, she decided that kiss was what she wanted. She wanted more of them. There was an adventure to be had with Mike, and she wanted it.

Jason had a vested interest in this now too. He liked Mike, and Mike liked Jason. It was a win-win as far as she was concerned.

Trying to put her head back into her job, she realized she needed to be realistic. Jason was as taken with Mike as she was. It wouldn't always be a perfect ride. There were going to be hard times if this was what she chose. And one of those hard times would be making Austin go away.

He'd never fully leave her life, and she understood that. But he had to leave her house. He had to never—ever—worm his way back into her bed.

Sickness washed over her as she moved behind the bar. That should have never happened again, she scolded herself. What had made her take him in that night?

It was because she'd turned Mike away. There had been a need to be loved, and she always turned back to Austin—who always disappointed.

As she pulled the orders from the printer, she silently promised herself that she'd never let that happen again. If it didn't work out with Mike, fine. She'd enjoy what he was willing to offer. But she would never go back to Austin.

CHAPTER 26

*I*t was nearly ten-thirty, and Mike assumed Chandra would be up any moment.

Jason had taken his invitation to lay down on Mike's bed until his mom got there. He'd been asleep nearly an hour and a half. It was understandable. Math was exhausting Mike humored to himself.

Turning on the TV, and making sure the volume was turned down low, Mike found a replay of Super Bowl XL. The Seahawks and the Steelers. He decided it was good TV. He couldn't even remember who won the game. This would have been the game for the 2005 season. That seemed like a lifetime ago he thought as he kicked his feet up on the small coffee table.

Fifteen minutes later, and a Steelers touchdown, there was a gentle tapping at the door.

Mike hurried up and to the door. When he opened it, he saw an exhausted woman standing there, though he wasn't sure how she was doing it.

"Looks like the evening was rough," he said pulling her inside and taking the liberty to envelop her in a hug.

She sighed as she rested her head on his chest. "It went to shit."

There was time to ask in a moment. For now, he wanted to hold her close and smell her hair. The need to just feel her breathe kept his arms wrapped around her.

After a few moments, he pulled back holding her arms as if to keep her near. "Let me get you something to drink. Maybe something to eat. You didn't get dinner did you?"

She winced as she shook her head. "Like I said. My evening went to shit after I was up here."

"Sit," he said as he let go of her and moved to the kitchen. "I want you to tell me everything. I'm going to make you a sandwich. I have sour cream and onion chips or Doritos."

A slight smile formed on her lips. "Doritos."

"Good choice. Ham or turkey?"

Her face contorted as she thought. "I love them both. Surprise me."

"Pepsi, Bud, milk, or water?"

Again she had to give it some thought. "I'll take a Pepsi. I'd love the Bud, but I have to drive home."

"Not for a while. I'll share the Bud with you," he offered and pulled it from the fridge.

Mike laid out the parts to the sandwich and began to assemble. "Homework is done. We even called Dane back to ask a few questions. You know, to get an opinion on how to do something I don't think I've ever seen before, but he knew how to work the problem. That lead to soccer talk, but I nixed that in ten minutes." He slathered mayonnaise on the bread and added a mix of meats. "I got one of the pretzels. So, I'll be taking one or two bites of this sandwich, because I'm hungry. And if we're going to kiss each other before you go, I might as well have some Doritos too, so we have equal breath."

She laughed, and he forced himself to not look at her. He wanted to calm himself first.

He was about to let her tell him about her shit night, and he wanted to give her his full attention. So much had happened, obviously, between their kiss and now. It had been hard to compose himself with Jason for the thirty minutes after she'd left. All he'd wanted to do was to chase her down and do that again.

Somewhere, his message of interested got through. Or so he hoped. But he needed that confirmation that it was only him. He wasn't going to kiss her like that and have her run back home to sleep with her ex.

Even the thought of it made his stomach tighten.

He pushed it out of his mind as he plated the sandwich and poured a hearty stack of Doritos on the plate.

With the bottle of beer tucked between his fingers, he carried the plate to the table and placed it in front of her. Opening the bottle, he sat down in the chair next to her.

"I can get a glass if sharing the bottle bothers you," he offered.

Her eyes, tired and sad, lifted to his. Then she raised her hand and rested it on his cheek before moving in closer to press a kiss to his lips. "I think we're past worrying about sharing a bottle."

And that was progress he thought. Thank God.

As she sat back in her chair and considered the sandwich, he reached over and took a chip. "Tell me about this horrible night of yours," he said as he crunched the chip in his teeth noisily and she smiled.

Instead of taking a half of the sandwich, she leaned back in her chair, crossed her arms in front of her, and took in a deep breath.

"About an hour ago I got a call from the police department. Austin was picked up on a DUI which resulted in an accident."

Mike moved toward her, taking her hand, and giving it a squeeze. "Everyone is okay?"

She nodded. "He's got minor injuries. It was a single car accident. They hit a pole. The guy he was with has a broken leg."

"I'm so sorry."

"He wants me to bail him out, but I don't have that kind of money."

"I can help you."

She lifted her head and shook it. "That's my dilemma. I don't want to bail him out."

That queasiness in his stomach seemed to settle when she said that. "So now what?"

"I have to tell Jason that I left his father in jail."

"That's okay, Mom." Jason's voice came from the doorway of the bedroom. "If he broke the law, that's where he should be."

Tears that might have been bottled up inside released the moment he spoke.

Mike nodded for him to join them. Jason rubbed his tired eyes and moved right to his mother to hug her. And that, he thought, was the compassion she needed. Her son loved her unconditionally. She'd done well with him.

"Don't cry, Mom. It's not worth it," Jason said as she clung to him.

"Why are you not sleeping?" she asked as she wiped her eyes and Jason sat in the chair to her other side.

"I heard you come in."

She gave Jason's hand a squeeze. "I can't help him."

"You've helped him enough. I love him because he's my dad. But, Mom, we can't take care of him forever. He's already stayed longer than normal. It's been nice, but you had to know it would be over soon."

Chandra batted her tear-filled eyes and looked toward Mike. "See, I got lucky. How smart is this kid?"

Mike nodded with a smile. "I'll let you two talk."

She reached for his arm as he tried to rise. "No. You're part of this. You don't have to leave."

He eased back in his chair.

For the next half hour, there were tears, and emotions moved from guilt to anger to sadness and back again. Mike sat silently as he watched her ten-year-old son console her. He was a prize, that was for sure.

"We'd better get home. You have school and need some sleep," she said wiping her eyes for what he assumed was the last time for the night.

"I don't want to go home tonight," Jason said. "I'd feel safer if we were both here. Dad isn't the kind to be violent, but let's just play it safe." He looked up at Mike. "Can we stay here?"

"Of course. I'll make up the couch for myself, and the two of you can sleep in my room."

Jason gave him a nod and turned back to his mom. "I'll go to bed. You can finish talking. Don't feel bad, Mom. We have Mike. He's a good guy."

Mike had to look away when he felt the tears sting in his eyes. He hadn't seen this coming when he'd moved to Colorado. The moment he'd seen the closed sign on his office door he was sure everything had been lost. How could he ever have known it was just the beginning?

CHAPTER 27

*M*ike heard the shower running in the other room. He winced when he realized that it was her normal time to start her day after they'd had a very long night.

He'd have liked it to have ended with more kissing, oh and his mind had wandered all night, but she'd kissed him gently and gone to bed. And that was the best, he knew.

Realizing that his morning ritual of getting up and having to pee was now interrupted, he focused on not focusing on it and headed to the kitchen to start some coffee. He had a few things for breakfast, but he didn't know what their routine was, so he'd wait. Though, he'd need to sneak into the bathroom soon. He wasn't sure how long he could hold on.

As the aroma of coffee filled the air, he heard the bedroom door open. At that moment he caught a glimpse of the most beautiful sight ever.

Chandra was freshly showered. Her hair, still wet, hung over her shoulder. She was dressed in a pair of his USC sweat pants, and a T-shirt he recognized from the back of his closet.

"Good morning," she said softly as she moved to him.

The thin fabric of his lounge pants didn't disguise his reaction to seeing her in the early morning light dressed in his clothes.

"I'll have coffee ready in a moment."

"I could use it. It's going to be a long day."

"I'll help. I'm going to sneak into the bathroom quickly. I'll be right back."

He'd wanted to scoop her up and press a kiss to that full, soft mouth, but some things just couldn't wait.

While in the bathroom, he took advantage of his toothbrush and remembered that he had some extras in his closet which Esther had brought him when he'd first moved in. He laid them out on the sink for both of them.

Chandra was standing by the window, a cup of coffee in her hands, looking out over the street.

He moved to her, he wrapped his arms around her, and she eased back against his chest.

Her hair was damp against his skin, but it shot heat through him which he hadn't felt in a long time. The length of her neck was exposed, and when he pressed a soft kiss to her skin, she moaned.

"You get up this early every morning?" he asked quietly.

"Since my mom moved out. I have to get him up and ready for school."

"I'll give him a ride."

She set her cup on the windowsill, and turned in his arms, wrapping her arms around his neck.

"I said I'd pick you up at Gabe's."

"You did." He stroked his hand over her cheek. "I have to say, I've never seen a sexier woman than you in my clothes."

"I felt as though I needed a change from yesterday. I hope you don't mind."

"Oh, I don't mind."

She lifted her chin so that her eyes met his. "Thank you for last night. You've been there for me at every turn for the past month. I don't know what I would do without you." She lowered her hands so that they splayed over his chest.

He wondered if she could feel the rapid beating of his heart in his chest.

"I don't know how to do this," she said. "Austin is the only relationship I've had since Jason was born. I'm out of practice."

Mike ran his hands over her arms. "I married my college girl-friend. I'm out of practice too. I guess we have to first admit that we've turned a corner here. Are we thinking we're entering a relationship? Or is this just heat and attraction?"

He held his breath and waited for her answer. They couldn't just have a physical relationship, not with Jason involved, he thought. It wasn't fair to him. But it sure would be hard to turn away.

Her fingers brushed his skin gently. "I'd like to explore this relationship. I mean, there is heat," her fingernails gently dug into his skin, and he moved his hands back to her back where they were safe. "I'd definitely like to feel that out." She bit down on her bottom lip and then ran her tongue over it. "I think there's more here, though. I see how you are with Jason, and how he is with you. He needs someone like you in his life."

Mike shook his head. "What about you?"

Chandra raised her arms again to wrap them around his neck. "I'd like to see what happens when I love a man who is good for me. One that's stable and secure in himself."

He swallowed hard. "When you love a man? That's a bold statement."

"I wouldn't bring a man into my son's life if I didn't think I loved him."

Mike moved lifted his hand to her cheek. "I think I fell in love with you the minute you looked at me that first day I walked in at lunch."

"You did?"

"Looking at you I thought we were on different planets, but there sure was a tug in your direction."

"Things are going to get sticky when Austin gets out of jail. You might want to rethink all this."

"What kind of relationship starts by one of the participants moving on when things get tough?"

"Oh, I should have taken that sign years ago." She chuckled.

"This is going to be different."

Chandra rested her head on his chest again. "What do I tell Jason?"

"He gave me permission to kiss you," he admitted, and she lifted her head.

"He did not."

"Oh, yes he did. I think he'll be fine with it."

The alarm on her phone rang in the other room. "I have to wake him up."

"Does he like Frosted Flakes?"

"He does."

"I'll pour us all some. We might as well all get started with our day."

MIKE PULLED UP IN FRONT OF GABE AND HOLLY'S HOUSE. THE truck must have been loud enough to stir the house's occupants, because as soon as Mike climbed from the truck, Gabe was standing in the doorway with the baby in his arms.

"Did you get all moved?" Gabe called out toward him as he walked up the front steps.

"I did. Thank you for the loan," he said reaching out to touch the baby's hand. "How's paternity leave?"

Gabe looked behind him and into the house. "I'm ready to go back to work."

"I heard that," Holly said as she walked toward them. "Actually, we're ready for him to go to work too." She wrapped her arm around her husband and looked down at their daughter. "I'm kidding. But I know he's ready to get back to normal."

"Well, when you get some time, come look at the apartment. Just a few more touches and I think it'll be done."

"Really? I didn't expect you to get done so quickly."

Mike shrugged. "I have another project."

Holly smiled. "I heard. You're buying a house. Tracy told me all about it."

"We close this afternoon. Then my son comes to visit. It's a big week."

He heard Chandra's car pull up behind Gabe's truck. "There's my ride."

Holly waved. "I'm sure she's ready for Gabe to be back too. She's been invaluable."

Gabe waved too. "Can't wait to see her face when I give her that bonus I have for her." He turned to Mike. "Don't tell her I said that."

Mike chuckled. "I wouldn't dare. Thanks for the loan. I'll talk to you soon," he said as he walked toward the street to where Chandra waited for him.

"I didn't know they were going to be at the door waiting for you," she said as he climbed into the car.

"I think he heard the truck."

"They probably think I'm in a mood. I didn't want to get out wearing your clothes," she offered as she pulled from the curb.

Mike reached over and took her hand in his, interlacing their fingers. "The other option is for them to see you out of my clothes, but me first."

A flush spread across her cheeks. "Is that where we're at now? Sex talk?"

He relaxed in the seat. "Let me just say you're damn sexy in my clothes. I'm not going to deny that I haven't thought about you out of them."

She gave his fingers a squeeze. "Jason, asked me if you'd kissed me again," she said as she turned at the stop sign.

"What did you tell him?"

The smile on her face enhanced the glow in her cheeks. "I didn't know what to tell him."

"He gave me permission to kiss you. I didn't think it would be you kissing me."

She sighed. "I didn't know it's what I wanted. Things are so complicated in my life."

"They don't have to be, Chandra. I'm not complicated."

"Sure you are. You're too good."

"My ex-wife might argue."

"I don't think she would," she said as she pulled up in front of her house. She put the car in park and sat for a moment. "I've seen how you talk about her. You're not sure you were in love with her, but you don't hate her."

"You don't hate Austin."

She winced. "I can't hate him. He gave me Jason. But I've learned, very recently, I don't like myself when I'm with him. He doesn't bring out the best in me. I think you might."

Mike reached for her face and placed his palm on her cheek. "My one stipulation to a relationship is that it's just me. I don't play the field."

"I don't either."

He nodded in agreement. "But I'm talking about you cutting ties. I don't mean that Jason shouldn't have Austin in his life. I'm talking about you holding on as you have been. There's no need to go into detail or tell me what's happened since he's been back. I'm telling you that I want this, but I don't want any competition."

"You don't have any. I promise."

He leaned in and pressed a kiss to her lips. "I want you to

consider staying with me, both of you, until Austin is out of jail and on his way."

"He'd never hurt me."

"I'd like to make sure of that," he admitted. "I care about both of you too deeply to see you get hurt."

"I need to go in and change my clothes. I'll grab a few things to stay tonight then. Come on in and have some coffee. I'll only be ten minutes."

He lingered his gaze on her until the corners of his mouth turned up into a smile. Perhaps he could bring out the best in her. Damn, he'd sure like to try.

THERE WAS NO DENYING THAT AUSTIN WAS OUT OF JAIL. CHANDRA looked around her house and wanted to burst into tears. He'd gone through everything and left a trail. No doubt he was looking for money, and by the looks of it, he'd found all of her stashing areas.

"Maybe you should call the police," Mike said as he pulled his phone from his pocket to hand it to her.

"No, he's gone."

"He broke into your home and trashed it."

"Can't say too much when he has a key." She let out a breath. "He came for money. He has what he needs. Now he can move on."

"I don't like this."

"You can trust me. He's moved on." She walked further into the house, toward her bedroom. The box which had housed a substantial amount of money laid open and on the bed empty. Wincing, she turned to Mike. "Go make some coffee. I could use some."

He agreed and left her standing in her shambles of a bedroom. Pulling her phone from her pocket, she pressed the speed dial for the school. They needed to know that Austin might try to pick up

Jason before she could get to him. In her heart, she knew he'd never, ever hurt him. But looking at the mess he'd left her, she was afraid that this was more than alcohol and weed. Somewhere he'd lapsed into something bigger. He'd done it before.

Okay, she admitted to herself as she hung up the phone, maybe she was a little scared.

CHAPTER 28

*B*ecause Gabe had somehow gotten word about what had happened to her house the day before, he came in to take over Chandra's shift.

"You can argue all you want, but you've been working non-stop for nearly two months now, and you need some time off," he said as he threw the towel over his shoulder and pulled the order off the printer.

"I don't have anywhere to go. Jason is at school. My mom, Tracy, and Mike are closing on that house. And this is where I belong."

"Then sit your ass on the other side of this bar and order lunch. But get out of my way."

He went about pouring drinks and setting them on trays that were picked up by the wait staff. In true Gabe style, he moved around her as if she didn't exist to make his point.

There was no use to argue with him, she thought. Making her way around to the other side of the bar, she sat down.

"What can I get you?" Gabe asked as if she were a regular customer.

"A glass of water. I'm on duty."

"No, you're not," he said as he pulled a tall Blue Moon from the tap and garnished it with a wedge of orange. He pushed it her way. "I have a prime rib sandwich already in the works for you too."

"Gabe…"

"Don't Gabe me. You have always taken care of me and what's mine. Let me give back a little, Chandra. You can't carry the world on your shoulders." He took an envelope from his pocket. "I was going to give this to you when you were walking out the door. But since you won't leave." He slid it toward her.

"What's this?" She ripped it open. "Gabe this is a check."

"You're right. It's for you, and you can't give it back. You can't tear it up, or I'll deposit it right in your damn account." He turned to her, placed his hands solidly on the bar. "Not many people step up like you do. God, I got to see my daughter be born. I didn't miss anything in her first few weeks. That's because you gave up everything to be here so I could do that."

"It's important to be there for that."

"Yeah, and now it's important for you to let me swing back into my routine."

"This check is nearly an extra two months' pay."

"It's exactly two months' pay. Go on vacation for spring break. Get your car fixed. Buy Jason something nice."

She ran her hands over thighs. "I want next week off to take him skiing."

"Good. Done."

"You're too good to me."

"We're a good team."

They were, she thought, as her lunch was delivered from the kitchen.

She listened to the bustling around her. All familiar sounds, but sweeter somehow when she was on the other side of the bar.

Aware that the table behind her had been seated, she kept her focus on the TV over the bar. She nearly jumped out of her skin when a set of hands gripped her shoulders and spun her around on the stool.

A moment later her mouth was covered, and the familiar feel and taste of Mike had her relaxing until she realized he was kissing her in front of Gabe.

Her hands came between them, and she pushed him back. It wasn't hard to figure Gabe saw what had happened. He stood just on the other side of the bar, his mouth gaping open.

Then he smiled. "So this is new?"

Mike laughed, and she felt the heat from the anger brewing, but couldn't justify it. "Got a problem with it?"

"Not in the least. Think it's a great thing actually." He moved down the bar and Mike continued to grin at her.

"What are you doing?" she asked.

"We're celebrating. So bring your beer and your lunch to the table."

It was then she noticed the grinning pair of ladies seated at that table behind her. Tracy and her mother beamed from what they'd seen. Well, she thought, there was no easing into it now.

Mike picked up her plate, and she her beer. He set it at the table, and she kissed her mother on the cheek, then did the same to Tracy.

"So, you all own a house, huh?" she asked, hoping to ward off any questions about Mike nearly sticking his tongue down her throat in public.

"We do," her mother said. "1904, all brick, hardwood floors, solid as the day it was built."

"Good. You won't have to do too much to it, right?" She looked at Mike.

"Still plenty to be done. It's been abandoned for a long time, but it has potential. Even if I gutted it, we still have a heck of a prize on our hands."

Gabe brought drinks to the table. He knew what he was serving to each of them, and that was part of his charm, she thought. There was a beer for Mike, and one for her mother. He set a mug of hot water in front of Tracy, who then pulled out a homemade tea packet, which Chandra was sure she'd concocted herself.

"Mike told us that Austin got a DUI and rummaged through the house," her mother confronted her before they could even dive into the possibilities of their new purchase.

"Yes. And you don't have to tell me what a mistake it was to…"

Her mother placed her hand over Chandra's. "I wasn't going to. It's quite evident to us that you've moved on," she said smiling up at Mike.

Mike cleared his throat. "We're trying it out," he offered.

"Good." She turned toward Chandra. "And so that you know, I'm not moving back in with you. You and Jason will be fine. Mike says he'll be helping him with the house after school. Gabe is back, and you won't be working all the time. It'll be good to get back to normal."

"You're always welcome in my home—our home—your home," she corrected.

"I know, but I'm having a great time being a free woman."

The way her cheeks blushed, and so had Tracy's, Chandra didn't even want to ask what that was about.

A runner from the kitchen brought out three entrees and set them on the table. She'd never heard them order, but then again, she could have placed those orders out of memory too.

"Oh, and I'll be picking up Jason today after school, and he's staying with Tracy and me for the night."

Chandra frowned. "Why? I can do it."

"It's all planned. You have a date." She grinned, and that had Chandra turning toward Mike, who was smiling equally as wide.

"I've had a big day. I want to celebrate. Jason will be alright with your mom. She's only a phone call away if anything happens."

She wasn't worried that he'd cut his finger or choke on a Lego

—not anymore. She was worried that Austin would go looking for Jason. She'd wanted to be the one there to pick him up.

She kept her eyes on Mike's face. Those soft dark eyes and the glow of his smile resonating in them, how could she possibly refuse?

"I'm not sure it's a good idea. But okay," she agreed.

Mike's hand rested on her knee under the table. The heat that transferred to her turned her insides to absolute mush. They were right. Jason would be okay. This thing with Mike might be new or at least acknowledged, but she wanted to find out what kind of heat it held. And from the flutters in her stomach, she was damn sure it was going to be a very good night.

CHAPTER 29

*C*handra had confirmed that her mother had indeed picked Jason up from school and that he was starting in on his homework. She was pleased that it had annoyed him that she even asked about homework. Her job was done, she thought as he told her about his day and about the substitute they'd had in gym.

She listened as she tidied up the kitchen in Mike's apartment. Not that it needed it. He was a fairly neat housekeeper, but she was going stir crazy just sitting there.

Gabe had kicked her out of the restaurant, and Mike had borrowed her car to run an errand. She was stranded.

"Be good for Grandma," she said one more time.

"I will. Hey, Mom," Jason said, his voice dropping in volume. "Is Dad okay?"

She let out a long breath. "I don't know, sweetheart. I don't know where he is or what has happened. I only know, you're safe with Grandma, and until I hear from him, I don't want you to go with him, okay?"

"I get it, Mom. I do. I just hope he's okay."

"I know you do. I'll talk to you in the morning before school."

She blew a kiss through the phone and disconnected.

Again, she looked around the small apartment. He wouldn't be living there much longer, she supposed. Once he got a room in the old house done, he'd live and work there. She'd grown accustomed to him being only a few feet away.

Brushing her braid over her shoulder, she pulled it back and ran her hands over it.

Perhaps she'd make herself up a bit before her date. Obviously, it hadn't been too important to Mike that she was glamorous or not. She certainly didn't hold a candle to his ex-wife, she thought, recalling the photo he'd shown her. But it didn't mean she couldn't look a little put together.

Chandra walked into the bathroom and stared into the mirror. In her bag, she knew she had some lip gloss and mascara. There might not be too much more to it.

Pulling the band from her hair, she brushed her fingers through the braid to release it into waves.

Her dark hair, only slightly speckled with the new gray she'd been finding, flowed over her shoulders in waves. For a moment she looked in the mirror admiring herself. She didn't need all the fancy makeup and such. Her mother had always told her she was a natural beauty, and for the first time, in a long time, she actually believed that.

"You're beautiful," Mike's voice came from behind her, and she turned to see him leaning against the doorjamb.

"I thought I'd try to look nice for our date, which, so that you know, I hate surprises."

He moved to her, moving his hands from her shoulder down her arms to capture her hands. "You might have to get used to them. I like to do them."

"Where are we going?"

"I want to show you something."

"I only have jeans and T-shirts," she warned.

"Don't ever think that's not okay." He raised his hand to run his fingers through her hair. "When you wear your hair down, you seem delicate, and that's not saying you're harsh. It's saying that it's different."

"I am harsh. You've met my mother. Hippie on the back of a Harley. I'm not much different."

He smiled. "It's part of your charm." Taking a step back, he kept his gaze on her face. "Where we're going, it doesn't matter what you wear. You might need a coat, though."

"I have one."

"Good. Oh, and we have to take your car."

"Of course," she laughed.

"I might need to look into getting one. Though Denver has a lot of mass transit options, I'm finding that it just isn't convenient enough."

"True."

Mike found that Chandra didn't say much when she was unsure of a situation. But she was mindful of every turn they took and every word he said.

No doubt some self-defense mechanism, though he couldn't help but wonder who would mess with her. Just her attitude alone said don't mess with me. The usual braid, sculpted arms, and tattoos would ward him off.

He chuckled to himself. Who was he kidding? They'd turned him on, which was a first. Usually, he didn't go for that type, but damn, wasn't it a great surprise to find out that he actually did like it? And to her credit, an older nerd didn't seem like her style either. But once she'd let her hair down, so to speak, he shined in her eyes. He saw it—and he loved it.

"Why are we near my house? You're taking me home to clean my house, aren't you? I'm not as neat and tidy as you are."

He laughed as he drove down the street, then through the alley, and parked behind the abandoned house he'd bought with her mother and Tracy. "No. You're not going back until we know it's safe, and then we can talk about cleaning up. Not because you're messy, but because a mess was left for you."

"You're good with words."

"I try," he smiled in the dark.

"So why are we here?"

"I want to share this with you. I want to walk through the house and tell you all my plans. At least pretend you're excited."

She laughed. "I can't wait to hear what you have in store."

MIKE TURNED OFF THE ENGINE, CLIMBED FROM THE CAR, AND BY the time she'd opened her door, he was standing there. Chandra wasn't sure she'd ever get used to his gentlemanly ways. Though after so many years of just being a discarded partner, she decided it was worth trying to get used to it.

He took her hand and walked with her to the back door. Fishing for the keys in his pocket, in the dark, he finally found the key and unlocked the lock. When he pushed open the door, he reached his hand inside and flicked the switch which turned on a single light in the room.

"This is like a mud room next to the kitchen. I'm not sure about keeping it," he said as he stepped in and then waited for her to cross into the house.

The smell of vacant house filled her nose. Dust, dander, and water stained wood. She saw and smelled, old house. Now she was curious what her mother, Tracy, and Mike saw.

With her hand still in his, he shut the door and began to guide her into the house.

"The kitchen will be a complete demo job. Everything in here is too old, and the electricity will need to be redone."

He continued to the front of the house which consisted of a large living room and dining room.

"The wood in here is amazing. Carved original work on the

mantel and railing up the stairs. I think a few comfy couches and chairs. Perhaps a book case of different kinds of books," he said as he pointed to a wall where the wallpaper curled away from the wall. "I'm juggling with a big family style dining table or little two or four person tables. I can't decide, but it's bottom of the list right now."

"How many rooms are upstairs?"

"Five bedrooms upstairs. There is one on the main floor too. Lots of rooms for guests. I'll have to work the bathroom situations. Honestly, the one thing my parents found was that guests liked to have their own facilities. It might cost me a room, but I can live with that."

As they continued their tour, he came to the room at the bottom of the stairs. Ornate wooden French doors closed off the room behind them.

"This is really what I want you to see." Mike pushed open the doors and turned on the light. She could only assume her shocked silence was what he was expecting.

The room was clean. It had been dusted, and the wood cleaned, as much as possible. The lemon scent gave that away.

In the middle of the room was a large wooden spool covered in a lace table cloth. There were place settings of china and crystal glasses.

"Mike, when did you set all this up?"

He placed his hand on her back. "Just a little errand I had to run."

She laughed as she turned into his arms. "I can't believe you did this." She turned back to look at the table. "I assume you planned to eat here?"

"Shortly. Nothing fancy, except the china which is your mother's."

Now she moved from him and went to the makeshift table. "I would have figured that out," she said with humor lit in her voice.

"I ordered pizza. One of the first things I did was replace the light bulb out front. Hopefully, they'll find us and deliver."

"I have to admit, when I met you, I never would have pegged you for the optimistic kind."

"It was a bad day."

"Was it?" she asked and the words caught in her chest.

His eyes grew dark as he pulled her to him. "No. No, it wasn't bad at all," he said as he gently brushed his lips over hers.

She let the sensation linger there a moment. His breath on her mouth, his hands on her back. God, if just a kiss from the man, and the simplest touch, could make her swoon as she was, what might the full package do to her? She'd be drunk for days she supposed.

Pulling his phone from his pocket, he swiped the screen and pushed something that sent it playing gentle music. Mike set it on the table, then spun her back into his arms, into an easy dance.

"I don't know how to dance," she argued as he swayed with her.

"Seems like you're doing a good job."

And like that, she felt like an entirely different person. Her hair swayed just as her body did. Mike's heartbeat drummed against her cheek, and he kept her close. Yes, she could get used to being treated like a princess. This man was a Godsend.

CHAPTER 30

No fancy restaurant would ever be as impressive as dinner on the old wooden spool in the library of a decrepit old house, Chandra thought as Mike drove back to his apartment.

They had danced to music on his iPhone, dined on pizza and wine, and they'd kissed. Oh, they'd kissed until she thought the heated breath in her lungs just might make her explode.

There was no miscommunication as to what the night might bring. They were two adults, falling in love, with a night alone in an apartment.

Perhaps she should have had him take her to Tracy's, but she couldn't resist seeing what might be next.

At what point over the past few weeks had she fallen in love with this perfect stranger? And perfect seemed to be the keyword.

Though every nerve in her body wished he'd just pull the damn car to the side of the road and take her there, she knew that perfect meant patient. There would be no quick pleasure. It would be slow, drawn out, and appreciated.

And even though it sickened her to think that she'd been with someone else only a short time ago, she knew that this romantically entranced version of her was still a virgin—and Mike had not even touched her yet.

His hand rested easily on the seat next to him. Unable to not touch him, she tucked her hand into his. As he stopped at a light, he slid a hot glance her way, and she melted with it.

They were four blocks from his apartment, and she didn't know if she could last.

Silence filled the space between them, and she assumed each of them weighing what was bound to happen in their own minds.

Sex was always a turning point, and it scared her a little bit. Mike was important to her, her mother, her son, and Gabe. If she messed this up...

She just wouldn't consider that it was going to get messed up. It was time she found something true in her life, something that brought her happiness. Mike possessed that something.

Still, no words were spoken as he pulled up behind the restaurant and parked her car. They each sat for a moment before opening their doors and stepping out into the alley. Mike moved to the door, his keys in his hand, and unlocked the lock.

In the dim glow of security lights, he lifted his eyes to her. Did he see what he needed to see? Or did the worry in her head cloud the need she felt in her body?

He pushed open the door to the stairwell and turned on the light. She passed through and heard him close the door behind them, and lock it as she started up the stairs. He met her at the top and unlocked his apartment door.

Pushing it open for her, Chandra crossed the threshold, and that was when the silence subsided.

The moment she heard the click on the door closing she turned, and he pulled her to him, turning her and pushing her up against the door. His mouth was hot and on hers, sucking out any reserve she'd had.

Chandra went to work on peeling off his jacket. He reciprocated by managing hers off without ever leaving her lips. Then, with frantic need, they both began to undress the other.

She fumbled with the buttons on his shirt as he pulled the hem of her T-shirt and pulled it over her head, only to return right back to her mouth.

As his hands touched her bare skin, she found it harder to breathe or to focus on the task at hand. When his hands moved to her back and unclasped her bra, she was sure she'd felt her knees buckle, and she pressed against the door as he touched her, so as not to fall.

Mike's mouth moved from hers to her neck. And she thought it should have given her a moment to catch her breath, but it did the opposite. Her head was spinning in the pleasure of his hands roaming over her sensitive skin, and his mouth—his breath—doing the same.

If he didn't lay her down, she was going to slide to the floor in a pile of goo.

As if he knew what she'd been thinking, Mike hoisted her up, her legs instinctively wrapped around him. He carried her to his bedroom, his mouth planted firmly on hers, and laid her on his bed.

Their lips separated, and she opened her eyes to see him looking down at her in the dimly lit room.

She was afraid to ask why he'd stopped.

"You are the most beautiful woman I've ever met."

"I've seen pictures of your ex-wife," she reminded him and thought it was certainly the wrong time to bring that up.

He shook his head. "Your beauty doesn't need enhancement. It's visible and shines from your soul. I've never been able to stop looking at you, even when I was irritated with you."

"I irritated you?"

"Only because you're so headstrong, which is sexy too." He accentuated that with a kiss on her collarbone which had her moaning. "I might have been irritated because I think I fell in love with you the moment I laid eyes on you. You sealed it with that tattoo with Jason's name."

Why was it she would cry around this man? Tears welled in her eyes when he said her son's name with love and warmth. "You fell in love with me?"

"I am in love with you."

There was security and certainty in the words, and she felt them hug her like a warm, comforting blanket. "I love you, too. You make me feel whole. You're very important to those that I love, and that means a lot to me."

His mouth took possession of hers again, and she wrapped her arms tightly around him, feeling his skin pressed to hers.

"I want to take this slowly," he said, his words strained against her throat. "I don't know if I can."

Chandra pushed her fingers through his hair, wrapping her legs up and around him again. "Then don't. I'm not leaving this bed all night. We can do this as many times as we want to."

Even in the shallow light, she saw his eyes grow dark with passion, desire, and need. With that, they each freed themselves from the bits of clothing they had on, and let the moment take over as they both gave themselves to one another in a passionate eruption of lovemaking.

∼

CHANDRA WOKE FROM WHAT FELT LIKE A DRUNKEN SLEEP, TO FEEL Mike's finger tracking the lines that had been drawn on her arms in ink. Sunlight now filled the room, but she wasn't sure she'd managed more than a few minutes of sleep all night.

She'd lost count of how many times they'd made love, and at that moment too, she realized it hadn't just been sex. It was so much more.

When she could manage it, she turned her head toward him. "Good morning."

"It is indeed," he said pressing a kiss to her shoulder. "Why the dreamcatcher?" Mike asked as he traced the lines of it on her shoulder.

"To always remind me to chase my dreams and never forget them."

"What are your dreams?"

She had to think. It had been so long since she didn't just go through motions that the tattoo's reminder seemed to have been lost.

"They've changed over the years. "I used to want to be a singer, but that was in elementary school. Many years before I realized I didn't have a voice. Then I wanted to drive semi-trucks like my parents. I was young then too, but I thought it would let me see the world. Every year my dreams changed a bit. Lately, they've been more focused on raising a great kid, making sure he's whole, and sending him in the right direction. I love what I do, so I can't say I settled, but I don't know. How do you dream bartending into being something bigger."

"If you're happy, why does it have to be bigger? But from an outsider's perspective, you're not just a bartender."

Now she rolled to face him. "What am I?"

"First of all, you run the joint. Yeah, even when Gabe is here. Everyone trusts you in that role of authority. I've seen you with the employees. You're not disliked at all, and they all do what you need them to do. You're a leader, who happens to pour the perfect drink."

"Thank you."

"You're also your son's role model. Don't forget that. He's not afraid of hard work. Trust me. I've worked with ten-year-olds before. They don't have the attention span for tasks like he does. You're raising an amazing kid. If that's your dream, you're following it."

Because she felt herself getting sappy again, she rolled so that she was perched atop of him. His hands came to her hips, and she rested hers on his chest. "You know what I'm dreaming of now?"

He grinned wide. "More sex?"

She returned his grin with a smile. "Breakfast. Biscuits and gravy."

"I could make that dream happen. Shower first?"

"Most certainly," she said as they both raised their heads when they heard a pounding on the outside door at the base of the staircase.

Mike scrambled up. "What are the chances that's some homeless person?"

"Knocking like that?" She watched as he pulled on his pants and she searched for any piece of clothing. "God, what if it's Jason." Then she looked up at him feeling the blood drain from her face. "What if it's Austin?"

"I'm going down. Be at the top of the stairs with your phone ready," he ordered as he headed out of the apartment, shirtless.

Chandra scrambled to find her shirt and tug it on, then somehow managed to jump into her pants as she followed him out the door.

The banging continued as he hurried down the stairs. As instructed, she held her hand on her phone, poised to call for help if they needed it.

Mike looked through the eye piece on the door. "Holy shit!"

"What? What?" She began to dial as he worked the lock and pushed open the door.

The stairwell was dark enough she couldn't manage to see much. But whoever was on the other side of the door had wrapped their arms around Mike, and now he was laughing. There were more than their two voices, but he didn't seem to be distressed.

As Mike pulled the man in, two more followed and they all looked up at her. She realized then, her hair was wild, and her shirt had barely been pulled over her unbuttoned pants.

She lowered the phone and adjusted the shirt. She felt the flush over her face as she squinted at the face of the man standing next to Mike, shadowed by the dim sunlight coming from beyond the metal door.

"Ah, I thought this would be different," Mike said shaking his head and chuckling. "But, Dane, I'd like you to meet Chandra."

CHAPTER 31

*C*handra was sure she was going to be sick. Being raised by the man and woman she had been, she usually didn't see confrontation as a bad thing. But right now, she was about to be face to face with Mike's son and his friends, as they ascended the stairs, and she knew what she looked like.

Managing to wipe her sweaty palm on her pants before shaking Dane's hand, she said, "It's very nice to meet you."

There was a grin wanting to surface on the young man's face she could tell. Surely it would match the ones on the other two standing down a few stairs behind them.

"It's nice to meet you too. I've heard a lot about you."

She shifted a glance in Mike's direction, and he grinned. "Well, let's go inside."

Chandra walked in first, and Mike followed with his arm around Dane, and then the other two.

"Oh, I should introduce you all." Dane turned to the other two men behind him. "This is Doug and James."

"Nice to meet you," Mike shot out his hand to shake those of the men who accompanied Dane.

Dane looked at his father. "We thought it would be fun to surprise you," he said, his lips twitching to smile wide.

"You surprised me all right. Us that is." Because he was an upstanding man, she decided, he moved in next to her and wrapped his arm around her waist. "We were just discussing breakfast. Would you guys be interested?"

"Most definitely," Dane said.

"Sit down and make yourselves at home. We'll get ready and be out in a few."

He turned her toward the bedroom and closed the door behind them.

She felt the blood rush to her cheeks. "Oh, God. That was horrible."

"He's nineteen."

"What does that matter? He knows what we were doing. Did he know about us? Me? I'm not usually one to get embarrassed but…"

He gripped her shoulders and pulled her in for a quick kiss. "He knew I had some feelings. He's been waiting for this, I think. I'm not going to be embarrassed by it. No reason to. Remember, he's the one that surprised us, not the other way around."

"You can't convince me that's true. He's surprised."

"And I'll have a good conversation about it with him while he's here. For now, we're going to jump in the shower, get dressed, and take my son and his friends out to breakfast."

He nipped her lips with another kiss before walking to the bathroom and starting the shower.

MIKE HURRIED THROUGH HIS SHOWER, BRUSHED HIS TEETH, AND dressed before going out to the living room where the three young men sat on the couch, bunched together, watching an old western, which surprised him.

"Roy Rogers?" he asked.

"It's a phase, Dad. Bonanza was a ritual in the dorm last year."

Mike laughed. "At least they're teaching you some culture. Want some coffee?"

All three of them nodded.

He moved to the kitchen to brew the coffee, and Dane followed him. He leaned up against the counter next to him as he filled the pot with water.

"You're dating the biker chick?" he asked softly since there was hardly a dividing wall between the kitchen and the living room.

Mike laughed. "It's brand new. It's not as if I kept it from you."

He noticed his son's smile, and it warmed him to think it was genuine. "I knew it was coming. I knew it."

"You're a genius," he joked as he poured the water into the machine. "It feels right. She has a lot on her plate, and so do I. We'll see what happens."

Dane rested a hand on his shoulder. "I'm happy for you. Just remember that when you know you know. Don't wait too long to have what you want."

When he lifted his eyes to see the humor in his son's, he realized there wasn't any. Dane was speaking from his heart, and it squeezed at his.

They heard the bedroom door open, and a moment later Chandra was standing at the table. Her hair was still damp, but braided as it was most of the time. She had on a tank top, which she was about to throw a denim shirt over when Dane halted her.

"I want to check out your ink," he said moving toward her. "Dreamcatcher, compass, and Jason's name. Oh, that's rad."

"Thank you." She pulled on the shirt. "He's very excited to meet you."

"Me too. We have a game planned against these losers," he said, and the other men on the couch both flipped him off in good humor. "He seems like a good kid. Dad really likes him."

He caught her eye as she looked his way. "He likes your dad too."

~

THEY'D GONE TO A NICE DINER, JUST A FEW BLOCKS FROM THE house Mike and his lovely investors had purchased. After they'd eaten, they'd taken the boys for a tour of the house.

The consensus was that it was haunted, and more than once, one of the boys jumped out from behind a door or wall to scare one of the others.

Chandra hadn't realized just how old she was until she was subject to the adolescent silliness of nineteen-year-old boys, but she found she loved it.

Because there wasn't enough room in her car, she took them all back to Mike's and drove to Tracy's to pick up Jason.

Tracy opened the door, and the smell of burning incense filtered out. "Good morning, Chandra. Have a nice night?" The grin on Tracy's flickered between casual and wide.

"It was very nice. Thank you."

"Come in. Jason and your mom are washing the dishes."

Chandra shook her head as she walked into the small house which was boldly decorated with eclectic items from around the world, and bright tapestries on the walls.

"How can she get him to do dishes and I can't?"

Tracy laughed easily as she wrapped an arm around Chandra's shoulders. "It's a grandmother's gift. You too will possess it someday."

As they entered the tiny kitchen, both her son and her mother turned their heads to look at them, their hands still submerged in the soapy water. "Hey, Mom. Where's Mike?"

There was no hitch in his voice, no condemning look in his eyes. Perhaps he was more ready for her to move on than she was.

"He's at his place. Dane and his friends arrived early to surprise him."

Water flung from Jason's fingertips as he swung around, his eyes wide, and his smile wider. "No way. They're here already?"

She laughed as she nodded and her mother handed him a towel to mop up the floor with. "Yes, they're here. They look forward to meeting you."

"Can we go over now?"

Her mother cleared her throat. "When you're done," she said firmly, and that had Jason turning back to the sink.

When they were finished with the dishes, Jason scurried off to gather his things. Her mother turned to her, resting a hip against the counter. "Well, it was a good night?"

She felt the flush creep along her cheeks and her neck, and a smile tugged at her mouth. "It was a good night."

"He's good people, Chandra. He loves you and he loves Jason."

She knew that too. Even better, she'd heard him say it, and she'd returned the words. "I know." The thought warmed her throughout. "I know," she repeated.

"Get him and go. He's so excited to meet Dane it's all he's talked about."

Chandra moved to her mother and kissed her cheek. "Thank you. I didn't see this coming," she admitted.

"I did. The moment I met him." She patted her cheek. "Now, go."

Jason loaded his bag into the car and pulled on his seatbelt. "What did you have for dinner?" he asked as he settled in.

She laughed. "I had pizza on Grandma's good china in Mike's new house."

Jason wrinkled up his nose. "It's dirty there."

She laughed. "He cleaned up one room so we could have dinner."

Chandra watched him fidget with the zipper on his jacket. "Did you stay at his house all night? Sleep there? With him?"

Taking a slow cleansing breath, she thought about her answer. She wasn't going to lie to him. "We stayed at his apartment. And yes, I slept there, with him."

He nodded slowly. "Are you going to live with him?"

That brought a smile to her lips. "He didn't ask me to live with him, honey. I don't know what will happen between us."

"Do you love him?"

Again, she thought about her answer. "I do."

His shoulders dropped, and she caught the smile that nearly took over his face.

"That's okay?" she asked as she pulled behind the restaurant.

"Oh, yeah. It's perfect."

CHAPTER 32

Chandra wasn't sure why it surprised her that the moment she turned off the engine, Jason jumped out of the car and bounded in the back door and up the staircase. She laughed as she followed, after locking the door, and checking it again.

By the time she'd reached Mike's apartment, she could already hear her son's voice rising over the others in excitement. Dane had him engaged in conversation with his friends, and he fell right in place.

"Mom, look what Dane brought me," he squealed as he held his arms out and donned a new University of Southern California T-shirt.

"That's awesome. Did you thank him?"

Dane nodded. "A million times before you even walked in," he said laughing. "It's a little big."

"He'll grow into it," she said as she walked toward Mike, who stood in the kitchen. He wrapped his arm around her waist and pecked her lips with a kiss.

"Did he quiz you about last night?"

"A little. He's okay with everything."

He kissed her again. "I knew he would be."

THEY SAT AT THE KITCHEN TABLE SIPPING COFFEE WATCHING THEIR sons bond. Dane had quickly fallen into the role of older brother, but then Mike had felt that tug when he'd held up his phone to the glass at the soccer game, and they'd watched Jason score his goal.

The boys were busy playing the Xbox that James had brought with him, and each of them included Jason, and surprisingly enough kept their mouths clean.

Mike watched as Chandra checked her watch for at least the fifth time in an hour. "It's killing you to not be downstairs, isn't it?"

She chewed her bottom lip. "I'm just getting used to the idea of having a day off again," she said. "And I can't get over the feeling that Gabe should be home with his baby."

Mike ran a comforting hand down her back. "Gabe will be fine."

"I know he will." She picked up her coffee and sipped. "He wants to go skiing with you when you go."

Mike leaned back in his chair. "I'm fairly sure Dane isn't going to go anywhere without him." He placed a hand on her thigh. "You'll go with us?"

He watched her think about it for only a moment. "I have some money set aside for us to do something for spring break. Can I still get a hotel room?"

Mike laughed easily. "We have a suite with three rooms. You and Jason are welcome to one of them."

She smiled at him, flecks of gold shimmered in her eyes only enhancing the smile. Perhaps she understood how much he'd like to share a room with her, but it was too early for that. Jason was more accepting that he would have been had his mother started staying with men. But just the thought of going away with her, even with all the boys, stirred him up.

When she looked at her watch again, he laughed. "Why don't you go down and check on him."

"I think I'll do that." She leaned in and kissed him gently. "I'll be back in a few minutes."

He doubted that very seriously.

THE RESTAURANT WAS STILL QUIET WHEN SHE WALKED THROUGH the door. Gabe was at the bar, the remote control in his hand poised toward the TV on the wall.

"Getting much sleep?" she asked, and he spun around.

"Hey," he said with a grin. "No. None at all. That's why I'm here. I can sleep on my feet."

Chandra slid onto one of the stools at the bar. "I'm a little itchy this morning. I feel as though I should be here."

"You should be on that vacation we talked about." Gabe set the remote down and leaned in over the bar. "Your car was here all night."

She narrowed her eyes on him. "How do you know that?"

"Security camera out back."

She snorted a laugh. "So what."

"Is it serious?" he asked as if he were an older brother and she was the sister who might need help.

Chandra tucked her lips between her teeth and thought for a moment before lifting her eyes to him. "I hope it is."

"Let's cut to the chase. Is he serious about you?"

"I think he is."

He gave her a slow nod. "I think he is too." Placing a hand over hers, he gave it a pat. "I think he's a good man."

"He is. I'm going on vacation with him this week. Skiing," she added. "With Jason and his son and some friends." The words rattled out as if they floated on the nerves that buzzed in her stomach.

"Yep, that's serious."

"I'm worried I'm going to mess this up for you and my mom. There are more people involved here than just me."

"You know what your problem is?" he asked as the first order printed out on the printer next to him. "You think too much. Try not to be in control for a little bit and see how that feels. Close off your mind a little bit and have a good time."

And just like that, Chandra felt those nerves subside. "Thanks," she said as she stood from the stool.

"Hey, while you're off this week, maybe you could stop by and see Holly. She's nursing and doesn't like to get too far from home. I think she's tired of her mother and me. The best conversations she's had in the past month have been with Madison. So, you know, anyone else who's not two-years-old would thrill her."

"I'll do that," she agreed.

When she turned around, she heard the muffled voices near the stairwell. Jason stood among the older boys, and Mike had just pushed through them. "They want to go kick the ball around. I told them Metro State had a field just a few blocks over. Care to take a walk? I brought your coat."

Her body warmed just looking at him and feeling the love that beamed from his eyes. "I'd like that."

The boys all carried on a conversation a few feet ahead of them, while she and Mike walked hand in hand. She searched her memory for a time when a man walked with her and held her hand like this, but she was coming up empty. His thumb gently brushed hers, and he'd give a little squeeze once in a while. When she'd look up at him, he'd be smiling down at her. Her heart jumped a bit each time, and all she could do was hope this ride would last for longer than a few months. Even though she and Austin had sort of been together for Jason's ten years, they'd only ever lasted a few months at a time. And none of it had ever been sweet as it was with Mike.

"I called the hotel, and we can leave for Breckenridge a day early. They had a cancellation on the room, and we can have it for another day. Are you free tomorrow?"

She smiled up at him. "I'm free."

"We'll leave at six. I'm going to rent an SUV. I have my eye on one, and this will be a good test drive, I decided."

"I'll go by my house this afternoon and get packed. I know I have a fridge full of food too."

Mike stopped walking. "You're not going alone. I'll go with you. Jason can stay with the boys."

She nodded in agreement. "It might upset him to see the mess his father made."

CHAPTER 33

*W*hen Chandra pushed opened the door to her house, she sighed. It was going to take a week to put her house back together, and here she was considering taking a vacation.

Mike put his hands on her shoulders. "The moment we get back, we'll clean this up. All of us."

She shook her head in disbelief as she looked around. "I just can't believe he did this. Mike, I'm ashamed."

He turned her toward him. "You can't feel any blame for this. It's who he is. Not who you are."

"I seriously thought he was going to be different," she admitted. "This is bigger than an alcohol binge."

"Call the police."

She shook her head again. "It's just some money. I can't do that to Jason."

"You think he'd care? He's the smartest kid I've ever met. You heard what he said. If he broke the law, he deserves to be in jail."

Chandra bit down on her lip until she tasted blood. "It hurts."

"Then think of it as doing something good for Austin. If they catch him, he can get some help. He stole your money, Chandra. He trashed your house. This isn't normal."

He was right, and she knew it. Taking a long cleansing breath, she pulled her phone from her pocket and placed the call to the police.

AFTER NEARLY TWO HOURS OF TALKING TO THE POLICE, AND GOING through her house, they finally walked into Mike's apartment. All four boys looked up from their game controllers, and then back to the TV as they played soccer from the couch.

Jason, however, kept his eyes on his mother.

He put down his controller and stood from between James and Dane, and walked to her. Not one word was said. He simply wrapped his arms around her and hugged her tightly.

"Let's go into the bedroom for a moment," Chandra said and led him through the door and closed it.

Jason sat down on the bed and looked up at her, his eyes full of wisdom. "Something else happened to Dad," he said, instead of asking.

Chandra sat down next to him. "I'm afraid something will."

"This is because of his DUI?"

She took his hand in hers. "Jason, he must be out of jail. He went to our house and took all the money I had stashed away. The house is quite a mess."

His lips grew thin, and his nostrils flared. "Why would he do that? You always take him in and let him see me. I thought this time was going to be different."

"I did too. Or at least I hoped it was going to be." Chandra brushed his hair back from his forehead, then placed a kiss there. "I had to call the police. If they come across him…"

"They'll arrest him?"

She nodded. "I'm sorry."

Jason shook his head. "Never apologize for him, Mom. He is

who he is. I'm not the only kid in school whose dad is messed up. Lots of my friends' dads are too. Some of their moms too. He's never hit us or hurt us. He has addictions, and I know that. You've always been there for me, Mom. I appreciate that."

"Thank you," she said softly willing back the tears that were stinging her throat.

"James's parents are divorced too. He said that his dad used to beat his mom and his brother."

Her heart squeezed. "He told you that?"

"Yeah, we were all talking about dads. Dane loves his dad, a lot. The guys started talking about their dads too. Doug's mom and dad are still married, and he has four sisters. That's all he said."

She smiled. "That says a lot."

"James said that his dad was a mean drunk. His mom called the police, and they took him away. He was twelve. He hasn't seen him since."

"And how does he feel about that?"

"His mom remarried, he said. He was," he rolled his eyes to the side as if to remember, "fourteen. He said this guy she married is super. His mom had another kid with him, so he has a little brother too."

"That's very special."

"It made me realize that you and I are okay without Dad. Maybe if he gets his life together, he'll be okay. And I was thinking, maybe if you married Mike, I'd have a dad around. A stepdad. And Dane would be my brother."

She felt the heat forming in her cheeks. "That's a lot of thinking. Mike and I are just," she thought for a moment, "dating."

"Yeah, but dating leads to marriage. And I'd be okay with that."

She kissed his cheek again. "We'll see how it goes."

THEY'D ORDERED PIZZA, WHICH HAD SURPRISED MIKE. HE WAS SURE college kids would want anything but pizza, but it had been their idea. Chandra had ordered up some appetizers from the restaurant, and Gabe had joined them for a slice before he headed home for the night.

When Mike and Chandra could no longer keep their eyes open, it was decidedly bed time.

"I'll sleep out here with the boys. You and Jason take my bed," he offered.

Jason looked at him, his frown full, and his eyes sad. "I want to sleep out here with these guys."

"I guess you could sleep with all of us. Your mom can have the bed to herself."

Jason looked around. "You can sleep in there with her," he said. "I'll be okay with these guys, Mom. I swear."

The older boys were exchanging looks and holding in their grins. They knew what they'd walked in on that morning, but Jason's innocence kept them from saying a word.

"He's okay with us," Dane said. "That is if you don't mind. And Dad can sleep in there with you. He snores anyway, so we don't want him to keep us up all night."

Mike let out a snort. "I do not snore."

Dane laughed and looked at Jason. "He does. Trust me."

"Fine. I'll sleep in my own room," Mike said as he stood from his seat. "And I'll take her with me. If you need to use the bathroom you'd better do it now," he warned. "I don't want to hear peeing in the middle of the night."

Jason roared with laughter, and his mother followed suit.

Ten minutes later he was climbing into his bed with Chandra, for the second night. This time, however, they were clothed, and the door was unlocked which was disappointing. Though, he was fairly sure she wouldn't be interested in anything but sleeping with her son in the other room.

As they settled into bed, Mike turned off the light on the

nightstand. Chandra moved her hair so that her neck was exposed, and he slid up next to her.

"I'm glad you have a kid who argues with you," he said as he pressed a kiss to her neck.

"I'm nervous about this," she said. "Since Austin, I've never slept with a man. Well, except for you last night."

"It's different because he's around. I've never slept with another woman but my wife either. We're all getting an education I suppose."

Chandra rolled in his arms and faced him. "He's okay with me calling the police on his father."

"I was sure he would be."

"He also thinks it would be great to have Dane as a brother."

Mike smiled in the dark. "I like your kid. Have I told you that?"

"That makes me very happy."

"You make me very happy." He nipped her lips with a kiss. "We'd better go to sleep. I can't have you this close without wanting you."

She rolled back so that his chest was pressed to her back. As they lay there silently, he thought about Jason and Dane. They'd be great brothers. Perhaps in time they'd be able to pursue that. Right now, he'd hold Chandra tightly in his arms. He was very sure he never wanted to let her go.

CHAPTER 34

*M*ike had rented a Suburban. He loved driving something bigger than Chandra's car. It plowed through the snow and made him feel nearly invincible in it.

Even with the extra room in the back, he was surprised how cramped they all were. But then he had to consider that there were six of them with luggage, extra food, and ski gear—no wonder a huge truck felt so small.

The noise behind him assured him that the three boys, all of which were over six-feet-tall, and the ten-year-old were just fine, even with bags at their feet.

He reached over the console and gripped Chandra's hand. "There is something very comfortable about all this," he said quietly. "I could get used to it."

She looked behind them. "He's going to be devastated when Dane and the boys go home."

He was going to be devastated too, he thought. "Skype is the best thing for homesick dads, and new friends."

She eased back in her seat and closed her eyes. Finally, he thought, she'd relax. No one deserved time away more than she did.

The room was perfect for them, and once again it was the boys who had decided on sleeping arrangements. Who was he to argue when he got to curl up next to the woman he'd fallen in love with every night.

They'd gone to the grocery store and purchased some essentials for the week and mixed with what Chandra had brought from her house they might squeak by with only eating out a couple of times.

Mike had arranged for Jason to take ski lessons, and because he was stepping right into the role of big brother, Dane had waited out his lesson before he had hit the slopes himself.

For three days they skied, had snowball fights, and ate dinner in front of the fireplace exhausted from the day's activities. Each morning, they'd rise as if they weren't so tired they couldn't move and do it all over again.

ON THE FOURTH MORNING, CHANDRA ROSE AND STARTED PANCAKES for the bunch. After having watched the older boys eat all week, she realized she'd need to get a second job to pay for the food Jason was going to consume in the next few years. She and her mother were small eaters, but she knew she was in trouble with a growing boy in the house.

The condo was still quiet when she began mixing the batter. Mike had been showering, and he walked out into the kitchen, dressed, but his hair was still wet. He eased in behind her and kissed her neck.

"I could get used to you in the kitchen all rumpled from quiet sex the night before."

She moaned. "I have some guilt over that."

"Don't. How do you think parents do it? Quietly." He kissed her neck again, and she felt her body become soft against him.

She heard the ringing of her cell phone from the other room, and her head snapped up from the sound. "Who would be calling me at seven-thirty?"

"I'll get it for you."

Mike hurried to the other room. She heard his voice as he answered her mother's call, as he'd called her by name. Then his voice changed, and when he walked through the door with the phone pressed to his ear, his face had gone white.

"You and Tracy stay with the officer. We'll be down within two hours." He listened for a moment more and then disconnected the phone.

Chandra could already feel her heart being to thud in her chest. She set the whisk down and wiped her hands on the towel which sat on the counter.

"God, Mike, what happened? Is Mom okay? Tracy? Gabe and Holly? What?"

He set her phone on the counter and took her hands in his. "I have to go back. You have to go with me," he said, his breath labored.

"Mike, you're scaring me."

He looked at their joined hands and then back up into her eyes. "The police called your mom. They arrested two men squatting in our house. The one we just bought," he said as if he needed to explain.

"Okay, so they got them?"

"Because they caught fire to the kitchen cooking meth and got caught in the house."

The breath in her lungs became thick and hard to push out. "There's more. You're not telling me something."

Mike wiped the back of his hand over his brow. "They arrested Austin. He's severely burnt, but the other guy is worse."

Her knees grew weak and she wobbled back, but his hands came around her.

"Let's sit down. It's a lot to take."

BERNADETTE MARIE

She shook her head, willing herself to stand up and face him. "This is all my fault."

"Like hell it is. You had nothing to do with this."

"I took him in. I coddled the asshole again. He's hurting the people I love. He's hurting you and my mother and Tracy. He could have burnt down the whole god-dammed house."

"And he didn't."

"What if we hadn't been up here? What if you and Jason had been working on the house and they broke in?" She pressed her hands to her chest as if to hold in her heart that felt as if it might explode.

"He'd never hurt Jason. I know this."

She moved her eyes to meet his. "He might hurt you. Meth? Oh, God! He could have tried to kill you. Obviously, he's out of his mind."

"Not now." He pulled her to him, but she pushed away. "They're going to help him."

"How can you be so calm about this?"

"Because none of us got hurt and you're right here with me. All of the people I love are right here with me and safe. You can't keep going through life thinking he's going to ruin it for you because you were in love with him once and you had a child together. It's going to ruin every relationship you try to have."

"I can't help it." Her voice grew in volume as her anger boiled. "Because of me, your investment is ruined."

"And I was going to have to fix it up anyway."

"Mike, he's always going to come back."

His eyes went dark as they fixed on hers. "And what you're telling me is you're always going to let him."

She knew that wasn't right, but she couldn't argue it because she'd always let him come back.

He raked his fingers through his hair and turned to find Dane and Jason standing in the doorway. Jason's eyes were filled with

262

tears, and Dane, with his hands on Jason's shoulders, only shook his head.

Mike rubbed his hand over his unshaven face and looked at his son. "I have to go back to Denver. You guys can stay up here and finish your vacation." He shifted his eyes to Jason. "I'm sorry, kiddo."

Jason's lips quivered as he looked past Mike and locked eyes with her. "Mom, Dad wouldn't really do that, would he? That's really bad, Mom."

She wiped her eyes. "I know. Baby…" She started, but Jason turned from Dane's grip and slammed the bedroom door, only barely missing Dane. Then she heard it lock.

CHAPTER 35

$\mathcal{M}$ ike stood in the middle of the room and looked around. The kitchen was a total loss. They'd been cooking on the stove, which had to be jimmied to work in the first place. He figured Austin was lucky to be alive. According to the fire marshal, most of the time, in situations like this, there were usually explosions.

Esther kicked a charred piece of something across the floor. "The water damage alone is enough to have to nearly demo the entire bedroom above the kitchen now. That little..."

"We will demo it back and make it perfect."

She crossed her arms in front of her. "You're not mad?"

"Oh, I'm pissed as hell, but it's not going to get me anywhere. This year hasn't been what I've expected, so I'm going to roll with it."

She chuckled. "No wonder she loves you. My girl isn't stupid. She knows a good thing."

"Yeah, well you'll have to convince her of that. She thinks she's to blame for all of this and that couldn't be farther from the truth."

"Why does she blame herself?"

Mike paced the small space with his hands tucked into the pockets of his coat, his lift ticket still clasped to the zipper. "She took him back. She let him back into their lives. But I know she didn't realize it went this deep. This has nothing to do with her."

"You have to tell her that."

"I did. A million times." He pulled his hand from his pocket and brushed it under his nose to distract his senses from the smell. "An hour in the car with your daughter when she's having a pity party is a long hour. She's stubborn. She looks tough, and don't get me wrong, she is. But seriously it all stems from her being a softy at heart. If she was the bitch she tries to be, Austin would never have come back the first time."

Esther laughed hard. "You know her pretty well, I'd say." She kicked another charred piece of wood. "What do you do now? I don't know a man in the world who would put up with her shit, and I'm her mother. So I can say that."

He narrowed his eyes on her. "Why would you say that? She's hurt. She needs us more now than ever."

Esther smiled as she walked to him and took his hands in hers. "I knew that's what you would say." She squeezed his hands. "What are your plans, Mike? In the long term with Chandra, what are your plans."

He didn't have to think of an answer. It was on the tip of his tongue. "I want to marry her. I want to tattoo her name on my god-dammed arm," he said laughing.

"Don't wait for her to come around. She'll put up that facade again, and you'll have to start all over."

"I don't think she'll say yes."

"I guarantee it. So don't be upset when she doesn't. Ask again."

Mike kissed Esther on the cheek. "I'll be good to her —to them."

"I knew that the moment I met you. And that's why I bought into your investment. I didn't want you to get away."

～

CHANDRA HAD THE HOUSE BACK IN ORDER. IT CERTAINLY HADN'T been how she wanted to spend her vacation. She'd managed to avoid Mike for the past three days, and she dealt with the moping child because of it.

But that morning, Dane had called and asked if he could take him to play soccer one more time before they headed back to California.

With Austin still in the hospital under custody, she figured it was safe enough. Besides, she didn't have the heart to see her son's eyes go sad again.

An hour after Dane had picked up Jason, the doorbell rang. Chandra stood frozen in the kitchen. She wasn't expecting anyone, and at that moment she wished she hadn't been alone in the house. Who was to say that Austin didn't have more friends lurking around in the neighborhood. What if he owed someone money or... the doorbell rang again.

Without making a sound, she walked toward the window to look out to the street. Parked on the street was a black Honda crossover with a new sticker in the window. She didn't know anyone who drove it, but then she saw movement at the door.

Cranking her head, she saw that her visitor was Mike.

Tears instantly stung her eyes and anger began to fuel heat through her. Why, she wasn't sure. Her anger wasn't aimed at Mike, but he seemed to bring it out.

Moving swiftly to the door, she yanked it open.

"What do you want?"

He didn't flinch, smile, or even frown. He only stood there calmly, those blue eyes focused in on her.

"I want you to marry me."

Seriously? She kept her eyes on him, but he didn't react at all. "Are you kidding me? What in the hell..." she stopped and then noticed a suitcase at his feet. "What's that for?"

"I'm moving in. I hear you have an empty room."

The anger seemed to be defusing into confusion. "You have an apartment. Hell, you have a house."

He nodded. "The apartment was rented out this morning. Gabe's cousin is moving to town next week. Since I was done with the remodel, I told him he should rent it out."

"Then go live in your house," she spat out the words, leaving Mike standing on the porch in the cold.

"You might have heard. We had a kitchen fire."

Chandra pursed her lips. "That's not funny."

"It's a fact. So, are you going to marry me?"

"No, I'm not going to marry you. You're crazy."

He nodded again, this time slower. "It's really cold out here. Can I come in?"

She wanted to tell him no. He didn't need to be in her house. Having him there would only confuse her, and he'd already done that with that whole marriage question. But it seemed as though she really did want to have him there, though just for a moment.

She stepped back and let him through. He set the suitcase on the floor, and she shut the door behind him, then pushed herself against it as if in defiance.

He cast a look at her, then walked into the kitchen.

"What are you doing?" she asked following him.

"I'd love some coffee. It's freezing out. Dane will probably have Jason back soon. Even sensible boys know to come in from the cold."

"Mike, you don't need coffee, and you don't need to be here."

"I need to live here."

She clenched her jaw and tossed her braid over her shoulder. "How long do you need to live here? This is stupid. Why don't you have my mother move back here, and you live at Tracy's?"

He wrinkled up his nose. "I'm not attracted to Tracy. Besides, your mom will move out of Tracy's when the house is finished. She's going to run the place."

Seriously, he was making her head spin. She pulled back one of the kitchen chairs and sat down. "Now my mother is your partner, and she's running your B and B?"

"Peter still has that business opportunity for me. I'll need to have time to explore that."

She pressed her palm to her chest as she watched Mike open her cupboards looking for mugs and coffee filters.

Finally, she stood up. Pushing him out of the way, she gathered the coffee and the filters. "Sit down. Let me do this."

He didn't move. Instead, he leaned against the counter casually and watched her make coffee.

"So about that room you have."

Chandra growled as she pressed the button on the machine and set it to brew. "I never said I had a room. My mother just can't tell you to come over here and…"

He cut her off by grabbing hold of her hips and pulling her to him. The air whooshed from her lungs as she found herself pressed against him. Her hands came to his chest by instinct.

As mad as she was, she needed to push free, but she'd missed him dearly. A moment of this wouldn't hurt a thing, she thought, as he took her mouth with his and swept her under with it.

Nothing made sense now in the jumbled mess of her brain. She loved this man, and he was decent and kind. But her mistakes had cost him dearly. She couldn't let him live with her bad judgment for the rest of his life.

His tongue flicked against hers, and her legs were weak again. Oh, to have this every day of her life, it was nearly worth it.

But something finally broke through her senses, and she pushed back from him.

"We can't do this," she said brushing the back of her hand over her warm lips.

He leaned back against the counter and crossed his arms in front of him. "We do it well."

"Mike, my life is a mess."

"No," he said easily. "Your head is a mess. As soon as you sort it out, you'll marry me."

She spun and planted her feet firmly where she stood. "Why do you keep saying that to me? When did we ever talk about marriage?"

"We didn't. I'm asking you about it now. Will you marry me?"

"And I said no."

He was grinning now. Why was he grinning?

She stomped out of the room and down the hall to her bedroom, shutting the door behind her. She paced a circle around the bed and back again. Each drawer to her dresser was opened and closed as if she thought there was something she could be looking for. The point was, she was mad. She was confused. She was in love with the man, and he'd asked her to marry him.

The thought came to her as if she'd only now heard it.

He wanted to marry her after all that had happened.

Chandra fell to the bed. Looking up at the old sculpted ceiling, she heard him ask again, in her head.

She didn't know what made her the bigger idiot, pushing him away because she'd once loved Austin, or keeping him forever, because who knew what might happen.

Sitting up, she pressed a hand to her stomach which had tightened with knots.

A few minutes later she walked back to the kitchen to find him sitting at her table drinking coffee and looking at his phone.

"The boys are on their way back. I'll have to take the rental back when I take them to the airport."

"You'll need a ride."

He nodded. "I will. You can drive my new car out and pick me up."

She looked out the window to the car parked on the street. "You finally bought yourself a car?"

"I did. Can't rely on you to drive me everywhere," he said taking another sip of his coffee.

Chandra picked up the rag that was draped over the side of the sink and wiped down the counter. There wasn't any mess to be cleaned up, but it gave her a moment to think.

Replacing the rag, she then turned to him. "Why did you keep asking me to marry you when I kept telling you no?"

He set his cup down and leaned back in his chair. "Because your mother told me you'd tell me no. Then she said to keep asking."

A smile tugged at the corner of her mouth, but she fought it. "You talked to my mother about this?"

"Of course."

"When?"

"Days ago."

Wiping her hands on her pants, she studied him. Cool, calm, and oh so handsome, he sat there gazing at her. After all that had happened, he still looked at her, and it was a gaze.

"Why do you want to marry me?"

"I have a million reasons," he said as he stood and moved to her. "But I only need one."

He put his hands on her waist and pressed his forehead to hers before she lifted her arms around his neck.

"I love you, Chandra. I love that kid of yours too. I'm not a shabby husband. And I think I'm a pretty good father figure. I just don't see why you won't marry me."

"Because I..." She stopped and lifted her head. At that moment she didn't have a reason in the world. "I didn't see this coming, Mike. I wasn't prepared to fall in love with you."

"Yeah, I wasn't prepared either. But in the past few months, I've learned that sometimes that door that slams in your face is a blessing."

Chandra raked her fingers through his hair. "I don't know if I can marry you. You have no ink. It says to me that you can't commit." She grinned up at him, and he puckered his lips.

"Let's go. I'll get your name tattooed right over my heart."

The sentiment squeezed her own heart until she thought she'd fall to the floor in a puddle of goo.

"You win. I'll marry you."

"Finally." He blew out a breath. "Now, why don't you go open that back door and let your boys in then. They have got to be freezing by now having had their ears pressed to the glass for nearly forty minutes."

She felt the wave of laughter flow through her as she did as he said.

Standing just beyond the door, Jason and Dane sat on an old tree stump in the back yard. Jason held a bouquet of flowers and Dane a ring box open with a gold band inside.

There was no stopping the tears now as she turned into Mike's arms. "Thanks for walking into the bar that day."

"Thanks for not saying no when I said I'd like to stay for the conversation."

She pressed a soft, warm kiss to his lips. "I'll never say no again."

"You'll marry me?"

"Yes."

"I can live here forever?"

"Forever," she said pressing her hands to his cheeks and pulling him in for a kiss, realizing that she'd be able to do that any time she wanted. Now this man who still looked like a cross between Bill Gates and a college professor, with no ink on his body, would be hers forever. She would never have guessed that this was exactly how she wanted it.

MEET THE AUTHOR

Bestselling Author Bernadette Marie is known for building families readers want to be part of. Her series The Keller Family has graced bestseller charts since its release in 2011, along with her other series and single title books. The married mother of five sons promises Happily Ever After always...and says she can write it, because she lives it.

When not writing, Bernadette Marie is shuffling her sons to their many events—mostly hockey—and enjoying the beautiful views of the Colorado Rocky Mountains from her front step. She is also an accomplished martial artist with a second degree black belt in Tang Soo Do.

A chronic entrepreneur, Bernadette Marie opened her own publishing house in 2011, 5 Prince Publishing, so that she could publish the books she liked to write and help make the dreams of other aspiring authors come true too. Bernadette Marie is also the CEO of Illumination Author Events.

We hope you enjoyed
NEVER SAW IT COMING by Bernadette Marie.
For your pleasure, here is another excerpt from one of
Bernadette Marie's collection.

CANDY KISSES

A NOVELLA

Part of the Denver Brides Series

CANDY KISSES CHAPTER 1

*T*hree hundred more truffles needed to be rolled and Tabitha's hands had long gone numb. On any other day, she'd take the time to stretch her fingers or even run them under warm water to relieve the cramping. But it was February, and that meant no stopping until the fifteenth. It was also spontaneous wedding season where people jumped at the thought of marriage, and that always made for a lot more work.

She blew a loose strand of hair from her eyes and kept making perfectly round balls from the batter before setting them on the lined tray to her side. She couldn't remember a year when she'd had as many wedding chocolates to make. Her biggest client Claire Banks, an esteemed wedding planner, must have booked every day in February with a wedding or party. And she had chosen Tabitha's Chocolates to tempt the guests at every table.

It was work that Tabitha lived for but added to her already heavy workload before Valentine's Day, she was feeling a bit pinched for time, and her mood was sinking fast.

"Okay, it's done." Brie darted into the prep area of Tabitha's small Cherry Creek store, waving a work order. "We just picked up the Johnson-Carr wedding."

Tabitha squished the dough ball in her hand. "How are we going to get this all done? We might need to start saying no," she grumbled as she rolled yet another truffle through the cocoa and then set it on the tray to dry.

"Hey listen, Ms. Valentine and Wedding-Scrooge. I've been planning a tropical vacation with grass huts and fruity drinks with umbrellas. We need all the weddings we can get so I can make the big bucks and get out of this icebox for a while." Brie hung the order on a clipboard on the order wall.

Tabitha scowled as she scooped out a dozen more truffles and set them on the tray to roll through the coating. "Scrooge, huh?"

"You work too hard. You forget what it's like to have men fall at your feet at least one day a year."

"Yet you and my mother seem to think it should happen all the time. I mean how many times can the woman get engaged and married on Valentine's Day? Doesn't it take away the special meaning?"

"Maybe she does it just to piss you off." Brie grinned, and Tabitha wondered if she and her mother didn't just plan to make her crazy on purpose.

Tabitha shook her head as Brie went back to answering the phone at the front counter. Sometimes your best friends shouldn't be the people you hire.

She blew out a breath and thought of the upcoming holiday. She couldn't help but be cynical in February. People turned starry-eyed and lovesick all because of a greeting card holiday. She, for one, knew better than to believe in such fanciful dreams.

Her mother had fallen head over heels in love on Valentine's Day. Who thinks that meeting the man of your dreams is possible when selling flowers on the street corner? And how asinine is it to run off with a man whose tongue dripped satin words? Marriage after four days of shacking up in a hotel room did not make for a lifetime of happy memories, Tabitha thought as she dusted her hands off on her apron. She hopped down from the stool, on which she'd been perched for hours, and sought out a cup of coffee.

As she washed the cocoa from her hands, she gave thought to the phrase "love at first sight." The idea was ridiculous, but people fell for it all the time. And there she was, making money off of their sentimental dreams.

She opened the cupboard and pulled down her favorite green, oversized mug. She poured strong black coffee inside and rested against the counter. She wasn't sure why she was worried who fell in love. It paid her bills, and it appeared that love would soon send Brie on a tropical vacation.

By late afternoon, Tabitha had rolled thousands of truffles. She had rolled some in cocoa and others in milk chocolate. Another batch was set aside for a variety of white and dark chocolate. Prepping strawberries for tomorrow's dipping would keep her busy for the rest of the night.

Brie poked her head into the workroom. "I locked up and am going to head out. I have a date." She wiggled her eyebrows and Tabitha shook her head. When did the girl not have a date? "Would you mind cleaning out the display?"

"Of course." Tabitha laid a long stem strawberry out on a tray to dry.

"I closed out the register." Brie pulled her coat from the rack and slipped it on.

"Who are you going out with?"

"Video store guy. And he is so fine. I think I've fallen in love."

Tabitha shook her head. Did this new love know Brie had fallen in love already three other times since New Year's Eve?

With Brie gone, Tabitha turned on the radio to fill the silence. She'd laid out the strawberries and set them on the rack, then pushed it into the cooler.

The storefront was dark, and the sign had been turned to

closed. Tabitha began the process of removing the few unsold chocolates from the display and boxing them to sell on the shelves the next day. It was rare that she discarded any chocolate. Her business had been voted one of the best stores both in Cherry Creek and in Denver, and her chocolate was ordered online all over the world. She laughed to herself when she thought about how sweet business had been for her.

Tabitha bent over and pulled a tray from the case. When she stood, she saw the face of a man, his gloved hands cupped around his eyes, looking into the store. She nearly dropped the tray of petit fours to the ground. When he'd seen her, he'd stepped back and waved.

Her heart beat at an uncomfortable pace. This was one of those times she wished she'd taken her mother's advice and planted a gun under the counter. The idea was as stupid as the grin on the man's lips that told her he wasn't dangerous. Or at least she hoped so.

She set down the tray and walked to the door, her hands shaking from the startle he'd given her. The man stepped back, still grinning widely as Tabitha pointed to the CLOSED sign.

"Please." She could hear him plead through the door.

It wasn't like her to open the door to a stranger, but this one had a familiar look to him, though she was sure she'd never seen him before. She looked around the streets, and people still walked between the stores. If she had to scream, someone would likely hear her.

She unlocked the door and opened it slightly, keeping her foot blocked behind it. "We're closed."

"I know. I'm so sorry. I just flew in from a convention in New York. My flight was late, then the bus to the parking lot was—"

"Sir," she cut him off, holding her hand up. "You'll have to come back tomorrow."

"Listen, I'll pay double if you help me out. It's my mother's birthday, and I've already missed the party. If I don't walk

NEVER SAW IT COMING

through the door with a box of Tabitha Chocolates and bat my big brown eyes at her, she'll have my head."

She considered him for a moment. "Batting your eyes won't work on its own?" The trick seemed to be working on her.

"I don't think so. Not this time."

His short brown hair had tunnels where his fingers must have raked through dozens of times. Dark circles shadowed under his eyes, which when fully alert she assumed would burn into a woman with their dark brown warmth. The collar of his shirt was open, and his tie hung loosely around his neck. The long wool coat, which should have kept him nice and warm in the bitter cold of Denver's winter, gaped open across his chest.

Against her better judgment, Tabitha moved her foot from behind the door and let him into the store.

She walked around the counter quickly to put space between them. "I'm afraid I don't have much of a selection. A week before Valentine's Day we're usually sold out of the favorites."

The man stopped and looked at the bare shelves in the display as he pulled his hands from his gloves. "You probably know my mother. She comes in often enough. Maybe you could help me throw together something."

"Who is your mother?"

"Claire Banks."

"Your mother is Claire Banks?" The image of his mother crossed her mind. Looking at the handsome man across from her, she found it hard to believe that Claire's son was such a head turner.

"You do know her."

"Of course I know her." Half of her order board had the woman's name on it, thankfully. "I mean no disrespect, but really, do you think a box of chocolates is what she needs for her birthday?" She hated how it sounded the moment it came out. But when the corners of his mouth turned up into a smile, which sent an alarming sizzle through her, she realized she hadn't offended him.

He leaned his arms on the top of the case. "My father tried to buy her flowers once. She said she didn't get any joy out of looking at pretty things. She'd rather eat pretty things. I prefer to appease her and think of her health later."

A giggle grew in her chest, and she kept it forced down. This man was keeping her at work even later than she'd anticipated. She just wanted his money and wanted him out. "She enjoys the petit fours quite a bit. I could probably spare some of the truffles I dipped a few hours ago, but I won't have the strawberries until the morning."

"Dear Lord, how much time does she spend in here?"

"Client confidentiality." She smiled, and it almost hurt, which made her realize she'd been doing her fair share of scowling lately. Februarys were usually for profit and hard work, not for smiling at handsome men.

"You have the most beautiful eyes."

The comment had her swallowing back the smile. Her spine stiffened. "I beg your pardon."

"Really. They're the color of milk chocolate with swirls of caramel. It's no wonder you're so good a being a chocolatier. It must run through your blood."

"This isn't going to get you a price discount or strawberries in that box."

That smile crossed his lips again. "Oh, I didn't mean any disrespect." Humor filled his voice. "I appreciate fine art the way my mother appreciates fine chocolates. Your eyes, like your chocolates, are beautiful. I'm sorry that you mind that I told you that."

"I don't mind." She turned and pulled a white pastry box from the shelf behind her. Inside she adjusted the paper doily. "I'm just not comfortable with strangers looking at me the way you do."

"Well then, I suppose we should fix that." He reached his hand over the counter. "Preston Banks. Son of Claire Banks, the distinguished wedding planner."

Hesitantly, she shook his hand. "Tabitha Knight, the wedding planner's choice for her chocolates. Privately and professionally."

His eyes widened. "You're Tabitha? As in Tabitha Chocolates? As in owner of the store?"

She pulled her hand from his, uncomfortable with his reaction. "You seem surprised."

"Well, I wouldn't have pictured you as the entrepreneur type."

"You wouldn't?"

"I mean …" He raked his fingers through his hair, deepening the channels where his fingers had traveled before. "What I meant to say was that I expected the name only to be a name. How many young and attractive women have their handmade products in some of the most exclusive shops and on the trays at the most elegant weddings?"

She swallowed back the urge to gasp at the attractive comment. She was out of her element. These were the kind of comments Brie usually received. "You seem to know my work well."

"Claire Banks is my mother, remember?"

Tabitha gave into her smile again. "She has been a substantial help in my business. I do tend to be on her list of people to call when she's planning a wedding."

"Then with Valentine's Day around the corner, you must be extremely busy."

"You have no idea." And, she thought, if he'd only finish his purchase she could get back to work on those orders his mother had placed for clients.

"That's why I cut my trip short, and I'm headed to her place. Not only is it her birthday, but this year it seems she's bitten off more than she can chew. She's booked one too many weddings this year, and now the entire family is in charge of seeing they all go off without a hitch."

"Awfully nice that you could help her out."

Tabitha began filling the box with items she knew Claire Banks would enjoy.

Preston looked around. "How did you get into this?"

"Chocolate?" He let out an agreeable hum, and she shrugged. "It was something I always loved. I fell in love with my Holly Hobby oven and making those little cakes."

"Were you one of those girls who wouldn't share? My sisters never would share Easy-Bake cakes with me."

Tabitha added a few more candies to the box. "I made one of my mother's first wedding cakes in my oven. Soon it turned to cookies and decorating the tops. Then I learned the fine art of a double boiler and a chocolatier was born." She counted out the items in the box silently. "And with my mother's affection for getting married every few years, it seemed a good hobby to acquire."

"And how many times has she been married?" The humor in his eyes raked on her nerves when he asked.

"On Valentine's Day, it will be her fifth."

"Fifth?" His voice rose in pitch.

Tabitha hated reactions like that, but that's what she got for opening her big mouth. She shook her head in disgust as she added a few more truffles to the box. He was irritating her, and he was going to pay for it as the box was getting heavier.

He shook his head. "All I can say is wow. Is she using my mother to plan her wedding?"

"If I were only that lucky. No, as if I weren't busy enough, she's somehow designated me as her bridal planner." Tabitha added the last petit fours from the tray she'd taken from the display and closed the box.

"Where do you find time if this is your busy season?"

"A question I've asked myself." She laid the box atop the display. "This is sixty dollars' worth of Tabitha Chocolates. Do you want me to dig up more or do you think she'll be fine with this?"

"I think she'll be delighted." He handed her a fifty and a twenty, not once blinking at the price. Perhaps she should have added quite a bit more.

"I'll be back. I've closed the drawer, so I have to get you change." She turned to walk to her office.

"No," he said, and she stopped. "Consider it my thank you for opening the door."

"I appreciate it, but that's not necessary."

"I insist."

At that, she turned and pulled a ribbon from a spool that hung on the wall. Carefully she lifted the box and tied the ribbon around it.

Preston watched her intently and lifted his eyes to hers when she finished with the bow. "Are you busy tomorrow night?"

"I'm sorry. What?" Her tone carried her impatience, and she just wanted to get back to work so she could finally get home.

"I'd love to take you to dinner."

She adjusted the bow atop the box and added a gold foiled sticker with the name of the bakery. "Mr. Banks, thank you, but ..."

"Preston," he reminded her with a smile. It did its job in calming her, but she wasn't comfortable with a stranger asking her out. She was in unfamiliar territory.

"Preston. I don't go out with men I've only met."

"Why?"

"Why? It's that simple. I don't know you."

"No, but you could if you have dinner with me. Unless you're married." His brows drew together, and the creases around his lips deepened. "I didn't think about that."

"I'm not married."

"Great," he said. "I'll stop by here after you close. If you're not done, I'd be happy to help you."

"You talk fast." She held her hands up as if to stop him. "Do you sell used cars?"

"No, only the finest BMWs and Jags." He smiled when she scowled. "I don't have to do a lot of talking. The cars sell themselves. But if I keep talking the buyer can't walk away from the sale."

"I'm walking away."

"No, you're not. You're going to let me take you to dinner tomorrow because now you're intrigued. And because my mother is not only one of your biggest customers with her business, she's a great fan of yours as well." He reached over the counter and grabbed her hand. He lifted it to his lips and brushed her knuckles with a kiss. "Tabitha, it certainly was my pleasure to meet you. Thank you for helping me out. I'll see you tomorrow." He picked up his box and walked out the door.

Tabitha stood still, rendered speechless by the man who had waltzed in and out of her store. Apparently, she was having dinner with the man. Had she said yes?

She wouldn't go. No one talked her into things like that. The last thing she needed in February was some man taking her to dinner. She was much too busy.

As she folded the money he'd handed her and shoved it into her pocket, she thought of Preston Banks and his playful smile. He was right. She was definitely intrigued.

Other Titles from 5 Prince Publishing
www.5princebooks.com

Never Saw It Coming *Bernadette Marie*
Blissful Disaster *Amy L. Gale*
Victory *Bernadette Marie*
Chasing Her Heart *J. L. Petersen*
Alone *M.J. Kane*
Goodnight Kisses *Wilhelmina Stolen*
The Deja Vu House *Doug Simpson*
We Are From Atlantis *Doug Simpson*
Prez *Lissa Jay*
The Train Robbers *James P. Hanley*
Walker Revenge *Bernadette Marie*
Lest We Aren't Forgiven *Railyn Stone*
Broken Hearts *M.O. Kenyan*
Goodnight Kisses *Wilhelmina Stolen*
The Three Stones of Bethany *April Marcom*
Wanderlust *Bernadette Marie*
Holiday Past *Jessica Dall*
Christmas Blitz *Amy Gale*
A Christmas for Chloe *Susan Lohrer*
Restored Hearts *Railyn Stone*
Last Christmas *Lisa J. Hobman*
A Romance for Christmas *Bernadette Marie*
The Fall of Undal *Katrina Sisowath*